Born and brought up in Kolkata, **Suparna Chatterjee** devotes her time to concocting mysteries for her protagonists to solve. When she's not dreaming up whodunits, Suparna is either reading, or meditating, or travelling the world, or taking care of her family. A theatre enthusiast, her musical 'Anand and Benaifer' has been staged in Mumbai and Bengaluru.

Suparna currently lives in Bengaluru with her husband and daughter.

Praise for *The All Bengali Crime Detectives*

'A combo of Blyton, Christie and Ray!'— *The Sunday Guardian*

'Suparna Chatterjee presents the latest slew of super-sleuths, the rising stars of detective fiction...'— *The Telegraph*

'Suparna has crafted endearing stories of individual characters... Most readers are waiting for the sequel…'— *The Hindu*

'There may have been many books released over the past few years that were set in Kolkata, but only few have been able to portray its nuances and quirkiness so beautifully.'— *The Times of India*

'What one enjoys immensely is Chatterjee's humour, more precisely, the quintessential Bengali humour.'— *The Statesman*

THE ALL BENGALI CRIME DETECTIVES–II

The Mysterious Death of Probhat Sanyal

Suparna Chatterjee

RUPA

Published by
Rupa Publications India Pvt. Ltd 2015
7/16, Ansari Road, Daryaganj
New Delhi 110002
Sales Centres:

Allahabad Bengaluru Chennai
Hyderabad Jaipur Kathmandu
Kolkata Mumbai

This is a work of fiction. Names, characters, places and incidents are either the product of the author's imagination or are used fictitiously and any resemblance to any actual person, living or dead, events or locales is entirely coincidental.

ISBN: 978-81-291-3590-2

First impression 2015

10 9 8 7 6 5 4 3 2 1

Printed by Parksons Graphics Pvt. Ltd, Mumbai

For Kanchan

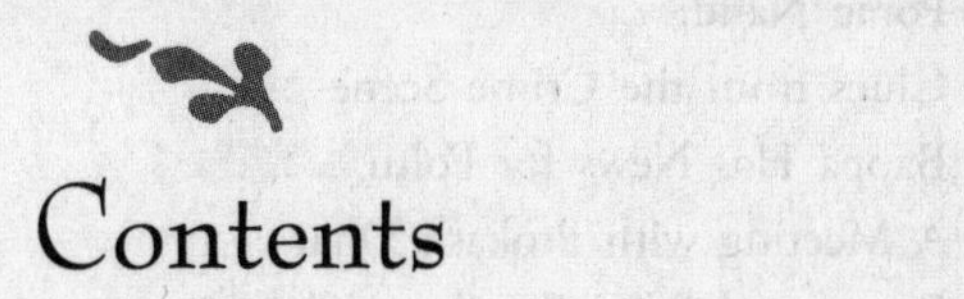

Contents

Debdas Guha Roy Enjoys a Cup of Tea

Debdas Guha Roy reclined on his armchair. A steaming cup of tea rested on the stool by his side, its enticing aroma inviting him to take a sip. There was a slight nip in the air, typical of early December mornings in Calcutta, when the sun, it would seem, was in no particular hurry to dispel the gray haze of dust and fog. He held the hot teacup, not by the handle, but by wrapping his cold fingers around it, and relished the warmth it brought. A loud voice, in the otherwise quiet street, made him sit up straight and crane his neck to search for the source. A mother was warning her son—dressed in trousers and bright school cardigan—they'd miss the bus if he didn't walk faster. It would be a common sight these days, thought Debdas Guha Roy, when the temptation to stay inside the warm *lep* would far outweigh getting up early for school.

In his school-going days, in a village in Birbhum, where temperatures were always a few degrees lower than that in the city, he and his brothers would be made to take a bath in the cold waters drawn from the village well, before walking a kilometre to reach the ramshackle structure that was to be his primary school. The thought of those cold morning showers sent a shiver down his spine, and he quickly gulped some more hot tea as if to replace the memory with his current, more comfortable existence. He had come a long way, it was true, from a little known village in Bengal with no electricity or access to any modern amenity, with its dusty roads tainted a permanent red—that colour of his soil—that made its long winding way into the green paddy fields, the hide-outs of many a childhood game. How often had he held the red earth, the *rangamaati*, in his palms, and wondered what it was that gave it the colour of sunset.

Today, he was a retired professor of geology, had a loving family, occupied most of his post-retirement days by giving private tuitions—and, as if all this was not enough, he was now also a member of the previously secret, but now fairly well-known club called 'The All Bengali Crime Detectives'. Indeed, it was he who had coined the name, cleverly taking the initial letters of the club members—Akhil, Bibhuti, Chandan and Debdas. And, if one put sufficient thought into it, *his* part in solving the previous case was really the most crucial. In light of all of the above, perhaps it would not be too presumptuous to think, that should there be a call for the President of the club—regardless of how unofficial the aforesaid club was, consisting as it were of four senior citizens who met every morning on a bench in the local Sabuj Kalyan Park—then, his name should come forth as a very strong possibility. Though, naturally he will decline the generous offer. 'Joj Saheb', or retired High Court judge Akhil Banerjee, being the most prominent figure, should be made the President, he would insist.

The thought, nevertheless, did bring a smile to his lips. Back in his college days, his name had come up for the position of the Treasurer of a literary club. But then, Prodip Biswas, who had clearly wanted the coveted position for himself, had launched a verbal attack on his fellow club members. The battle had turned ugly. Rabindranath and Sarat Chandra were forgotten, and in their place, tiresome speeches highlighting the general incompetence of the members were being read out. Debdas Guha Roy had decided that he no longer wished to be the Treasurer of such a club and had withdrawn his candidature. But now, perhaps the time had come when such a post was inevitable.

His fame as a detective was already spreading. Only the other day he had run into Debotosh Bagchi, professor of chemistry and his former colleague. '*Ki byapar,* DGR?' he had asked. 'It seems retirement has opened up newer career options for you? Were you always interested in this sort of work? *Hya?* Working undercover all these years, *moshai*?' They enjoyed a hearty laugh. Debdas Guha Roy had tried his best to appear humble. But he had not been able to help the swelling feeling inside. Professor Bagchi had filled him in with news of his former college: the usual inter-department politics, the frequent disagreements between the heads of departments over sharing of lab resources by the ladies' section in the morning and the boys' section during the day, the speculations of who was going to replace the principal, once he was up for retirement in six months.

'*Moshai*, I can't wait to retire,' Professor Bagchi had declared eventually. 'I have plans of going back to my village, build a small house there and look after the farm…I need a break from this mundane routine. I envy you, *moshai*.'

True, life after retirement was good, if not better.

There was still the question of finding a suitable match for his elder daughter Piya. Thus far, it had proved to be difficult. Piya had the habit of speaking her mind. That is the way she had been brought up, of course. In his days, children never dared to question their father, just dutifully accepting what was asked of them. They would not look in the eye of an elder when spoken to, it was considered insolence. But these were different times. Children were being brought up in a fiercely competitive environment, they were being taught to think for themselves. They questioned, opined and if required voiced their protests. And in some ways, it was necessary too, thought Debdas Guha Roy. Otherwise, one might find oneself thoroughly ill-equipped to deal with the myriad challenges that surfaced every day in the modern way of life. Humility and docility did have a place, but armed with just those, one could well find oneself being trampled all over.

Had he done all he could for his two daughters? As a parent, you could never be sure. No matter how much you did, it never seemed enough. Perhaps, Piya could have gone abroad to study. She certainly had the merit. But Debdas Guha Roy could not have afforded that. He had not given them a lavish childhood, pampering them with expensive toys and dresses, or signing them up for tennis, ballet and piano lessons like parents did these days. But he had given them a happy one, he hoped. And most importantly, he had given them the right values. Somewhere, he believed, was a boy who would appreciate these, and agree to marry Piya and keep her happy. Somewhere…

The newspaper flew in and fell on the floor with a thud. Debdas Guha Roy got off the arm chair, walked over to the gate and bent down to pick it up. Bhombol, the pudgy paperboy, had worn his blue sweater again. Right-side out today, Debdas Guha Roy noted.

Akhil Banerjee Runs into an Old Friend

The minibus blew a thick cloud of fumes and sped away. Akhil Banerjee covered his nostrils with a handkerchief and craned his neck to see if the flow of traffic had thinned. He had been standing there, at the corner of Hazra More for almost ten minutes now. On either side of him young men and women boldly stepped on to the road in spite of the oncoming traffic, and managed to deftly cross over to the other side with practised agility. In his younger days, Akhil Banerjee too would have done the same. But now, somehow, he was not so sure. What if the bus driver did not see your hand signal? Or what if you were not fast enough to avoid the auto that came whizzing behind the Maruti? Reflexes were slow, and one couldn't trust oneself the way one used to. He would simply have to wait till the pedestrian signal turned green, indicating that it was now absolutely safe to cross.

'*Arrey,* Akhil, isn't it?'

The voice made him turn around. A tall man about his age, with a large squarish face was smiling at him. He had thinning grey hair neatly parted on the side, a large nose on which rested a pair of dark-rimmed spectacles. His eyes, black and beady and slightly slanted towards the outer edges, bore an amused, impish look.

'*Ki*? Couldn't recognize me?' he smiled teasingly.

Akhil Banerjee hesitated. The man had used the informal

pronoun. Was he perhaps someone he had known in his childhood?

'Biren...Biren Ghoshal. Law college '66. *Ki?* Can you place me now?'

'Oh ho!' smiled Akhil Banerjee, slapping his forehead. 'Biren! My God! Did not recognize you at all...'

'Thank God! You saved me from a lot of embarrassment. I was beginning to think...'

'What?'

'*Nah*... Perhaps it was audacious of me to call you by the first name like that. I mean, you are a High Court Judge and I am a simple family lawyer.'

'*Arrey, dur, dur*,' Akhil Banerjee waved away the apology. 'All those titles are for inside the Court. Besides, I have retired now. Tell me Biren, do you still play cricket?'

Biren Ghoshal smiled, shaking his head. 'You remember?'

'Of course, how can I forget? Last match of the tournament at Maidan... We were tied 1-1 with Presidency, and playing for the Cup. Their bowlers looked like they were there to avenge some past wrong...not one of our batsmen stayed on the crease for longer than two overs. Then you came, and started hitting fours and sixes almost at every ball. We needed five runs off the last ball...and sure enough you hit a six, and we won! What a day it was!'

'Ah, yes, yes. I still talk about that to my grandson,' Biren Ghoshal chuckled.

The pedestrian signal turned green. Scores of people shoved their way to the other side. Akhil Banerjee hesitated.

'I was saying, Akhil, are you in a hurry?'

'*Arrey*, no, no. Retired folks are never in a hurry. Tell me, what do you have in mind?'

'How about a cup of tea? *Ei toh*, there's a tea shop right

around the corner. The ambience won't be what you are normally accustomed to perhaps, but the tea will be good. That much is guaranteed.'

'*Chol na*, let's go.'

They made their way through the crowded pavement, walking past small, crude shops that sold cigarettes and betel leaves, the edges decorated with colourful pouches of chewables that hung from the top like garlands.

As with most sweet and tea shops in Calcutta, Sri Hari Mishtanna Bhandar was never quite empty even on a weekday. Akhil Banerjee and Biren Ghoshal walked past the array of sweets—round, square, rectangular, oblong, some dotted with cashews and raisins, some as white as milk, some golden from a dash of saffron, some a deep brown from being fried in hot oil—displayed neatly in rows. They made their way to the rear end of the shop where a few tables had been placed for customers. A young boy arrived to free the table of the remnants of the previous meal.

'What tea do you have?' asked Biren Ghoshal.

'All kinds, babu,' replied the boy. 'Assam, Darjeeling, tulsi-cha, masala-cha...'

'Darjeeling,' said Akhil Banerjee. 'Two cups.'

The boy nodded and left.

'So Biren, what have you been up to?'

'Not much,' replied Biren. After graduating from law college he had joined the family firm. They still had the office in Loudon Street, though he had officially 'retired'. He had two sons—the older one went abroad to study and chose to settle down in the UK. The younger one looked after the family business. He had run into Bijoy and Shudhanshu and Ronojoy—old classmates whose names sounded familiar to Akhil Banerjee, though he had to confess he was unable to put faces to those names.

The boy arrived with two cups of tea. Biren Ghoshal brought his cup close to his face and allowed himself a whiff of the heady aroma, before quickly putting the cup down. The steam had cast a screen on his glasses.

'This "Darjeeling tea",' he said, wiping the glasses on his cotton *panjabi*, 'reminds me of a strange incident.' He paused before continuing. 'Umm... Have you heard of Makaibari?'

'Of course, Makaibari is one of the oldest tea gardens in Kurseong,' said Akhil Banerjee. 'It produces one of the world's most expensive tea-leaves. Silver Tips Imperial. Only 50 grams can cost as much as a thousand rupees!'

'My God! What are you saying?'

Akhil Banerjee nodded. 'Anyway...you were saying?'

'Uhh...yes. Don't know what to make of it, really,' he shrugged. 'Last month I was admitted to Kothari for a few days. Chest pains. Nothing serious, but wife and sons insisted that I get it checked. A slight block in one of the arteries... Doctor said, no need to operate, just take these medications and restrict your diet.

'Anyway, I was sharing the room with another gentleman. About our age, maybe slightly younger. He would lie quietly in his bed, reading a book or watching television. One night, after the nurse had taken our blood pressures and given us our medications, we got talking. His name was Sanyal, Probhat Sanyal. Has a house in Behala. He had the strangest story to tell.'

Probhat Sanyal's Story

I was a manager at a tea garden in Kurseong called Makaibari. You might have heard of it.

Have you ever been to a tea garden, Mr Ghoshal? I tell you, if you haven't, you have missed seeing something. Imagine—acres and acres of lush green rolling hills enveloped in a cloud of mist much of the year. A surreal landscape, you couldn't but be mesmerized by the sheer beauty of it. Even a city-bred man like myself could feel oneness with earth—the earth that was the livelihood of thousands of people, right from the workers to the estate managers.

My bungalow was a little up the hills. A huge colonial house with high ceilings and wooden floors that creaked when you walked. It was nestled amidst towering oaks, maples and birches. A variety of ferns and rare orchids grew in the wild all around. It was a plant lover's paradise. Early every morning, I would wake up to the sounds of birds—the bulbul-like fairy blue bird, with its two-note 'glu-it, glu-it' calls, or the soft cooing of the emerald dove. The workers would start coming in very early, women with slit eyes and flattened faces, a large conical basket tied to their backs, would pluck the tea leaves with the care of a mother tending to a newborn, often a song on their lips. Sometimes they would bring their young babies, and place them in makeshift cradles under a canopy. All the babies under one canopy. And they would take turns to come sit by them, and sing lullabies and rock them to sleep.

I am a confirmed bachelor, Mr Ghoshal. Family life was not for me, I was sure of that. I had a Nepali servant, Raju, who stayed with me, and cooked and cleaned. I divided my time between work (which wasn't all that challenging, to be honest) and nature. Every now and then, I would take off for a few days, losing myself in the idyllic little-known villages far away from the touristy circuits, walking down narrow roads that disappeared into the clouds. I often stayed with the locals, in their simple huts, enjoying their hospitality and their generosity. They welcomed me as one of their own.

Have you seen the Kanchenjunga, Mr Ghoshal? I would pity the tourists who came to see her. They would spend so much money and meticulously plan a vacation in this land to catch a glimpse of the majestic peak, only to be cruelly tricked by the treacherous weather. How often have I seen tourists extend their stay, day after day, so that they may be able to see her. She's elusive, that one. She shows herself when she wants to, preferring to play hide and seek behind the clouds on most days. Yet, I have had the enormous fortune, again and again, to see her, to marvel at her, to wonder at her beauty. Even now, when I close my eyes, I can see the Kanchenjunga, as if she had just risen from behind the veil of clouds.

You must be wondering, if I loved the place so much, why did I choose to leave and return to Calcutta? It is because of one incident that happened some twenty years ago.

Life in the tea estate is extremely lonely. Once the sun is down, and the workers have left for their huts, you had nothing but the company of your thoughts. In the evenings, I would often go to a local club. Some of the managers from the adjoining estates would come, too. We would play a few rounds of poker, share a few drinks—little distractions that helped you survive till the sun was mercifully up again.

One evening, it had gotten later than usual, I was returning home from the club and had probably taken a few more drinks than intended. There was a fairly thick mist, but I was not concerned. I knew the road like the back of my hand, every turn, every hair-pin bend.

I steered the jeep around the last bend. I could see the lights of my bungalow flickering between the tall trees, when all of a sudden a man in a bicycle appeared right in front of the jeep. Before I realized what was happening, there was a crash and I saw him fly off the cycle and land on the road.

I completely froze, Mr Ghoshal. My limbs went numb, my mind switched off. I did not know what to do. I turned off the ignition, turned off the lights. And trembling, I got off the jeep and stumbled towards him. He was lying with his face down. His twisted cycle lay upturned a little further away, the wheels still in rotation. I called out to him. He didn't move. I did not know what to do. I should have taken him in my jeep to the hospital, but it was clear he was already dead! I would fail the alcohol test, for sure. My life, my career was ruined. I am not proud of what I did, but I had no choice. I lifted the bicycle and threw it off the edge. Then I dragged the body by the leg to the edge of the road, and gave it a push, just enough to get it off the road. And I drove away.

I reached the bungalow and poured myself some brandy. My hands were still shaking. I realized my shirt was wet with sweat, in spite of the cold. Anyway, the next day, I called in sick. Stayed in my room most of the day. By evening I was feeling much better. I thought of grabbing a bite, but there was no food in the house. The servant had taken leave for a week. Apparently his mother was sick or something and he needed to go to his village urgently. He had promised his brother would fill in during his leave—but obviously the brother was nowhere around. I managed to make myself a sandwich, watched some TV, then took sleeping tablets before retiring for the night.

In a few days, the incident had already retreated to the hidden corners of my memory. Life was back to normal. I could almost pretend the incident had not occurred at all, and that it was all a part of a distant nightmare.

Then one night, maybe a week or so after the accident, I had almost dozed off, when I thought I heard a rap on the window. Softly first, then louder. Who could it be so late in the night? I wondered. I slipped on my housecoat and slippers, went to the window and parted the curtains.

I am a rational man, Mr Ghoshal. There is no scope in my mind for the likes of ghosts and phantoms. But what I saw that night, outside my window, made my blood curdle. It was as if I was staring at a spirit, its white face, deep beady eyes glaring back at me, his mouth opening and closing, as if uttering some omen that I was unable to hear. I wanted to scream but words would not come out. I drew back the curtains hastily, stumbled back into my bed and stayed up all night. You must be thinking I had imagined it all. But I didn't Mr Ghoshal, I didn't. Early next morning, at the crack of dawn, I took the first train back to Calcutta, never to go back again.

My younger brother Probir lived with his wife and daughter, in a small rented house in Calcutta. Our father stayed with them, too. Probir had never been a very bright student, and had had to struggle quite a bit. He eventually managed to find a clerical job in CESC and settle down. I moved in with them. It was tough for all of us in a small two-bedroom place, but his wife took good care of all of us, and soon things were looking up again. I started my own business—a small firm that procured teas from all over India, blended them according to flavour and strength, then re-packaged and sold them for consumption. I rented a small office space in Dhormotola. We started out small, with just two or three people. But soon I had twenty people working under me! In only a few years, I moved out of the old office into a much bigger place.

I have to thank the tea-loving connoisseurs of Calcutta for the success. As business grew, so did my product-base. I started keeping more expensive brands of tea. From Sikkim's Lopchu to Darjeeling's Orange Pekoe and Okayti Emperor Black Tea, to the more exotic Green and Jasmine teas. A few years later, I was in a position to construct a house in Behala. I asked Probir and his family to move in with me. Probir refused at first. He had his pride. But eventually he gave in.

The house has two floors. On the ground floor, we have two bedrooms—my father stays in one, I in the other. Probir's family lives upstairs. My father is now close to ninety and spends most of his days staring out of the window at the street outside. His television set is switched on almost throughout the day, loud enough for the whole neighbourhood to hear. You have to scream to get yourself heard in our house. *Jai hok,* we—all of us—settled down very well in the house. Apart from the occasional skirmish that is inevitable between brothers, I'd like to think we were all happy with the arrangement.

Then, last month, one evening I was reading a magazine and enjoying a peg of whisky. It must have been around 8.30. I could hear the familiar title song of a Bengali tele-serial coming from Baba's room, when suddenly I heard a rap on the window, a soft rap. I thought it must be the wind, and ignored it. Then the rap got louder. I got up to check. I drew the curtains aside and what do I see right outside my window? That same face, Mr Ghoshal, staring at me with that vacant expression. The phantom of Kurseong had returned!

I stumbled back on to my bed. Hands, trembling and cold with sweat, I picked up the phone and called Rajib. He is a young fellow who works in my firm. You would have seen him. He comes here every day to visit me. Very bright, talented chap. He came over immediately and calmed me down. Said I must have imagined the whole thing, there were no ghosts in Calcutta, etcetera. I guessed he must've been right. Maybe the alcohol made me imagine things.

But then again… Last Sunday, I had just sat down to dinner—I usually eat alone in my room—and suddenly there was a rap on the window. I had not taken a sip of alcohol that week…so for sure, I did not imagine this. I gradually got up and pulled aside the curtain only slightly. Sure enough, Mr Ghoshal…it was there!

I called Rajib again. He is the only one I could trust. Rajib came over and insisted that I see a doctor immediately. My blood pressure is anyway a little high. And you know what doctors are like. Once they find a patient, they don't let go of him easily. They make you do hundreds of tests till they are convinced you have a condition that needs treatment. Doctor Gupta advised that I get myself admitted here for a few days. I protested, there's nothing wrong with me, I said. But Rajib would not hear of it.

They tell me I will be discharged tomorrow. But I don't know if I want to go back home, Mr Ghoshal. The past has a way of catching up with you, doesn't it? My end is very near, my time is up. I'm convinced of it.

Bibhuti Bose Has a Problem

The morning air had a slight nip, enough to prompt cold-fearing Bengalis to pull out their sweaters, shawls, mufflers and monkey-caps from the forgotten corners of their wardrobes. Calcutta did not see a severe winter. Her winter was fleeting, transient, limited to a slight dip in temperature in those few days in January that felt the winds of Gangasagar blowing towards her. It was easy to miss it altogether, if one did not pay particular attention to the changing winds. It was perhaps this fear of missing out on the winters, that when the slightest inkling of a temperature dip was detected, Calcuttans wasted no time in bringing out an array of woolen garments, handwoven with utmost love by elderly female relatives—the *mashimas* and the *jethimas*, and collected over the years as a reminder of days when love and concern came in the form of multicoloured sweaters knitted in Bardhaman Wool.

Cold was something Bengalis refused to take lightly. Every cough and sneeze was a potential pre-cursor to pneumonia. *Thanda legey jabey!* (You will catch a cold!), was the most frequent warning issued to reckless children, venturing out into the 13 degrees Celcius of Calcutta cold in a mere full-shirt.

There was a case for being cautious, of course, thought Kalpana Mukherjee. No point in taking unnecessary risks. Yet at times, she could not help but wonder, if perhaps Bengalis had taken it too far. These thoughts crossed her mind while watching her husband, Chandan Mukherjee, empty the contents of an entire drawer on the floor, frantically searching for one missing item to complete his attire.

'Where is my *iye*?' he thundered.

He had at least three layers of clothing, woolen and otherwise, on his body, a muffler wrapped snugly round his neck, warm trousers and socks for his legs and feet. Socks, underwear, handkerchiefs, vests were strewn all over the floor. Try as she might, Kaplana Mukherjee could not arrive at which '*iye*' was missing. At times, it did seem incredulous, that *bongosontans*, the brave sons of Bengal, who had waged many a war against the British, could be so intimidated by the prospect of a mere cold.

'Which *iye*?' she demanded, eyeing the increasing pile of discarded clothes with growing irritation.

'*Arrey*, the *iye* that I bought last winter from Ballygunj Phari.' Now, *iye* could be anything—from buttons to blankets, and everything in between.

'How should I know?' she shot back. 'You are the detective. Go find out your own "*iye*"!'

*

Bibhuti Bose ambled towards the bench, brushed the seat with his tweed flat cap before settling down. There were fewer morning walkers in the park—only the very religious, for whom this morning ritual far exceeded in importance any inconvenience brought on by the changing weather. There were others who postponed their walk in these colder days, till the sun was well above their heads. And there were still others, like himself, for whom it mattered little how suitable or otherwise the weather was for any form of exercise. Walking was something he did, to get himself from one place to another—from the bedroom to the bathroom, from the bathroom to the living room, from home to the Sabuj Kalyan Park and back. What was the point in walking more than what was strictly required?

It was a rare morning that he, Bibhuti Bose, was the first to arrive at the park. Joj Saheb was usually the first, followed by, he guessed, Debdas Guha Roy and Chandan Mukherjee. Usually, by the time he reached Sabuj Kalyan Park, Joj Saheb's ten rounds of walking would have been done, and Debdas Guha Roy would have ordered the first round of tea from the local shop. For Bibhuti Bose, sleep came intermittently at night, plagued with nightmares and a myriad of unwelcome thoughts. It was not easy for him to be up and about as early as the others. Though lately, at the insistence of his family doctor, he had been reducing his dependence on sleeping pills. As a result, he often found himself wide awake at the crack of dawn. It became difficult to stay in the house, listening to his wife, Joyoti Bose, snore peacefully, while he sat in the living room waiting for first light to filter through the curtains.

The sun had come up behind him, its weak rays fell on his back like a light sweater that did little to lessen the cold. The blades of grass glistened with early morning dew. Hungry, excited birds—the myna, the papiya, the bulbul—chirped noisily alongside the cawing of the black crow. A lizard, clinging on to the bark of the gulmohar tree, inched ahead to the patch of sunlight, where it waited a while longer before beginning its day. A group of young boys carrying cricket bats arrived at the park. Bibhuti Bose watched them pile bricks, one on top of the other, in three neat columns that would serve as stumps.

'*E ki, moshai*? How come you are first today?' asked Chandan Mukherjee, swinging his walking stick as he approached the bench. 'Where are the others?'

'Joj Saheb is right behind you. And I think that is Char Podobi in the distance, near the gulmohor tree.' Char Podobi—the four surnames—was his nickname for Debdas Guha Roy, Deb, Das, Guha and Roy being four distinct Bengali surnames.

'Good morning!' Akhil Banerjee called out.

'Good morning, sir!' replied Chandan Mukherjee, rubbing his hands together. 'I dare say, the winter this time seems to be more severe than last year.'

'The cold is *jompesh, moshai*,' said Bibhuti Bose. 'Let's order the tea.'

'Bibhuti babu, I did not see you at the club yesterday?' asked Chandan Mukherjee, sitting down on the bench. 'Jyoti da was looking for a bridge partner. He does not want to take Bhotchaj—you know how he is hard of hearing and always gives a wrong call...'

'*Arrey, moshai*,' replied Bibhuti Bose, having signaled 'four' to the tea-shop owner, 'Have gotten myself into a bit of a situation.'

'What situation?' asked Debdas Guha Roy, approaching the bench.

'The other day, I ran into an old classmate of mine. Jotin Ghosh. We had studied in City College together. Naturally, we were very excited to see each other after so many years, and Jotin insisted that I visit him soon. He has a house on Lake View road. So I went there the following Friday, and there I met a few other batchmates. Shoibal Dhar, Ashit Ranjan Guha, Udaybhanu Roy. All fossils, by the way—one has had a cataract operation, one is hard of hearing, one has had an angioplasty done...anyway, the evening was very enjoyable, we indulged in old fashioned *adda*, we reminisced about our good old days, and we all agreed that we should meet again soon. Ashit Ranjan suggested that we meet in his house the following week. So again I went, and by this time the number had increased from five to twelve. Yesterday, Abhoy Kanti Chowdhury invited us to his house. There are many more of us now. Eighteen! Can you imagine? And Abhoy Kanti—well he has his family business, so obviously there is no retirement for him—has this huge house in Raja Basanta Roy Road. And instead of just tea and snacks, he served us a catered meal. Bijoligrill Caterers. *Fish chop, hinger kochuri, chholar daal, alur dom, roshomalai.* Very delicious, but quite unnecessary, if you ask me. So now, given the success of these frequent get-togethers, it has been suggested that each one of us volunteer to host one in the coming weeks. *Moshai*, now I'm finding it difficult to wiggle out of this situation. One or two others have already volunteered. Very soon, it will be my turn, *moshai.* The thing is, I wouldn't mind having a few close friends over to my house...but so many of them?'

'*Arrey*, Bibhuti babu, you worry needlessly. People tend to be enthusiastic about these reunions at the start, but very soon it fizzles out,' replied Chandan Mukherjee.

'Maybe you are right. And there is something else about these meetings that is beginning to bother me. Somehow, I always come home a little...saddened.'

'Saddened?'

'Well, perhaps saddened is too strong a word—what I mean is this: there was this time, when we were all young and believed we would do great things. We were so full of hope, full of confidence. You see that in young people today as well, don't you? You see it in the way they talk, the way they carry themselves, as if they own the world. At some point, we thought the same, didn't we? Did we think we would get old so soon? Did we realize that this energy, this hope, this belief was fleeting. That we'd blink and our time would be up? Kaushik Sen, one of my classmates, said the other day, "Bibhuti, we expected you to do something different. We thought you would be a writer." I was surprised to hear that, believe me. But it is true, I used to write articles and poems for the college magazine. I had completely forgotten about it! Yet, someone remembered. After all these years, he remembered those few insignificant lines that I had written in some magazine, and which, at that time, must have been such a rush of inspiration. But what did I make of my life, tell me? I took up a regular job, just like everyone else and lived an ordinary life.'

'*Arrey,* everyone has had those dreams, Bibhuti babu,' said Debdas Guha Roy, shaking his head. 'Being a poet sounds romantic, *moshai*, but real life is very different. One has to think of earning a livelihood, or else in our society you will be labelled reckless and irresponsible. After all, we were not born with a silver spoon in our mouths, were we?'

'It does not matter how and where you were born, Debdas babu,' continued Bibhuti Bose, with the remnant of that East Bengali accent that still laced his tongue. 'Life has a cruel way of playing the harshest jokes on you. That I can tell from experience. My father and grandfather were barristers in Dhaka. We had a sprawling house. At least twenty bedrooms. We would eat fresh fish caught from our own pond, and feed on mangoes grown in our own orchards. What happened to all that? Overnight, we had to leave everything and flee to India during the Partition. My father and my elder brother took a wad of money, few hundred rupees at the most, and hid it in the soles of their shoes. Somehow, we managed to reach Calcutta, and stayed with a relative here. Slowly, bit by bit, we had to reconstruct our lives from scratch. Dada studied medicine and joined the Army. Later, to fulfil the familial demands he got married and had a son. Things had started looking up for us, when one day came the news of his sudden death. He was posted in Rajasthan at the time. His son would be what—five or six years old at the time? Baba was in a state of shock. I was still in college and there were two sisters to be married off. One day, Baba's friend, Bishu Banerjee, whom we called Bishu kaku, came to our house. Said he wanted to speak to me. A British company, Andrew Yule, was hiring apprentices. Put in your application, he had said. What choice did I have?'

'*Moshai,* what is gone, is gone,' said Akhil Banerjee. 'Fretting and worrying about the past, is not helping the present, is it? Just remember, Bibhuti babu, you took the best possible decision at that time. With the family situation as it was, do you think you would have been happier being a poet? I doubt it. Our moral obligations, our social responsibilities come way before any personal indulgences, *moshai*. That is the way we have been brought up. Perhaps, the young people of today would call us foolish. Perhaps, many of them cannot see any value in sacrifice. And perhaps, when we see them giving their chosen careers utmost importance, we are quick to call them selfish. The thing, Bibhuti babu, is to trust that whatever decisions we have taken in the past, were the ones best possible under those circumstances. Otherwise, one can be caught up in regret for ever.'

'There have been instances in history, though, where men have defied all norms of society and followed their true calling with an unshakeable faith,' said Debdas Guha Roy. 'Take the example of our very own Swamiji. Swami Bibekanondo. At one time, after his father's death, his family was heavily in debt. He had a mother and a younger sister to look after. Pressures from all sides, to take up a job and support his family.

'*Moshai*, the story goes that he went to Thakur Sri Ramkrishna. And Thakur said to him, "Naren, something seems to be bothering you...just go tell Ma Kali. She will grant you anything tonight."

So Swamiji went to pray in the Kali Mandir. You would think, in such a situation, any man would ask for the obvious—job, money, security… But guess what Swamiji asked for? Three things—*gyan, bibek, bairagyo*. Knowledge, conscientiousness, dispassion. Can you imagine?'

'Swami Bibekanondo was a Mahapurush, *moshai*. Not an ordinary human being like you and me,' commented Chandan Mukherjee.

'Bibhuti babu, I completely understand what you are going through,' said Debdas Guha Roy. 'Back in college, I too had grand ambitions. Once I had almost become the treasurer of a literary club. I could give impromptu speeches in public, which to the casual listener appeared well rehearsed. Once or twice, I was even approached by various student political parties, believe me!' He laughed. 'But now I think, thank God I did not step in that direction.'

'I see the uselessness in dwelling in the past,' said Bibhuti Bose. 'Now, the problem is how to get out of this situation?'

'Just stop going to these reunions, Bibhuti babu,' offered Chandan Mukherjee.

'It may not be so easy,' said Akhil Banerjee. 'One point of advice I can give you, Bibhuti babu, is not to put your name down in writing anywhere. For example, if someone wants to make a list of who will volunteer when in future…if you put down your name, there is absolutely no escape!'

'Why is that so, Joj Saheb?'

'You see, most of these situations start small. First, there were only a few friends, a casual tea. Quite harmless and enjoyable. Naturally, if such a reunion happens again, you will go. But by attending the reunions a few times, you have created for yourself an image in front of your friends—an image of someone who enjoys coming to these meetings, someone who enjoys social gatherings. Now, even without being conscious of it, you will try your very best to live up to this image. Why? Because it shows consistency in your character. If you suddenly stop coming, citing whatever excuse, it would be considered inconsistent with your past behaviour. And inconsistency is not easy to live with. A lot of what we think of ourselves is really what others think of us, isn't it? And if others start seeing us in a light that is not entirely desirable, then it gives rise to further problems. Trust me, there have been many psychological studies on this, *moshai.*'

'But that part about writing something down?' asked Debdas Guha Roy. 'What is that about, Joj Saheb?'

'Hmm…human behaviour is quite interesting. There are two things at play here, consistency, followed by commitment. You don't want to come across as someone "inconsistent", but coupled with that, if you make a commitment of some sort—and usually written commitments are much stronger than verbal ones—it is almost impossible to slime out of the deal. Marketing professionals use this tactic very effectively.

'Have you ever wondered why companies selling toothpaste or washing powder or instant noodles or even credit cards, often announce these contests, where participants have to write a slogan or a short essay? Usually the best entry is promised a cash prize coupled with the possibility of having their slogan or essay used for the company's marketing purposes. Correct? Actually, there is something else at work here.' He paused. 'You see, for any such contest, there are usually thousands, maybe lakhs of entries. Am I right? Now, each of these participants will spend some time thinking about how best to write his essay or slogan. Naturally they will have highlighted the benefits of the product, maybe even compared it with other brands in the market. And then they would write it down. So, the next time they are in the market shopping for washing powder or toothpaste or instant noodles, which brand do you think they will choose?'

'Ah ha! I see,' exclaimed Chandan Mukherjee. 'Just because they have written good things about a product, they must now be consistent with their own behaviour, and buy only that brand.'

'Exactly!' said Akhil Banerjee.

'My God!' exclaimed Debdas Guha Roy. 'I had never thought this way.'

'There are many such interesting examples. During the Korean War, the Chinese communists used a very simple technique to make the American prisoners of war co-operate with them. The technique proved to be extremely successful, and hardened American soldiers found themselves co-operating with their captors wholeheartedly. As a result, escape plans were easily thwarted. Now, the question is: what did the Chinese do?

'An American psychologist by the name of Edgar Schein, who interrogated the soldiers returning after the war, found out details of the Chinese tactic. It seems, the soldiers were first asked to make a statement, that, on the face of it, seemed fairly harmless and not at all derogatory to their own country. It did not seem very pro-communist either. Like say, *America is not a perfect country.* Or something like, *in a communist country, unemployment is not a problem.* Once a soldier had uttered these seemingly minor statements, he was then asked by the interrogator to list some points why he thought America was not perfect. He would then be asked to write down the list, and sign on the bottom of it, maybe even read it out to fellow prisoners. He might then be asked to elaborate on the points he had listed in a short essay. His essay would then be broadcast on radio, not only to his camp, but also to other POW camps in both North and South Korea.

And before he knew, he had suddenly created for himself the image of a pro-communist, a collaborator. The most ingenious part of this technique is that the soldier is fully aware that none of these utterances have been coerced out of him. They were all pretty much voluntary on his part. And henceforth, he would try his best to remain consistent with the image his fellow prisoners and his captors have of him.

'Sometimes the captors conducted political essay contests—the prize would be something insignificant, like say a couple of cigarettes. More often than not, the winning essay would be something that was heavily pro-Communist. But again, the captors showed remarkable foresight. Once in a while, the winning essay would be one that was heavily pro-American, but with a few points mentioned here and there that were in favour of the Chinese. The outcome was exactly what the Chinese had wanted. The prisoners continued to participate voluntarily in these contests, for now they could remain completely loyal to their country and still win. But in order to increase their chances of winning, they would, perhaps unconsciously, write more and more pro-Communist statements. The Chinese were quick to use these to their advantage. After all, this was a completely voluntary exercise and that too in writing for all to see!'

'Hmm...interesting!' sighed Bibhuti Bose. 'So, if I have to get out of this, I have to do it fast. Before I am asked to volunteer my name in writing!'

Chandan Mukherjee let out a hearty laugh, slapping his friend lightly on his back. 'All the best, Bibhuti babu!'

'Talking of old classmates,' said Akhil Banerjee, 'I too ran into one the other day.'

Boys Will Be Boys

Piya Guha Roy waited at the bus-stop near Jodubabu's bazaar, with its endless shops that sold multi-coloured woollen caps, sweaters and mufflers alongside plastic Santa Claus dolls in red suits, garlands of Christmas lights and artificial trees of all sizes. She was half-tempted to pick up a tree and a Santa Claus, but she desisted. Perhaps she was too old for that sort of thing.

As a young child, she remembered coming home from school one day terribly upset with the fact that a certain someone called Santa Claus, who had apparently visited her friends' homes during the holidays with gifts, had not set foot in theirs. Diya, her younger sister, had burst into tears, having been told by a friend that Santa Claus only visited homes of children who had been good the entire year. *What was the point then, in getting up early every day, doing her studies, finishing her plate even when she was already full, when these apparent hardships went entirely unnoticed in the eyes of Santa Claus—whoever he was,* she had questioned between her sobs. Their father, Debdas Guha Roy, had attempted to explain that Santa Claus only visited Christian homes, and since they were Hindus, gifts would be restricted to Durga Pujo, provided, of course, they still remained good.

The logic had failed to hold good with his daughters. Sonali, Mithu, Debarati were NOT Christians, and not entirely 'good children' at that. This sense of having been grievously wronged had made them brood for two whole days. The following week, which was sometime in early January, their parents had taken Piya and Diya to a movie—*The Sound of Music*, playing in The Lighthouse. It had been one of the most memorable outings of their young lives. Not only did they get to watch an English movie in a movie hall, they were even treated to ice creams later in New Market. And as if all that was not enough, the following morning, on waking up, they had found a pair of discarded socks on their beds, filled with plastic goodies and candy. Santa Claus had come to their home, after all! Piya caught herself smiling at the memory. In their excitement, they had not once questioned the fact that both sisters had received identical gifts—plastic whistles, erasers, balloons, streamers—that looked suspiciously like the ones displayed in a shop near the ice cream parlour, with its large 50% OFF discount tags.

Piya checked her watch for the third time, and fanned her face with the loose end of her dupatta. Even December days, once the sun was well above our heads, tended to be hot.

It amused her to see people on the street—only a few, of course—sporting 'haat-kata' sweaters, a sleeveless woolen garment that somehow always bore an unfinished look. According to Piya, one should either wear a full-sleeve sweater or none at all. What was the point in telling the cold, *I'm prepared for you, but not fully!* The same argument could be extended to sleeveless kurtas or blouses as well, of course. But those attires, Piya reminded herself, were meant for the summers, where one was rather inclined to shed parts of a garment that were deemed not strictly necessary.

A sudden flurry of excitement forced Piya to come out of her reflections on the practicalities of seasonal garments. A bus had been sighted and seemingly normal people, who had been patiently waiting at the stop for the past fifteen minutes, instantly lost all sense of calm. A race to board the bus was followed by pushing, shoving, elbowing one's way inside in the hope of finding a place to stand.

She recalled... A cousin of hers had once remarked, 'Did you know, that there are people in Calcutta who have never seen what the inside of a bus looks like?' The thought had amazed Piya. It had seemed incredible at that time to think that there were people that rich in this city, where so many dwelt on pavements in every corner. She could understand how some people had never had the *need* to board a bus, having been born into luxury by fate, but not even knowing what a bus looks like from the inside!? Her cousin had, then, hastened to clarify, 'That's because they have been hanging from the door of the bus all their lives!'

Piya took a deep breath, clutched her handbag and prepared herself for the ordeal. Once inside, she elbowed her way through the standing passengers, found herself a spot to stand and held on to the back of a seat for support. Beside her stood a lady, probably in her late twenties, struggling with a baby in one arm and a Big Shopper bag in the other. Unable to hold on to anything for support, she swerved back and forth every time the bus halted or restarted. When the conductor approached her for the ticket, she had no way of fishing out her money, much to his irritation.

'Why can't you keep the money ready, *boudi*?' he snapped at her.

Piya shot him a look, held out a note and signaled 'two'.

'For you and...?'

'Her.' She pointed at the lady beside her, who, on realizing what Piya was doing, protested vehemently.

'It's alright,' assured Piya. 'It's not much.'

'Thank you, *didibhai*.'

All this while, Piya noticed that the seats right in front of them were occupied by two young men, who witnessed the scene without the slightest moral compunction. *The least they could have done was to offer the lady a seat*, thought Piya. She was half-tempted to tap the man sitting nearest to her and ask him to get up, but checked herself. There was always a possibility that the person might retort back in an unpleasant manner, *Ki, didi? You talk about 'equality' and 'gender bias' all the time! What happens when we have to keep standing? Do you ever offer us your seats?*

Piya was all for equality and women's rights. But at times like these, she wondered if perhaps the price of such movements was the fast disappearance of basic human courtesy. She remembered once, when she was much younger, she had been standing by the side of the street with her mother, who had been trying in vain to hail a taxi for a long time. Piya had pointed out to her mother, that it was not enough to simply wave a hand, she needed to yell 'Taxi!' at the top of her voice like the others were doing. Her mother had looked scandalized. *It is unthinkable for a lady to holler like a man*, she had said to Piya. *Sooner or later, some taxi driver will surely notice us*, mother had added. Eventually, a young man, a 'dada', with a half-filled glass of black tea in one hand and an unfinished cigarette in the other, baring his hairy chest under a thread-bare *sando-genji*, had come to their rescue. And the very next taxi that had come whizzing was made to halt. Chivalry did show its face once in a while, in the streets of Calcutta, even if it did not come clad in shining armor.

The bus turned right onto Middleton Row, her school '*paara*', and Piya got ready to alight. This was yet another ordeal. Often bus-drivers were in such a hurry to complete their routes that they did not even bother to come to a halt. They would simply slow down and expect the passengers to jump off. Most boys and men were adept at this, having jumped on and off buses all their lives. Piya braced herself as she neared the door.

On seeing her, the conductor of the bus announced, '*Aastey ladies!* (Slow down, we have a lady passenger),' followed by, '*Aastey ladies, koley baccha!* (Slow down further, we have a lady with a baby in her arm!).'

One should always be thankful, smiled Piya, as she got off—'gender equality' or not, women in Calcutta were not expected to jump off buses. Yet.

She made her way to the 'Success Language Training Institute: Self-confidence in 10 modules'. Piya had been appointed as a part-time teacher of spoken English with classes three times a week. The size of the class was small, hence manageable. And after some minor adjustments in the schedule of her other students, the ones she gave private tuitions to, Piya found that this job, temporary though it might be, was an easy way to triple her income. The students, mostly from humble backgrounds, having studied in vernacular mediums in the city suburbs, were not the brightest. But that was expected. And that was the challenge, Piya had told herself.

Now, making her way through the busy street, half-turning ever so often to allow passers-by coming from the opposite direction, Piya glanced at her wristwatch to check if she had time to stop at the cyber cafe around the corner. It would be tight, she decided.

It was then that for a flickering second the uneasy feeling that had been bothering her lately, returned. She glanced behind her shoulder briefly. Then turned around and quickened her pace.

*

Kanai stopped abruptly, unsure of whether to climb up the remaining stairs with Kortababu's cup of tea, or to climb down in order to answer the door. He hesitated a second, then decided on the latter. Leaving the cup and saucer on the marble-topped table in the hallway, he sauntered towards the door.

'*Iye*...is Akhil in?'

Kanai hesitated.

'Kortababu?'

'Yes, Joj Saheb,' clarified the visitor.

Kanai nodded and led him into the drawing room.

'What name shall I say, babu?'

'Biren. Biren Ghoshal.'

Biplab Maity smashed a mosquito that had quietly landed on his left thigh, then flicked it away like it was a striker on a carom board. He was seated on the sole table in the clubhouse, the table that—depending on need and availability—served as a platform for playing cards, carom, or chess. At this moment, which was close to 11 in the morning according to the cobweb covered wall-clock, however, no enthusiasts of the aforesaid games had come forward to claim their right on the table. Which was why, Biplab Maity, President of Sabuj Kalyan (Youth) Association, had hoisted himself on top of it and was now contemplating whether to have his third cup of tea.

A few feet away from him, seated on the floor, were Bappa, Soumen and Jishu, bending over, what Biplab could only presume to be, a film magazine. Bappa had the centre page spread open on his lap.

'*Ei!* What are you boys looking at?' he asked, feigning mild interest.

'Nothing,' replied Soumen, pulling himself back, eyes still glued to the photograph of the Tollywood actress, who the magazine claimed was the starlet to watch out for.

'Which magazine is that?' Biplab persisted.

'*Anandolok*.'

Biplab smirked. *Boys! They just cannot help it, can they? If not a picture in a magazine, then a damsel in the neighbourhood. What can one possibly do with this bunch of good-for-nothings, their brains occupied with but a singular point of interest!*

'Read something better, boys,' said Biplab in a disparaging tone. 'Something to enrich your minds.'

The words failed to produce any noticeable effect. The three continued to ogle at the pictures in the magazine. Beside them, Poltu, who bore the look of someone who had been denied entry into an exclusive club, sat digging out the contents of his nose, examining them all along with acute interest.

Biplab continued undeterred, 'Like...say...*Desh Potrika*, or *India Today*. Do you have any idea what is happening in the world today? Any idea at all?'

Some faint pricking of the conscience might have stirred the trio. Bappa shut the magazine and cast it aside.

'What's the point, Biplab da?' he asked, stretching his arms and attempting to speak while letting out a yawn. 'What difference does it make to us, what happens in the world?'

'You see?!' exclaimed Biplab. 'This is the very problem with you boys!'

Having made this pronouncement with a fair degree of conviction, Biplab allowed himself a moment of quiet reflection. It was, in all fairness, difficult to single out one problem with this lot. Indeed, there were too many.

First, their utter lack of interest in anything remotely intellectual—like, say for example, literature, or history or the sciences. Here Biplab reined himself back—science, or at least what was taught beyond Class X, was not his forte. He could never get his head around those complicated diagrams with arrows pointing every which way, hitting surfaces, then getting reflected back, then hitting something else. Or problems with those utterly unlikely scenarios—an iron ball going up on a pulley, and another coming down, then one being hit by a third ball somewhere en route. Try as he might, Biplab could never imagine, where on earth such occurrences took place. And hence, the usefulness of calculating the final momentum—once all the iron balls were done colliding—was completely lost on him.

Then there was mathematics. Just when you had mastered the integers and fractions and decimals, and the addition, subtraction, multiplication, division thereof, some mathematician with a twisted mind and a little too much free time on his hand, brought into the picture a whole new alphabet! Did it really matter, Biplab had often asked himself while struggling with calculus, if we did not know the exact instant of time when the car had changed velocity from 30 kilometres an hour to 32? What difference did it make? Yet so much time was wasted in breaking up moments into instances, then breaking them down further and further, till all you were left with was that infinitesimally small instant between one event and the next.

Only once, according to Biplab, had that tiny instance, that fleeting dot in the timeline of his life, had had any significance for him. It was an afternoon at the college canteen. Biplab, then a 2nd year student, had had a heated argument with Buro da over cold *singaras*. Buro da was close to sixty—really way beyond the 'dada' years—but the suffix had been handed down to him by generations of college students. And the increasing age difference between Buro da and a fresh batch entering the college had never been factored into the equation of familiarity.

Normally, Biplab Maity would not have created a ruckus. But that particular day—perhaps it was fate—he had been particularly flustered over the temperature of his samosas. Having expressed his dissent, he had turned to return to his seat, when Surochita Purokayastha, a fresher from History Honors, the girl whom everyone had been eyeing, had given him an empathetic look. A brief look—but a look none-the-less.

Biplab had noticed a half-eaten samosa on her plate, and presumed, rightly so, that hers too had been served cold. He would have gone back to yell at Buro da again, for serving cold samosas to Surochita Purokayastha (First year, History Honours), but she had left by then.

Throughout the rest of the day, and indeed the rest of that week, that instant—infinitesimally small though it was—came back to him, again and again. And Biplab Maity had found himself regaining respect for calculus, and the importance of breaking down moments, further and further, till one reached that exact point of time when Surochita's doleful eyes had met his own.

Next on the list of problems in general with the boys of Sabuj Kalyan (Youth) Association, was their constant pre-occupation with the female of our species. Where was the time to indulge in anything intellectual, when a large part of your brain—tiny in itself—was filled with thoughts of girls? Biplab knew that a significant part of their day was spent atop the boundary wall of Sabuj Kalyan Park. What view could it possibly offer? The slums of Haripada Das lane, the queue of rickshaw-wallahs smoking biris, vendors with their carts filled with vegetables? No. They sat there to ogle at the neighbourhood girls passing by. Biplab knew most of the girls in the *paara*, and frankly, not one of them came close to Surochita Purokayastha. That lissome body, those large round eyes, thick black hair that was braided at the back, the heady aroma of jasmine—doubtless from some feminine talc... His thoughts wandered yet again to that afternoon in the college canteen and the memory of that first time when his heart had skipped a beat, the memory that lay hidden in some obscure recess of his mind, and now suddenly brought back because of a stray thought involving a bunch of good-for-nothings.

Biplab forced himself to return to the situation at hand. He took a deep breath before continuing.

'Unless you expand your minds, broaden your horizons, how do you hope to achieve *any thing* in life?!'

Soumen, Bappa and Jishu gaped back, silenced by the sheer gravity of his words. Even Poltu was forced to momentarily halt inspection of his latest excavation.

'Do you boys know Shakespeare?' asked Biplab Maity, seizing the moment.

'Of course!' replied Soumen. 'Who here doesn't know Shakespeare?' He tilted his head sharply to imply the ridiculousness of the question asked.

'Really?' Biplab da was taken aback.

'*Bah!*' said Soumen, 'Shakespeare—Habul da's son! Don't you remember? He failed Madhyamik exams for the third time, then ran away from home. We all went looking for him. Habul da was sick with worry. Then Bhombol—I think it was Bhombol, I'm not sure—discovered a scribbling on the wall behind their house. "*Ami polai ni. Ashey pashey ghur ghur koritechi* (I haven't run away. I'm in and around here only)."'

'*Duss!*' exclaimed Biplab da. 'Not Habul da's son Shakespeare! I'm talking about Ouilliam Shakespeare, the English playwright. Though one can't help but snigger at Habul da...naming his son Shakespeare of all things! Was he expecting him to write literature?!' He allowed himself a chuckle.

'Who the hell is Ouilliam Shakespeare?' asked Jishu.

Biplab smiled. It was a smile of relief coupled with assurance.

His suppositions, regarding the utter ignorance of his audience, were still intact.

'Some may say he is the greatest writer that ever lived,' pronounced Biplab with elan.

'What are you saying Biplab da? Is he better than our own Robi Thakur? Impossible!' cried out Bappa, disregarding the fact that he hardly had any authority to comment, having read neither Robi Thakur nor Shakespeare.

'Ah! I'm not comparing, Bappa. I'm just saying Ouilliam Shakespeare was a universally acclaimed playwright. He wrote many dramas…mostly on *prem*—love.' His voice drawled more than he had intended. Bappa and Jishu stole surreptitious glances.

'Haven't you heard of *Romeo and Juliet*? The greatest love story ever written?' continued Biplab da. 'Juliet would stand on the balcony and Romeo, her lover, on the street below would call out to her.'

'Oh yes!' called out Poltu, hurriedly wiping his fingers on his shirt. 'Romeo! Now I remember…he comes in a song…doesn't he?' He squinted his brows trying to recall the exact lyrics.

I don't want to be Romeo
So please take your afternoon nap
No need to stand on the balcony anymore
Ronjona, I won't come again
Ronjona, I won't come again…

Biplab da, you've got the chick's name wrong. It's Ronjona not… not…'

'Idiot! The chick's name is Juliet!' cried Biplab da. 'At least, in Shakespeare's play it is Juliet. They are iconic lovers. Anytime, anywhere you think of…'

'If you won't believe me, I will play the cassette for you,

Biplab da,' protested Poltu. 'The chick's name is Ronjona. Anjan Dutta's album. I still have it somewhere in my collection.'

'Shut up, Poltu!' yelled Soumen. 'Biplab da is talking.' He shot Poltu a reproachful look. For once Biplab da had hit upon an interesting topic, and trust Poltu to ruin it.

Poltu looked deflated.

'Please go on, Biplab da,' urged Bappa, with as innocent an expression as he could manage.

Biplab da sat silently, as if trying to recall the train of thought before Poltu's interruption.

'Hmm, where was I? Ah yes! Romeo and Juliet.'

'Did you study English literature, too?' The question was asked by Partho who had just entered the clubhouse. 'I thought you had mentioned you were a science student?'

Biplab Maity half-turned his head towards the door.

'Feel like having tea,' he said in response. '*Ei* Poltu!'

Poltu looked away. This was so typical. Just when something interesting was about to be discussed, Poltu would be sent out on a useless errand. Why not ask Partho? He was closest to the door, wasn't he?

'*Ei* Poltu! Couldn't you hear? Biplab da wants tea,' called out Partho, in a tone that was almost proprietorial.

Poltu got up reluctantly and made his way to the door.

'And get some biscuits and potato chips for us as well,' added Soumen.

'What about mon...?'

'*Ki bolli*? What did you say?!'

'Umm...nothing.'

Biren Ghoshal Has News to Share

'*Arrey,* Biren?' asked Akhil Banerjee stepping into his living room. '*Bosh, bosh.* Sit.'

'I must apologize, Akhil. Dropping in like this, without calling up first…'

'*Arrey*, no, no. What are you saying?! Tell me, what seems to be the matter?'

Akhil Banerjee settled down in the armchair and asked Kanai, who was waiting at the door, to fetch tea.

'It is like this…' started Biren Ghoshal, settling back on the sofa. 'You remember my room-mate at Kothari's? Probhat Sanyal?'

'The manager at the Makaibari tea garden?'

'Yes, him. Well, he called up the other day. Last Tuesday, in fact. We talked about this and that, and he invited me to his place. If I am ever in that part of the city, I should just drop by. No need to inform beforehand. You know, the old Bengali way? No formalities, just drop by for *adda*.'

'Hmm, okay.'

'So, the other day—this last Friday—I was at Taratola on some work. Finished early, so thought why not go see Sanyal babu. The gentleman's house—I had noted down the address—was at James Long Sarani, not too far from where I was. So I simply boarded a bus, and got dropped off almost in front of his house.

I rang the doorbell and waited. No one came out for a while. So I rang the bell again. I could hear that the television inside was on. There had to be somebody home.

'I knocked and eventually a young man answered the door. I immediately recognized him—Rajib, he used to visit Sanyal babu in the hospital every day. He could not place me right away. But when I mentioned Kothari, he recognized me instantly.'

He paused the narration. Kanai had brought in tea and biscuits. Biren Ghoshal took a sip before continuing.

'He took me inside, to the living room, brought me a glass of water and then broke the news. Sanyal babu was dead. Died of a heart attack on Tuesday itself! I couldn't believe it, Akhil. He had called me up that very morning, we had spoken for almost twenty minutes!'

He put the saucer on the table.

'I guess death never takes a prior appointment, but still—as you can imagine—I was quite shaken. Probhat babu's brother, Probir babu, came to see me. He was still in the white attire, hadn't shaved for some days—their days of *"asauch"* were still not over. I offered my condolences.

'It seems on Tuesday evening, he was served dinner in his room as usual. Sometime later, Probir babu went to his room and his brother collapsed suddenly, before his very eyes. They did not even have time to call a doctor or an ambulance.

'I asked them, if Probhat babu had seen the ghost again—you know, the ghost of Kurseong that he had told me about—and Probir babu, well, he completely denied having heard of any such thing. He dismissed it as rubbish! I was quite taken aback, Akhil. I thought it was common family knowledge. But not only did Probir babu not know of any such happening, he even accused me of tainting his family name with such a cock-and-bull story.

His tone had begun to sound less and less polite. So what could I do? I apologized and left.'

He paused. Sounds of young boys playing cricket could be heard on the street outside. A water pump had been switched on nearby. Its low hum was interspersed by the high nasal voice of a vegetable vendor calling out the contents of his cart. 'Potatoes, beans, cauliflower…'

'This thing has been bothering me, Akhil,' continued Biren Ghoshal. 'Did Probhat Sanyal really invent the whole story? Or was it a figment of his imagination? And why, after almost a month, did he suddenly call me that particular day, only to die a few hours later? I have not been able to sleep well these past two nights. Kept recalling that night at the hospital, and how scared he was thinking that the phantom had returned. So finally, this morning, I decided that I should talk to you.'

Akhil Banerjee took his time to respond.

'Hmm…when Probhat babu called you that day, did he mention the ghost?'

'Well no…and I did not ask either…but you know what? I have a feeling he had wanted to tell me something. That's why he had asked me to come over. I can't be sure, though.'

'Did he say he was feeling unwell?'

'Well, I thought he sounded…anxious.'

'Hmm… It's quite possible that there is nothing sinister behind his death. His heart was weak, he had high blood pressure, was probably given to occasional drinking—it's difficult to kick out the habit once you've spent some years in a tea estate. In his condition, a heart attack is fairly common.'

'What about the ghost, Akhil? Are you saying he made up the whole story? What purpose would that serve?'

'It's always possible that he imagined the whole thing in an inebriated state. If you ask me, Biren, it is best not to dwell on this too much. There is probably nothing fishy about Probhat babu's death.'

'Hmm…I hope so, too, Akhil. But I have this feeling, this very uneasy feeling.'

*

Chhaya Guha Roy tossed the washed clothes absentmindedly on the faded, floral bed sheet spread out on the floor. She counted the items of clothing mentally: two shirts, three salwaar suits and a pair of her husband's trousers—faded and scuffed at the bottom from repeated wash. These would be bundled up and given to the ironing-man, the *istri-wallah*, when he came around. She hesitated a second or two. Should she give the Baluchori sari as well? The Gangulys were due to come see Piya this Sunday. A Baluchori would definitely make an impression. But one couldn't trust these roadside *istri-wallahs* with expensive silk saris. She should probably give it to the dry cleaners, but the one in their *paara*, James Bond Dry Cleaners, had the reputation of taking forever to do the job. And this being the winters, they were bound to be flooded with jackets, suits and shawls. She cursed herself for not having thought of this sooner.

It was difficult—if not particularly stressful—to have to shoulder the entire responsibility of finding a suitable match for Piya. In these matters, it always helped if the man of the house, the *korta*, took the initiative. Her husband, Debdas Guha Roy, though, would fail to recognize a prince if he came riding up to him on a white horse. Such were husbands, she sighed.

Why…only the other day, that ex-student of his, Subhrojit Dutta, had dropped by to pay his old teacher a visit. How many boys did that these days? That gesture alone spoke volumes about the family he had been raised in. Even though the purpose of the visit had become clearer only later, it did not take anything away from the fact that Subhrojit Dutta was as perfect a groom as one could have hoped for.

For one, he stood up the moment Chhaya Guha Roy had walked into the room with a cup of tea, and before she had had the time to protest, had stooped down and touched her feet. Her husband then introduced the boy as Subhrojit Dutta, Chartered Accountant, CA. Chhaya Guha Roy had promptly sauntered back to the kitchen to arrange a plate of *nimkis* and biscuits. Chartered Accountant—something about that degree (or was it a diploma?) had always fascinated Chhaya Guha Roy. Perhaps, it was the 'chartered' bit. Only 'accountant' suggested a mere clerical job. You could be an accountant with a B.Com. degree, and that was not something one necessarily wrote beside one's name.

There was this man though, in the Garcha road *paara* where she had lived before marriage, who had engraved 'B.Com.' on his name plate. *Abhijit Das, B.Com.* Everyone in the neighbourhood ended up calling him 'B.Com. Das'. In those days perhaps, a B.Com. degree was worth something, but these days you needed initials like CA for a decidedly better chance of employment.

In any case, qualifications that allowed you to write an array of initials after your name, without a doubt added a certain something to your whole persona. And in some cases, Chhaya Guha Roy had noted, the acronyms had succeeded in giving an otherwise unassuming name, a rather lofty aura: Komol Ray, F.M.C.S., or Dola Sen, MPhil., PhD.

So it was, that when she heard the name Subhrojit Dutta, and mentally added the CA after it, she felt compelled to serve him savouries alongside the tea. When she had stepped into the living room a second time a plate of crisp *nimkis* in hand, she had overheard Subhrojit Dutta mention he had recently been offered a job at a top corporation, KPMG. More initials! Chhaya Guha Roy had hastily placed the plate on the centre table and retreated to the kitchen hoping to find the last couple of *rosogollas* left over from a relative's visit some days ago. She had made a mental note of keeping the pantry well stocked, should such unexpected visits from successful (male) ex-students occur in the future.

While Subhrojit Dutta munched away the *nimkis,* Chhaya Guha Roy threw surreptitious glances at her husband. Could he really be this blind? Apparently, he could.

'What? What are you saying?' He had blurted out loud, completely oblivious of the eye-signals Chhaya Guha Roy was throwing his way. Husbands! If it was left to Debdas Guha Roy, Piya would stay a spinster for life!

'Where is your house?' she asked Subhrajit Dutta sweetly.

'At Bhobanipur, kakima.'

'Nice, nice. Who all are there in your family?'

'Just my parents and myself. My older sister got married two years ago. She lives in New Delhi now.'

Having thus apprised Chhaya Guha Roy of the members of his family, he had quickly added, 'Kakima, you must visit my home with Sir. My parents will be very happy to meet you both.'

'Yes, yes, of course, we will.' Chhaya Guha Roy shot her husband a triumphant look.

'I have to get going, sir,' said Subhrojit putting his empty plate down. 'Actually, I am in a bit of a hurry. Will be booking a car today. Have to pick up my father.'

'Stay for lunch,' offered Chhaya Guha Roy. 'It's almost ready.'

'Thank you, kakima. But another day, perhaps. And the next time I come, I will bring my wife along.'

'Wife?!'

'Well, yes…that is the main reason for my coming.' He had pulled out a wedding card from his side bag, and handed it over to Debdas Guha Roy. 'Next month. 21st January. Both of you must come.'

Chhaya Guha Roy had not intended for the long sigh. But she had not been able to help it.

Except for that minor glitch, Subhrojit Dutta would have been perfect for Piya, she told herself. And Piya too would have… she stopped the train of thought. Perhaps Piya would not have been as enthusiastic. She probably would have said—he was too short, or his glasses were too thick, or that his teeth stuck out even when his mouth was closed. A chartered accountant working at KPMG! What more could Piya want in her man?

It was difficult to comprehend girls of Piya's generation. In her time, all that mattered was that the boy's family background was respectable, and that he was earning a decent living. What else did one need for a happy life, really? But Piya said she wanted someone—what was the word she had used—'presentable'. Chhaya Guha Roy had struggled to comprehend the meaning. As long as one had eyes and ears in their proper places, one was presentable, wasn't he? Beyond that, it was unrealistic to expect every Bengali boy to look like Uttam Kumar.

And Piya herself was not exactly a wingless fairy, but she did have a pleasant face none-the-less. As Chhaya Guha Roy's mother-in-law had rightly remarked at the hospital, newborn grandchild in her arms, 'Despite the *suppressed* complexion, she is not that bad to look at.'

She set aside the Baluchori, and bundled up the remaining clothes. It would be an eventful week. There was that visit from the Gangulys. They had been postponing their trip to Calcutta, in spite of showing a lot of interest initially. It was perhaps understandable. For a boy like Dr Rajshekhar Ganguly, it was easy to imagine that there would be no dearth of well-qualified, beautiful brides. Just the fact that they had shown so much interest in Piya, wanting to come down to Calcutta all the way from Delhi, was surprising enough. But honestly, Chhaya Guha Roy was not too hopeful about this alliance. The boy was a cardiologist in a hospital in Delhi. His father was an IAS officer, currently in the Ministry of Human Resource Development, and his mother, a banker and an active social worker. Where was the match with their family? A retired professor of geology, a house-wife and an MA in English daughter who gave private tuitions and taught part-time in a language institute.

But still…you know what they say about marriages. It's all about what is written in your destiny.

Biren Ghoshal Has a Visitor

Biren Ghoshal slipped on his *panjabi* and patted his hair in place. The doorbell sounded, making him automatically glance at the wall-clock. 7.45. It's probably the paperboy, he thought.

The only people who came this early in the morning were the milkman and the paperboy, and they tended not to announce their arrivals unless it was time to collect their dues. One gave little thought to these arrivals, these little conveniences, except on rare days such as this one, when either the packet of milk or the newspaper was missing from the doorstep.

This morning when Biren Ghoshal had unlatched the door, he noticed, with mild irritation, that the paper was missing. Biren Ghoshal particularly hated not having the paper available first thing in the morning. It was a part of his morning ritual. He would unlatch the front door, then unlock the collapsible iron gate and push it to one side, and pick up the paper and the packet of milk that had been delivered earlier that morning. His eyes glued to the day's headline, he would leave the packet of milk on the dining table. By this time, his wife will have prepared a cup of tea—Goodricke—and he would be content to sit for the next half an hour or so, sipping the tea and glancing through the news.

It was not just that his morning ritual had been broken today—that was one reason for sure—but he did not, particularly, like the idea of starting the day without first having apprised himself of the situation in the world outside. It made him feel… unprepared, somehow.

'*Arrey*, Rajib?'

'Good morning, Mr Ghoshal. I am extremely sorry to drop in like this.'

'*Arrey*, no, no. Please come in.'

Rajib took off his shoes and followed Biren Ghoshal into the living room. He unwrapped his muffler, took off his denim jacket before settling down on the sofa. Biren Ghoshal called out to his maid to bring in two cups of tea.

'*Ki byapar?* What seems to be the matter?'

There was a brief hesitation before Rajib spoke.

'Sir, I have been thinking of coming to see you…ever since you visited the Sanyal house the other day. I knew you stayed in this neighbourhood, Sanyal babu had mentioned it.'

'My address?'

'I got it from the telephone directory.'

'*Oh achha*, I see.'

'Thing is…I have a feeling that Sir's death was not…may not…be due to a natural cause.'

Biren Ghoshal stiffened. 'You mean…?'

Rajib nodded gravely.

'But who? And how?'

'That I do not know. But I have a feeling something is not right.'

'Hmm…I've had this feeling too. I mean, Probhat babu had called me on 13th morning, had said he wanted me to visit him. At that time, I naturally did not give much thought to this. He was probably just being polite. But the fact that he passed away that very evening…did he want to tell me something specific, I cannot help but wonder.'

'There have been certain developments, of late,' said Rajib thoughtfully. 'I cannot really go into much detail right now. But something tells me there is more than what meets the eye.'

'Hmm...but why come to me?'

'I thought of going to the police, but what will I tell them? I have no proof against anyone.' He hesitated. 'Besides, I do not want to drag Sir's family into a mess unnecessarily. I was hoping you could give me some advice.'

'Do you suspect anyone in particular?' asked Biren Ghoshal.

Rajib nodded cautiously. 'But it's too early to point fingers at anyone...without proper evidence. You tell me, what should I do? '

'Me? But you hardly know me. Surely, there are other people...'

Rajib shook his head vigorously. 'I don't trust anyone,' he said. 'Besides, you are the only person, other than myself, to whom Sir has confided about the Kurseong incident. Even his own brother has no inkling about it.'

Biren Ghoshal felt a fresh pang of guilt. 'Yes, perhaps I was a little too hasty to mention that to his brother. Somehow, I thought it was common family knowledge. I mean, if Sanyal babu could confide in me, a complete stranger...'

Rajib made light of the accidental utterance with a slight wave of his hand.

'I think Sir trusted you. And that makes me want to trust you too, Ghoshal babu. Honestly, I don't know what to do. Should I let this matter rest? After all, Sir is not going to come back, is he? But then...this nagging feeling will haunt me till death. That perhaps someone did something terrible to him, and I did nothing to bring justice. You are a lawyer Mr Ghoshal. Tell me, what should I do?'

Biren Ghoshal thought for a moment before answering.

'I was thinking...would you mind meeting a friend of mine?'

*

It had not been a good start to the day.

It took Bibhuti Bose fifteen minutes or so to change into his informal wear of *lungi* and *fotua,* wrap an *alowan* over himself, settle into his favourite arm-chair and take a sip of the steaming tea. His wife had still not stopped grumbling.

'Carrots, snowpeas, brinjals…' he could hear Joyoti Bose mutter while taking stock of the contents of the *tholi,* the red and green striped nylon bag which Bibhuti Bose carried to the market every day. As far as Bibhuti Bose was concerned, it was not his fault at all. Yes, he did trust Jadu—the vegetable vendor at the market place—a little too much, perhaps. That much was true. It was a trust that had been earned over several years of acquaintance. It gave Bibhuti Bose a certain sense of comfort in 'knowing' who he bought his vegetables from…that man with a mole on his left cheek, and his unkempt hair, and his habit of touching the Rupee notes to his forehead every time a customer made a payment. A trust that, unfortunately, had not found favour with his wife. She insisted that Jadu and his friends had a nickname for her husband. *There comes Pocha-babu*, they said when they saw him coming. *Now all the vegetables that had been rotting all week will get sold!*

To say what happened today was Jadu's fault, was as unfair as comparing Messi to Maradona. When did Messi single-handedly tackle, dodge, dribble against eight outstanding players to score a goal? All these over-hyped players of today with their heavy endorsement deals…*Tchah!*

'What am I supposed to cook with this lot?! Will you tell me?' called out Joyoti Bose.

It was her fault to begin with, Bibhuti Bose had replied. He, as always, had dropped off his *tholi,* along with his wife's list, at Jadu's stall. And Jadu had—as always—read the list and stuffed Bibhuti Bose's *tholi* with the required vegetables. It was only when the contents of the *tholi* had been emptied at home that Joyoti Bose let out her first shriek of the day.

'*E ki?!*' Joyoti Bose had called out. 'Carrots, snow peas, brinjals, spinach…I had specifically told you *not* to bring these very things!'

'Huh?! What do you mean?' asked Bibhuti Bose, baffled.

'I had written it down in the list. Do you even read *the list*?' she emphasized.

'Of course, I do.'

'Where is it? Show me.'

'Here,' Bibhuti Bose had said, confidently waving a scrap of paper that he had fished out from the pocket of his bush shirt, now hanging from a hanger in his almirah. 'See this is your list. Carrots, brinjals…'

'Yes.'

'*Snow peas…*'

'Yes.'

'*Spinach…*'

'Yes.'

Bibhuti Bose stopped.

'*Ki holo?* Read on.' urged Joyoti Bose.

'*No need to bring…*' finished Bibhuti Bose.

Joyoti Bose had let out a long sigh.

'What is the point in sending you to the market, tell me?'

'Ah!' exclaimed Bibhuti Bose in an irritated tone. 'Whoever heard of a list of things *not required*? When you make a list it should be of things that you *require*!'

The arguments had gone on for a while. Other instances of

blunders made by Bibhuti Bose had been brought up. That time, many years ago, when they were going on a trip to Rishikesh and had an early morning train to catch and Bibhuti Bose had insisted on booking a taxi. They were all up and ready at the crack of dawn. The minutes ticked away, but the aforementioned taxi was nowhere in sight. Even though Joyoti Bose repeatedly insisted that they should go to the '*more*'—the junction of Uday Shankar Sarani and Haripada Das Lane—to hail another cab, Bibhuti Bose, confident of his taxi driver's sense of responsibility, had ignored his wife's rantings. They almost risked missing the train. When, weeks later, Bibhuti Bose had run into the taxi driver and had demanded an explanation, the driver had nonchalantly replied, 'But you never mentioned the date, babu.'

'Make the Botanical Garden dish!' Bibhuti Bose called out to his wife from the living room.

'Botanical Garden?'

'Yes, you know…the one in which you put every vegetable one can think of.'

'Oh! You mean *labda*?'

'Yes, yes, *labda*…goes very well with *khichuri*. The sky is cloudy today; perfect weather for *khichuri* and *labda*…maybe some *begunis* to go with it.'

'*Bah!* You've decided on the menu, I see.'

'Oh! And don't forget the tomato chutney…maybe some…'

The telephone ring interrupted his meal planning. Bibhuti Bose stretched his arm to reach for the receiver.

'Hello?'

'Hello, Bibhuti babu?'

'Yes, Chandan babu, tell me.'

'*Iye*…are you free this evening? Joj Saheb is calling us for tea.'

'Oh, is it?'

'Well, yes. It seems that friend of his, Mr Ghoshal—the one who was in the hospital—is coming to see him today. Possibly, Joj Saheb has an inkling that this is more than a casual visit. 5.30, okay?'

'Yes, yes. I will be there.'

Rajib Tells His Story

Piya got off the auto-rickshaw and instantly felt a gust of wind on her face. She paid the fare and wrapped the shawl tightly around herself. Light had faded in spite of the early evening hour, and the street, lit only by a flickering lamp-post around which insects buzzed in the hope of gathering warmth, bore a deserted look.

Piya clutched her handbag and made her way towards home. The temperature in these parts of the city—the quiet residential areas free of happening malls and sprawling corporate offices—was decidedly a degree or two lower than the busy 'office *paaras*'. The smell of roasting corn coming from the *thela* of a roadside vendor incited in her a fresh pang of hunger. She would be home in a few short minutes, and her mother would hasten to make her tea and warm her dinner, ask her about her day: How many students had come to class today? Are they taking interest in the lessons taught? That boy, Debojit, who had asked for a leave to attend his sister's wedding—was he back? Did Piya have to wait long for her bus back home? It was as if her mother, entangled in the web of domestic chores, had waited all day for news from the world outside. At times Piya wondered if her mother regretted, albeit in a small way, not having a career, not being able to go out there and prove her worth. That perhaps she was not perfectly happy shouldering domestic responsibilities all her life, looking after the husband, the daughters, their school, their extra-curricular activities—an entire lifetime gone in making sure the food was ready, the clothes were ironed, the books were packed, the fees were paid... Did her mother, while pursuing her master's degree in Bengali, think that all those notebooks filled with essays on the history of Bengali literature, right from its rudimentary beginnings, would be gathering dust in the attic? But the thought that her mother would rather have done something else had seemed so ridiculous that she had promptly waved it away. Yet, would Piya herself be ready to do this all her life?

And was she willing to give up the comfort of home, of having a freshly warmed dinner waiting for her when she returned each day, of making conversation, albeit about mundane things—people she had met, things she had seen on the street, a friend who had called—and settle for a life where she would return home to a stranger, too caught up in his own world to bother about which of Piya's students were doing well and which bus she had taken home that day?

The thought made her halt, briefly. A sudden, unexpected lump formed in her throat, and she blinked before tears could moisten her eyes. She took a deep breath and turned onto Haripada Das Lane.

There was the ironing man in the distance, humming a tune to himself, pressing clothes—a burning coal oven by his side served to keep him warm. The boundary wall of her home, atop which were pots of seasonal flowers—petunia, verbena, sweet william, phlox—came into view. A few short steps and she would be home.

It was then that she heard footsteps behind her and suddenly that uncomfortable feeling returned. Was she imagining it all, or did someone just emerge from the shadows behind? She quickened her pace, not daring to look back.

'Piya?' a voice, a whisper almost, called out.

She turned sharply and scanned the street, suddenly aware of her rapid heartbeat. The street was deserted. She turned around and quickened her pace. Half scampering, half walking, she did not stop till she had thrown open the gate and had run inside into the safety of her home.

*

'Perhaps you should start from the beginning,' said Akhil Banerjee, having introduced his guests Biren Ghoshal and Rajib, to the other members of The All Bengali Crime Detectives.

They were all seated in the retired judge's living room, tastefully decorated with furniture that had clearly lasted generations. The sofas had polished teak wood armrests and white cane that criss-crossed to form the seat and the back rest. An intricately designed red carpet—Persian perhaps—was spread on the floor, on which the guests could safely place their bare feet without the sting of the cold white marble floor. A large walnut wood wall-clock ticktock'd in the background. A pile of books on varied topics—impressionist art, psychology, world history, Bengali poems—rested on the centre table. Artefacts from all over the world—Masai hunter statues, Balinese masks, Australian aboriginal art—blended beautifully with the old-world furniture of the room, and gave it an understated *bonedi* charm, far from the ostentatiousness of the nouveau riche.

'Well, I have been working with Sir, that is, with late Mr Probhat Sanyal, for about seven years now,' started Rajib. His voice was soft yet had a distinguished quality about it. *Quite like the young man himself,* thought Akhil Banerjee. There was no ruggedness about his appearance, his features were soft. Yet it was clear he had seen more of the world than other young men his age. Youthful exuberance had been replaced with quiet dignity, and perhaps a trifle bit sooner than he would have liked. Like a bubbling stream that had suddenly lost its vitality on meeting the river. *He has responsibilities on his young shoulders, this man*, thought Akhil Banerjee.

'I graduated with a B.Com. from City College and soon after started hunting for a job,' continued Rajib. 'The situation of my family was never good. Both my parents had passed away when I was quite young, and I had been brought up by Pishimoni, my father's younger sister. She had decided she would not marry in order to be able to bring me up. She would do all sorts of odd jobs—sewing petticoats and blouses, doing embroidery work for neighbours, or even cooking meals and delivering them to bachelors who lived in the area. We live in a tiny two-room flat in Kasba, and I can still hear the sound of her sewing machine late into the night.

'We lived hand-to-mouth most of the time. There were days when Pishimoni would give me two rotis and lie to me about having eaten already. She would pop two *batashas* in her mouth, gulp it down with a glass of water and pretend she had had her dessert and was now full.

'Often I protested that I was old enough to find a job, but she would hear nothing of it. "Finish your studies first, it'll only be a few more years, and get a job in an office…then I will stop working," she would say.

'But finding a job was proving to be very difficult. There were no takers for a mere B.Com. graduate. I needed a higher degree or lacking that, at least a few years of job experience. But how was I to get any job experience if no one was willing to hire me in the first place? For almost three months I went from door to door looking for employment. My friends from college had already started preparing for CA and CS exams. Professional degree is necessary for getting a good job, they advised me. But I have seen people struggling to clear these exams…it could take anything from three to five years. I did not have that kind of time. Three months of visiting offices, and appearing for interview after interview, yielded no result. I was completely dejected.

'One day, after yet another rejection, I was sitting in a tea-shop, Kedar Da's cafe in Esplanade. I was completely drained out and tired, had no idea what I was going to do with my life, what I was going to tell Pishimoni…when I noticed a sign that said "Help Required". I looked around. There were maybe thirty tables, almost all were occupied. Young boys, 15-16 year olds in dirty shirts and khaki shorts were moving about, clearing tables, collecting bills and taking orders. I finished my cup of tea, and went straight to the manager. At first, he looked at me with scepticism. My appearance was not like the other waiters in the shop. I had clean clothes. I spoke like a *bhadrolok*, a gentleman. But I lied about my education, told him I was a high school drop-out and no one would hire me. I told him I can speak English and keeping an English speaking waiter would help him get business from foreigners. Esplanade had a fair share of foreign tourists who wanted a taste of "local" shopping in a relatively safe environment. I had seen a couple of whites in this very tea-shop. They had been struggling to explain their order to the waiter.

'Eventually, Kedar da agreed. I was to join the very next day at a salary of 2,000 rupees. I lied to Pishimoni. Told her I had a job in a very good office, and they were paying me very well. She was so proud of me, she went about distributing sweets to all the neighbours and telling them how this was the happiest day of her life.

'I started work at the cafe the following day. I tried not to think about how this was not what I should be doing. I just went through the motions all day, taking orders and clearing plates, wiping tables and collecting tips.

'There was a gentleman who came to the cafe often. And he would always order the same thing. Two pieces of toast, an omelette and a cup of Makaibari tea. The first time I heard that name, I said I will have to check if we had the particular brand. Kedar da had smiled and said, "Yes, we keep that tea especially for this client."

'He would come two or three times a week, usually around 11 in the morning. After the first few visits, he told me, "No need to come take my order. You know what to bring." I liked the gentleman. He was unlike our other customers. He never called me "waiter" or "boy". Always called me by my name. Unlike many other clients he never created a ruckus if the toast was a little burnt. And he always left me a big tip.

'Then one day, when I brought him his tea, he asked me to sit. I hesitated. He looked around the shop and said, "Look, there are hardly any customers now. Let's chat for a few minutes. I am sure Kedar will not mind." I was not very confident if Kedar da would be fine with this, so I declined. I did not want to lose the only job I had.

'So he asked me if I could take a break, so that we could go out somewhere and talk for a while. That I could easily do. So, I informed Kedar da and stepped out of the shop. We started walking towards New Market, and he asked me what I did before joining the tea-shop. I told him everything. My childhood as an orphan brought up by a spinster aunt, my college degree that was gathering dust. As I recounted my story I had a strange feeling that he had known all along that I was actually an educated man doing a menial job for the sake of putting food on the table. At the end of the conversation he offered me a job at his firm. He had a small company that acquired tea from different areas in India, then blended them. I told him I knew nothing of tea-blending, but he waved it aside. "You will learn what you need to," he said.

'I started work the following week. My salary was five times what I was getting at the tea-shop. Mr Sanyal (I finally learnt his name) said I was to be on probation for three months and then made permanent if I showed enough aptitude. Manohar babu, who was the senior accountant, took me under his wing. I was a fast learner, and I put my heart and soul into the job. Sir even offered to sponsor tutorials for my CA exam. He bought all the books I needed and pushed me to study hard. In three years, I had cleared the CA exams. I had become a chartered accountant! I could not believe my fortune. You should have seen Pishimoni that day! She couldn't stop crying. I bought her new saris, told her I will buy a scooter now so she need not walk all the way to and from the bazaar with heavy bags. It was perhaps the happiest day of our lives!

'I never believed in God. Or rather, even if God existed, I figured, He was really cruel to have taken my parents away so early, and for giving me a life that I felt I did not deserve. I felt that very strongly, when my friends would not think twice about spending money in a restaurant or going to the cinemas to watch a movie, while I had to walk my way back home to save the bus fare. I say all this just to let you know that for me, Sir was the closest thing to God. He would always tell me, "Rajib, whatever you do, don't leave this job. If you want money for anything, I will give it to you. You simply have to ask. But don't leave." And I would laugh and say, "Sir, I wouldn't dream of leaving even if I were offered three times my salary." Where would I get a boss as wonderful as him? When I met my old college friends, they always complained about their bosses. How horrible they were, how badly they treated their employees. I was thankful for the boss I had. He would take me out to restaurants for lunch, and we would spend hours in long conversations. We rarely talked about work at these times. It was always some story about his Darjeeling days—how he had spotted a leopard once while bird-watching, how he had felt when he had seen the Kanchenjunga for the first time... Sir was a bachelor, he had never married. And over time I figured he was not close to his brother's family, either. I guess, in some ways, we filled the void in each other's lives...his, to have a close friend or family, and mine, to have a father figure.

'Our business grew. We had offices, not only in Calcutta, but also in Mumbai and Chennai. Demand for exotic tea—from Sri Lanka, Japan, even South Africa—was increasing. Sir started giving me more responsibilities while he withdrew more and more from work. He had built a new house in Behala, where his father and his brother's family too moved in with him. I would visit his house often, perhaps to get a paper signed or to discuss an urgent office matter, and he never let me leave before having dinner.'

'Did he ever mention the ghost of Kurseong?' asked Akhil Banerjee.

Rajib nodded. 'Once, we were in his room. He was finishing his whisky. He usually had a peg almost every other evening. He would offer me a drink sometimes, and I would naturally refuse. But I always stayed on to ensure he did not overdo it. He started talking of this...accident. And how he had started seeing ghosts outside his window right after, and that made him pack up and leave the place for good.'

'And he had recently started seeing the ghost again in his Behala home, am I right?' asked Chandan Mukherjee.

'Yes, about two months ago, I had gone to Sir's place as usual. It was my birthday and I wanted his blessings. Sir insisted that I have dinner with him, but I knew Pishimoni had been cooking my favourite dishes all day, so I declined.

'I was on my way home—it was later than usual. Pishimoni had asked me to stop at the market and pick up some sweets on the way back. And then I get a call. It was Sir. His voice was choked with fear. He spoke in spurts as if he had difficulty in getting the words out…THE GHOST HAS RETURNED! THE GHOST HAS RETURNED! That is all he seemed to be able to say. I rushed back to his home immediately. He had calmed down considerably by the time I had arrived. Probably, had had a glass of brandy. But I insisted that he get a check-up done. He wouldn't listen. I suppose he was scared that his family would get alarmed.

'Then again, a month or so later, the same thing happened. I was on my way back home from the movies when he called. I went to his place immediately. This time, he was visibly more frightened, and I managed to convince him to see a doctor, at least to get his blood pressure checked. I assured him that his secret was safe with me. As it happened, the doctor saw that his BP was very high and suggested I take him to Kothari, get him admitted for a few more tests.'

'How were things after he returned from the hospital?' asked Akhil Banerjee.

'Health-wise, it was much better, I guess. He gave up drinking completely, was quite particular about taking his medications. Although, life for him had become quite stressful in that house.'

'Why is that?'

Rajib lowered his eyes ever so slightly as if in an implicit acknowledgement of guilt.

'I suppose I am partly responsible for that,' he said finally. 'His family, especially his brother and his brother's wife, had started behaving extremely rudely with him. His brother was after him to make a will. Heated arguments were a regular feature. I often embarrassed myself by walking right into one. They would stop talking abruptly, but you could make out from their faces that my entry had halted a tirade of unpleasant words. Once or twice, Probir babu's wife had even spoken out loud in my presence about blood being thicker than water, and that one should think things carefully and not take an impulsive decision. The house, the business belonged to Sir. I suppose, they were scared that he would leave everything to me, an outsider.'

'And did he?'

'Huh?'

'Did Sanyal babu make a will leaving everything to you?'

Rajib shut his eyes and nodded slowly. 'His lawyer, Mr Chowdhury contacted me yesterday. The house is not mentioned in the will, so I suppose that will go to his brother. But he has left the entire business to me.'

'And how did his family react?'

'They have not contacted me, but I can imagine they are not very thrilled. The business is now worth a considerable sum.'

'Hmm... What happened on the 13th of December? The day he died?'

'I had been to his house that morning. Those days I had limited my visits, going only when it was absolutely necessary. Even then, more often than not I would send another employee. Later, Sir would call up, and I would know from his voice that he was hurt. He would never say it out loud of course, but I knew. Beneath all the conversations about the workings of the company, he seemed to say, *I am sorry. Forgive me for my family's rudeness.* I would feel terrible and would go visit him the very next day. *It is Sir's house and it is for him that I come here,* I would tell myself.

'He was not quite himself that day, I think. Perhaps there was something else that was bothering him. We even had a bit of an argument. In the heat of the moment, Sir said some rather unpleasant things to say to me. That I should not forget who I was before Sir had taken me under his wing…a lowly waiter in a tea-shop…and all that.

'I cannot pretend it did not hurt. Sir had never spoken to me like that before. But I understood his anguish.'

'Any particular reason why he said such things?'

'It wasn't anything serious, really. He had made a proposition and I disagreed with it. Anyway, before I left, I managed to make him see my point of view and he had calmed down. He even apologized for his behaviour.'

'Hmm…What time did you leave?'

'Say around 1 p.m.'

'And what time did you reach home that day?'

'Around 8 p.m., I think. Was feeling quite disturbed, so had decided to watch a movie to take my mind off the morning's visit. It was about a half hour later, I guess. I was just about to sit for dinner when I got the call, *Sir had passed away.* '

The pronouncement hung in the air for a while. A lizard that had been darting about the wall announced its presence by the *tick tick* sound. Somewhere in the distance, an iron gate clamoured shut, the sound magnified by the stillness of a cold December night.

'Hmm…What do you want me…us…to do, Rajib?'

'I am not sure, really,' he confessed. 'I suppose Ghoshal babu has told you already, I went to see him this morning. I have a feeling that something is not quite right. I mean...I cannot point a finger at anyone but the way events have unfurled, first the sightings of the phantom, then his sudden death...'

'I feel the same, Akhil,' remarked Biren Ghoshal. 'I simply cannot get over the fact that I had spoken to the man that very day and...'

'Yes, but you must understand, Rajib, that murder investigations cannot take place based on mere "feelings"... As I had told Biren earlier, Probhat babu had a weak heart, he was given to occasional drinking, his stress level was high...all of these could have contributed to heart failure.'

'What about the ghosts?' Bibhuti Bose spoke for the first time. '*Moshai*, I can imagine ghosts in the deserted tea gardens in Darjeeling...but right here in Calcutta?'

'I am having a tough time believing that story, too,' quipped Chandan Mukherjee. 'If you ask me, he imagined the whole thing. I am sorry Rajib, that's just what I feel.'

'You may be right, sir,' replied Rajib. 'It is just that...well... if you had met Sir and heard him talk of those incidents, they might have seemed more real to you. Frankly, I do not know what to make of it as well.'

'My suggestion, Rajib, would be to let matters rest,' said Akhil Banerjee. 'I understand you were very close to Probhat babu and this is a huge personal loss for you. But sometimes, we have to simply acknowledge reality and let time take care of the rest. I am sorry, but I do not think I can offer any other advice.'

'Yes, perhaps you are right, sir,' sighed Rajib. He paused before adding, 'Well, anyway, thank you all for hearing me out. I feel much lighter already.' He allowed himself a smile and having thanked his hosts, got up to leave.

'Let me get going too, Akhil,' said Biren Ghoshal. 'I'll come again another time. *Elaam.*'

'*Aae.* Do come again,' replied Akhil Banerjee, according to the custom of the land where an invitation to a future visit is implied in the goodbye.

Debdas Guha Roy, who had been silent throughout the evening, suddenly got up from his seat.

'I'll be right back,' he said and hastily made his way to the door. Biren Ghoshal and Rajib had barely let themselves out of the main gate when they heard Debdas Guha Roy call out, 'One minute!'

'Umm...Rajib,' he said, walking up to him. 'I did not catch your full name.'

'Guha, Rajib Guha.'

'Kayastha?!' The word had rolled out of his tongue before he could help himself.

'Huh?'

'Oh nothing nothing...I was just thinking...' he hesitated.

'Tell me, kaku,' insisted Rajib.

'If I, if we...want to contact you again?'

'Oh yes, of course,' said Rajib, taking out a cell phone from his pocket. 'Tell me your number, kaku, and I will give you a missed call.'

'Huh?'

Contrary to Rajib's expectation, what came out of Debdas Guha Roy's *panjabi* pocket after much fumbling, was not a cell phone, but a scrap of paper, which he held out gingerly. Rajib obliged.

'Thank you, bhai,' said Debdas Guha Roy, taking the paper back. 'See you again...sometime.'

'Yes, sure, kaku. It was really nice meeting all of you,' replied Rajib. He folded his hands in a quick namaskar and walked away.

Debdas Guha Roy found himself lingering at the gate till the backs of the visitors disappeared around the corner. He folded the paper gently and put it in his pocket.

He couldn't help the smile on his lips.

*

'*E ki? Labda* and *khichuri* for dinner as well?!' asked Bibhuti Bose irritatedly. 'Repeat telecast?'

'What can I do?' shot back Joyoti Bose. 'Is there any space left in the fridge?'

'*Nah!* This hotel has gone from bad to worse! Could you not make *luchi,* sometime? With mutton curry? How long has it been...'

'Food! Food! Food! Do you ever think of anything else? At this age, people tend to be cautious. And all you can think of is what to eat next!'

'What else will I think about?'

'Can't you do a little *jop*? Chant names of Gods...like normal people your age?'

'*Duss!* That is not for me. Pour some more chutney on my plate.'

Joyoti Bose shook her head, and did as told. *Some people never change!*

'Why did Joj Saheb call you all today? Is there a new case?'

Bibhuti Bose shrugged. 'Maybe.'

'What is it about? Another theft?'

'Why?'

'Just asking. You can tell me, I will keep it a secret.'

Bibhuti bose shot his wife a disbelieving look.

'What? You don't believe me? Okay, never mind,' continued Joyoti Bose. 'Who needs to know? I have my own mysteries to solve.'

'You are solving mysteries?'

'Why not? You don't think I can be a detective? I tell you, women would make better detectives. If the police took help of more women, cases would be solved just like that.' She snapped her fingers to emphasize the promptness. 'There is so much going on that only women will notice. Like, tell me...have you noted anything strange about the paper boy?'

'Which paper boy?'

'Ah! See? You don't even know who the paper boy is. His name is Bhombol...lives in the other street, Haripada Das Lane. Fat, round, dark. Comes around every morning at seven.'

'What about him?'

'He wears the same sweater every day. But...' continued Joyoti Bose, before her husband could remark, 'On alternate days he wears it inside-out.' She paused for effect. 'Now that is a bit strange, don't you think?'

Bibhuti Bose shrugged. 'Maybe he is superstitious.'

Joyoti Bose shook her head. 'I don't think so...I think it's something else.' She paused before adding, 'Let us see who can deduce the reason why. You or I.'

A Visit to the Old College

Biplab Maity thumbed through the pages of *Anandolok*, the Bengali film magazine, that had been left behind by Bappa the previous day. It carried stories of break-ups and engagements, partnerships and scandals, new releases and box-office hits. Biplab briefly glanced at all the stories but for one, wherein he spent considerable time going through the alleged love affair between a starlet and an aged producer. No news was quite as entertaining as the salacious, he decided.

Having thus apprised himself of the news of the celluloid world, and having made a mental note of a film that was scheduled to be released the following Friday, Biplab cast the magazine aside, got off the table, stretched his arms in a prolonged yawn and made his way to the library. The 'library'—one of those useless endeavours by the 'seniors' in an attempt to promote reading among the youth—was modest at best. A couple of shelves filled with dusty, dog-eared English and Bengali novels that had been donated by people of the neighbourhood.

We have too many books in our house. They are gathering dust. No place to keep so many, Biplab could imagine one of the wives complaining. And that would have given someone the idea of making a library and donating all those books which no one would want to read anyway.

The senior citizens of their *paara* did these things. Came up with ridiculous projects from time to time to make their presence felt. There was that 'Tree Plantation' drive, not too long ago. Was there anything even remotely challenging about it? The local nursery delivered the saplings. Then Ganesh, the gardener who took care of the Sabuj Kalyan Park, was made to dig out holes at regular intervals. The prominent members of the neighbourhood gingerly lowered the saplings on to the holes and posed for photographs, while their wives fussed about getting their white dhotis soiled.

It is a good thing, Biplab reminded himself, that the seniors had been booted out—in the gentlest manner possible—of the Pujo Committee. Organizing a Pujo was no child's play—rather, it was no old man's play, Biplab chuckled at the thought. It required tremendous amount of hard work, commitment, enthusiasm, dedication…all of which it seemed, came in short supply as one advanced in years. The graceful thing would have been to realize this on their own, and voluntarily hand over the responsibilities to the younger lot. Like, when Sunil Gavaskar quit cricket or Zidane quit football. Did they not have many more years of the sport left in them? They surely did. But there was also this realization—*I have done the best I could. Now it is time for younger players to prove their mettle.*

Left to Biplab, he would have done this much sooner. But politeness and protocol demanded that he swallow his pride and allow the seniors to continue sitting on the Pujo Committee. Their actions—or lack thereof—had cost them the Sharad Samman Awards for all these years. The seniors were perhaps not even cognizant of such an award! They weren't the ones facing the humiliation. Why would they even care?

And all this while, Milonee—the club in the next *paara*—with its young, hip, office-going residents came up with brilliant ideas (and more importantly, the funds to implement those ideas) and won the award hands down. Sudhir Bagchi, president of Milonee

Club, did not let pass a single opportunity to taunt Biplab about the same.

'*Ki* Biplab? What are you doing for Durga Pujo this year? Same old, same old?' he would ask aloud from the other side of the road, sipping tea at Ramu's tea-shop with his cronies—a bunch of young, energetic and decidedly better-informed boys than the lot Biplab had to put up with.

Well, he had had enough! Last year, he and his boys had made it amply clear that they were in charge now. The seniors had taken it rather well, he thought. Perhaps, secretly, they were only too happy to let go of the responsibility. It gave them more time to…to…what was it that retired people did anyway? Haggle with fish-sellers, argue with taxi-drivers, mull over constipation and the various discomforts associated with it? Some, he had come to hear, had created a detective club! Of all the…Biplab caught himself laughing in mid-thought as the image of a dhoti-clad Chandan Mukherjee floated into his mind, waving his walking stick at the culprit, screaming, '*Ei, ei…roko! Palata kyon hain?*'

And what cases would they solve? The fast disappearance of the ever-popular winter gear of yesteryears: the monkey-cap? Or the mysterious case of Bhombol, who Biplab had come to notice, wore the same blue sweater every day, but wore it inside out on alternate days. Biplab had been meaning to ask Bhombol, but had brushed it aside. It did make a curious case: 'The Mystery of The Man Who Wore His Sweater Inside Out on Alternate Days'. Or perhaps 'the detectives' could help him unravel the stupefying mystery of why Sabuj Kalyan Club could never come close to beating Milonee Club at Durga Pujo, no matter how hard they tried? Somewhere deep inside he knew he needed to dwell on this, dig a little deeper, zero in on the exact issue at hand; but it was an uncomfortable, disturbing thought. He shook his head in an attempt to wake up before a nightmare could arrive.

Well, at least getting the seniors out of the way had given Biplab and his boys a lot of flexibility. They could now boldly pursue their ideas without having to appease anyone. The last Durga Pujo was definitely bigger and better than any of the previous years'—if one did not count the unfortunate fiasco involving a certain wild animal. Biplab was not going to let such minor incidents hold him back. *The next Pujo too will be grand. And different. It will capture the imagination of the young and the old.* It was tough, thought Biplab, that in these regards, he received such little help from his fellow club members. A bunch of callous, uncouth boys, who had neither education nor any sense of culture! High school drop-outs, who would much rather spend their time ogling at girls and devouring film magazines, than educating themselves about the finer things in life.

If only there was some way of instilling some sense of culture, some finesse in his boys! His fingertips picked up dust as he ran them lightly over the books. He wasn't really reading the titles. His brows were knitted in concentration. The seed of an idea—vague and indistinct—formed in his mind. He pulled out a book and began to leaf through its pages.

*

Debdas Guha Roy got off the bus at Hazra More and walked the remaining distance to Ashutosh College—the institution where he had spent thirty-five long years teaching geology to undergraduate students.

The familiar sight of young boys and girls lingering on the footsteps—books and backpacks in hand—welcomed him. These young kids had not seen him teach. Engrossed in conversation, they barely looked up when he came by. Debdas Guha Roy made his way through the steps, requesting the students to make way for him to pass.

He made his way up to the second floor. Jogomohon, the *darwan*, saluted and flashed him a broad smile, which got even broader when Debdas Guha Roy slapped him lightly on the back and asked after his family.

'Is Principal sir in?'

'Yes, yes. He is waiting for you,' replied Jogomohan as he knocked and let Debdas Guha Roy in.

The principal, Subhomoy Ghosh, was on the phone and, from the looks of it, was not having a particularly pleasant conversation. He acknowledged Debdas Guha Roy and motioned him to take a seat.

'*Ki byapar*? Did I come on a bad day?' asked Debdas Guha Roy once the receiver had been put down.

'*Arrey*, no, no, Debdas babu. It is the same every day. If it's not this, it is something else. Is there any end to life's hassles, tell me?'

Debdas Guha Roy had to agree with this statement. Life, it would seem, was a continuous play of fixing one thing after another.

'*Moshai*, I can't wait to retire like you,' continued Subhomoy Ghosh. 'Being a principal is the most thankless job ever, I tell you—nobody is happy with what you do! Not the students, not the faculty, not the Unions, not the Ministry… Anyway, these things are part of everyday life, *moshai*. You tell me…how is retired life treating you?'

'*Oi*, same old.'

'*Ta*, are you doing something these days?'

'Nothing as such…I give private tuitions to some neighbourhood boys. Just a way to keep myself occupied, that's all.'

'Hmm...yes, yes of course.' Subhomoy Ghosh waited. He tapped lightly on the desk, occupied for the most part with tattered files held together with rubber-bands.

Debdas Guha Roy looked about the room. It had not changed much from the last time he had visited the office. A photograph of Mahatma Gandhi hung on the wall in front. The remaining walls were occupied by calendars given by publishers of text books, or booksellers from College Street.

'*Iye*...,' Subhomoy Ghosh spoke presently, 'I heard you are also doing some... *detectivegiri* on the side?' His tone was casual, eyes still on the desk.

'*O babba!*' exclaimed Debdas Guha Roy. 'How did you hear of that?'

'Professor Bagchi, from the chemistry department was saying something. Is it true?'

'It is nothing serious,' Debdas Guha Roy hastened to explain. '*Oi*, a bunch of retired friends having a little fun snooping around, that's all.'

'Hmm...good, good.' He hesitated. 'Actually...' He cleared his throat, 'There is a reason why I asked you to come see me, Debdas babu. I do not know if you can help me in any way, but...there is this matter...'

'Yes, sir. Tell me.'

'It is like this... Recently...' He stopped. Jogomohan had entered with two cups of tea. Subhomoy Ghosh waited till Jogomohan had placed the cups on the table, and closed the door behind him as he left.

'Recently...' resumed Subhomoy Ghosh, offering Debdas Guha Roy a cup, 'there have been some thefts in our college.'

'What kind of thefts?'

'Chemicals.'

'Chemicals?'

Subhomoy Ghosh nodded, taking a sip from his cup. 'From time to time, the boys do pinch a few chemicals from the lab... to try out experiments at home, I'm sure. Small quantities of fairly harmless compounds. But this time, Kapil, the lab assistant, informed me that one sachet of arsenic oxide was missing from the cupboard. About 100 grams. I'm a bit concerned, Debdas babu. I am told that is a lethal dose.

'You know how students are these days? A few marks less in a paper or a relationship gone wrong, and they will not think twice before ending their lives. Is one of my boys planning a suicide? If this has come to my notice, I want to do everything I can to stop it.'

'Sure, sure,' Debdas Guha Roy nodded understandingly.

'You cannot begin to imagine the legal hassles, *moshai*... especially if something happens inside the college premises.'

'Hmm...I understand. So how can I help, sir?'

'I was hoping you could give us some idea about how to find out who has stolen this. The matter is rather delicate. I do not want publicity by calling the police right away. And I do not want to alert the boy, either. Who knows, if he feels we are on to him, he might do something drastic sooner than he had planned.'

'When was the theft discovered?'

'Two days back. Kapil normally takes a stock of all the chemicals at the end of each week. He needs to place an order before the supplies get over. That's when he noticed that one packet was missing.'

'Do you suspect anyone in particular?'

The principal shook his head.

'As you know, there are so many students in each department, it is almost impossible to know anyone well enough to be able to pinpoint who is going through an emotional crisis. I have thought of individually summoning each one to my office for questioning, but I fear that will create more harm than good. Besides, once the Students' Union gets a whiff of this, you never know how far the matter will escalate. Whatever has to be done, has to be done with utmost caution, and without making things glaringly obvious.'

'Hmm…I understand. Well…let me see what I can do. But sir, if he really wanted to harm himself and if he already is in possession of the poison, why has he not done so already?'

'It is possible that he is waiting. The exam results will be out in two weeks. He probably knows he has not done well in the exams and just wants to confirm before taking such a drastic step? Professor Bagchi is re-checking the papers. He will have a list of students who are at the bottom of the class, but frankly, I don't know if that is any good. It is all about reference points, Debdas babu. More often than not, the boy who missed getting a first class by one or two marks, is the one most tempted to end his life.'

'True,' agreed Debdas Guha Roy. 'So, were they stolen from the chemistry lab?'

'Yes. Kapil keeps all the dangerous chemicals under lock and key. And all experiments are done under strict supervision. During the lab periods the cupboard is usually open, but it is only Kapil who takes out the required chemicals. No one else is allowed to take things from there. A couple of days back, the boys had just left after finishing their lab work. Kapil began taking stock of the chemicals. That is when he discovered the theft. It is worrying. Do you think you can help, Debdas babu?'

Debdas Guha Roy assumed a serious expression.

'I will need to speak to Kapil,' he said finally.

A half-hour later, armed with a list of names of the Chemistry Honours students of the first, second and third year, Debdas Guha Roy stepped out of the college building and hailed a taxi. Once inside the cab, he thought over his conversation with the lab assistant. The latter had shown him the cupboard, placed in one of the smaller rooms adjoining the main lab. The lock had not been broken, hence whatever was stolen was stolen during class.

Debdas Guha Roy had ventured to ask a pointed question or two, on whether Kapil had locked the cupboard properly, or whether he was around the whole time. Kapil seemed to have taken it personally. His attitude had become shifty. He was the only lab assistant for so many students, he had said by way of explanation. He had so many things to take care of. He had to keep an eye on everyone handling chemicals—somebody could burst a test-tube by over-heating it, someone could be measuring acid in a pipette in spite of repeatedly being told not to. He was not complaining, he had added hastily, but he was only human. If he had known one of the boys was up to something, he would have ensured that the cupboard was locked.

The bottom line was, that the cupboard had probably been left open, which meant anyone who had the intention to steal, had only to wait for the perfect opportunity.

The taxi stopped with a jerk. Lost in thought, Debdas Guha Roy had not noticed that they had hardly moved. A weekday afternoon, apparently an off-peak time, and yet the traffic was appalling. *What will happen to the city in another ten years? It seems to be bursting at the seams already.*

Large hoardings of film and theatre festivals, of youth and handicraft fairs, of classical music concerts and the yearly book fair loomed on either side of the road. There was so much to do, it seemed. So many places to go to. Wherever the eyes fell, there were people crossing the street in the midst of moving vehicles, running after a bus that had just left the stop, haggling with a taxi-driver who refused to go to your destination.

It was just as well, thought Debdas Guha Roy with a smile. If suddenly one morning, one woke up to find that everything was in order in a city that thrived on chaos, most people, deprived of their daily sources of stress—the squabbles, the traffic jams, the honking, the dust and the sweat—would lose their minds, he suspected. A roadside priest approached Debdas Guha Roy's taxi driver and offered to do a short puja so the day would turn out good. The driver nodded his approval.

It was a wonder of sorts, thought Debdas Guha Roy as he watched the priest sprinkle flowers and chant mantras, that in spite of the insurmountable odds, this city worked at all. There was—there had to be—an underlying order to this maddening chaos, a perfectly drawn blueprint, where there was place for each one of us, with an allowance for all our idiosyncrasies and our human frailties. Each of us in our own place, connected by invisible spider webs that held us together and helped us survive. Perhaps these little prayers, these paltry offerings of a flower and an incense stick to the divine, helped in some mysterious way to keep it all together.

Do Ghosts Really Exist?

'*Moshai*, do ghosts really exist?'

The question was asked by Chandan Mukherjee who seated himself on the bench, hooked his walking stick on the arm, and rubbed his palms together in an attempt to warm his hands.

It was a little before seven in the morning, with the sky just beginning to change colour from pink to blue. A gentle breeze, cold but not biting, ruffled the hair. The grass below the feet, wet with dew, glistened in the first rays of the sun. A cacophony of birds, crows mostly, but also the occasional woodpecker or the hungry baby mynahs surrounded them. A squirrel darted up the nearby gulmohar tree to the higher branches, perhaps in search of warmth.

Ramu, the tea shop owner, who had a ramshackle arrangement at the corner of the street just outside the park, came over with four earthen mugs of tea—two mugs balanced delicately on the rim of two others. The gentlemen fished out coins from their pockets and wrapped their cold fingers around the warmth of the mugs.

Bibhuti Bose took a sip and let out a long, contended 'Aah!' before continuing. 'Didn't I tell you what happened to me once? It was sometime in the sixties. One of my distant uncles owned several tea gardens in Jalpaiguri. That summer, my cousin, Bubu da, who was several years older to me, invited me and Dada over to their tea garden. They lived in a big zamindari bungalow—marble floors, high ceilings, dinner served in brassware by uniformed servants—that was as good as royalty to me, *moshai*.

'Anyway, there was a servant, Jagannath. We called him Joga. He had a knack for telling ghost stories. At night, when the power would be out, and the large living hall illuminated only by candlelight, we would gather around him to listen to spine chilling tales of ghosts that were sighted wandering in the mists of the tea gardens. Stories of how once he barely escaped his neck being wrung by a *petni*, a witch; or how the ghost of an Englishman who had been murdered by his wife, who later committed suicide, still screamed in agony in the dead of the night. As entertaining as the stories were, going to bed at night was frightening, I tell you, with everything around shrouded in darkness and Joga's words still ringing in the ears.

'One day, Bubu da and I went for a drive in his jeep. He knew the area well, having stayed there during every school vacation. We were returning home after a long day at the neighbouring town, when suddenly his jeep stuttered and shut down completely. He tried coaxing the engine back to life, but it groaned and refused to oblige further. We were stranded in the middle of nowhere, and it was beginning to get dark. For miles on either side you couldn't see any sign of habitation. Those days, of course, there were no cell-phones. So we waited, hoping for a lift in a passing jeep or car. For a long, long time, nothing came our way.

'It had become dark. And honestly, I had started to panic. Then suddenly, we thought we saw something in the distance.' Bibhuti Bose bent forward, knitted his eye-brows and pointed in front to mimic his action in the story. Headlights!

'Our hopes went up. But the car was taking an inexplicably long time to arrive. It almost seemed like it did not move at all. Then, after what seemed like hours, it came in front of us and halted. We wasted no time in scrambling on to the back seat. It was only after the car started moving again—very slowly—that we realized the driver's seat was empty!

'What to tell you, *moshai*? My blood froze. I nudged Bubu da (he mimicked the action by nudging Debdas Guha Roy sitting next to him with his elbow), too scared to speak, then realized, he had noticed it too. I contemplated jumping out—after all, the car was moving at a snail's pace—and pointed to the door (he pointed to his left). I was about to say "Jai Ma!" and go for it (he pretend-lunged forward), when suddenly the car stopped. Can you guess what happened?'

'Hmm…I think I can, Bibhuti babu,' said Akhil Banerjee, an amused look on his face. 'But I would much rather hear it in your words.'

'What happened? What happened?' asked Debdas Guha Roy eagerly.

Bibhuti Bose did not respond immediately. His face turned into a mock-serious expression.

'A voice called out from behind,' said Bibhuti Bose. '*O dada! You've been sitting for a long time. Now, how about I sit and you push*?'

Akhil Banerjee joined in the laughter. He was sure he had heard a similar story somewhere before, from a different person in a different scenario. These were the kind of stories that had assumed a rightful place as a true event in one's life, where the line between truth and fiction had been blurred through repeated narration in family gatherings and dinner parties.

'*Moshai*, I can still swallow ghosts in the eerie tea gardens,' said Chandan Mukherjee. 'But right here? In the heart of Calcutta?'

'What are you saying, Chandan babu?' said Debdas Guha Roy. 'Have you not heard of the ghost of National Library? Sounds of a horse-carriage screeching to a stop, the continuous tapping on a typewriter all night, sighting of apparitions have all been reported by guards. And surely you know the story of Hastings House? The old residence of the Governor-General? Now, of course, it has become the Calcutta Womens' College. But students swear they have seen the ghost of Hastings walking about! It seems there was a freaky accident once, long time ago, where a young boy died of sports injuries, and his spirit too haunts the place. There is hardly a heritage site in Calcutta that does not have a ghost story associated with it, *moshai.* National Library, Park Street Cemetery, Race course...you name it!'

'*O moshai*,' quipped Chandan Mukherjee, 'I suppose there is a ghost in Writer's Building as well. That must explain why everyone is so quick to escape the instant the clock chimes 5.30 p.m.'

'Yes, yes, Writer's Building, too. Once a government clerk was working late...' Debdas Guha Roy had started in all earnest, when the joke dawned on him, and his face broke into a smile. 'Oh ho! I see what you mean...'

'I do not personally believe in ghosts and spirits,' said Akhil Banerjee. 'But during my long career in the Court, I witnessed one case that was bizarre to say the least.

'It was a case of "suppression of facts". A couple had bought a recently renovated heritage house and claimed that it was haunted. And that this fact was purposely not disclosed by the real-estate agents during the sale of the property. Several details surfaced during the trial, and the final story was eerie to say the least.

'Now this is what had happened. An elderly couple, Mr and Mrs Roy Chowdhury, had recently moved to Calcutta after spending many long years in Benaras. They purchased a renovated heritage house in north Calcutta, in the Baghbazar area. They had two grown-up sons. The older son married a city girl and they all lived together in the same house. Everything was absolutely normal. Then one day, some six months after the marriage, the whole family decided to go out for the movies. At the last moment, the young bride complained of headache, and decided to stay back home. When the family returned later that evening, they found to their horror that the young bride had committed suicide by jumping off the terrace. The matter was dismissed as an unfortunate case of suicide, though no one could fathom the reason behind it. She had not looked troubled or disturbed in any way and the neighbours found her very friendly and pleasant to talk to.

'Anyway, some years later, it was the turn of the younger son to be married. Again, for a few months everything was fine. Then the family started to notice that the young bride would be missing for hours together. She used to say she was going to take a bath and then was not seen for more than two hours. They had to knock on her door several times, before she responded. Though not a cause of major worry, it had begun to bother the husband. One day, it seems, she had gone to the terrace to hang washed clothes to dry, and had not come down for hours. The husband went looking for her, and found her standing in the middle of the terrace, muttering something to herself. She seemed totally oblivious of his presence. As he neared her cautiously, he realized that she was talking…it appeared, to someone else. She was nodding her head and gesticulating, as if having a real conversation. When he called out to her, she did not answer at first, then he called out louder and suddenly, as if snapping back from a trance, she looked at him and smiled, and said, "Oh look how late it is. You must be hungry." That sort of thing. As if nothing was out of the ordinary.

'This bothered her husband and he kept a close watch on her, even forbidding her to go to the terrace, which angered his wife. "Who are you to tell me where I should go and what I should do," she would yell back at him. Then one night—it was during the summer months, the power was out—the husband woke up from sleep. He turned to face his wife and noticed that she was not there. He called out to her, thinking she must be in the bathroom. When she did not reply, he got anxious. Getting out of the mosquito net and fumbling for the torchlight, he went looking for her.

'When he reached the landing of the stairs, he felt a draft of breeze and realized that the door of the terrace upstairs was open. He climbed up the stairs cautiously, and found to his horror, his wife, standing with one foot on the parapet and one foot in mid-air, about to jump off. He lunged forward and managed to pull her back in the nick of time, thus avoiding yet another tragedy.

'Based on the above facts, the Roy Chowdhurys filed a case against the seller of the home, claiming the house was haunted and this fact was not disclosed at the time of the sale. Their lawyers produced the most intriguing evidence in court.

'It seems, many years ago, during the times of the Raj, the house was owned by a zamindar by the name of Benigopal. Like many other zamindars of his time, Benigopal frequently hosted parties for his friends, with liquor and performances by *baijis*, the nautch girls. These *baijis*, as you are probably aware, lived in the Bow Bazar area, and Kathak and Thumri teachers from Lucknow, Benaras, Delhi would come and train them. At that time—this was before the social reform movement of 1892—these performers were exclusively patronized by the cultured elite of Calcutta.

'Some of these girls had permanently moved into Benigopal's house. Once, he was to host a huge party, probably during some festival or the other, and his guest list consisted of not just local babus, but also British officers. Benigopal spared no effort to make it as grand as possible. At that time, one *baiji*, by the name of Girija bai, had created quite an impression on many of our zamindar babus. They spoke at length of her beauty, her gracefulness and her divine talents. So Benigopal had decided that she must perform at his home.

'Girija bai turned out to be much more than all the superlatives that were being said of her. Benigopal, hopelessly smitten by her charm, asked her to marry him. She moved into the house and was treated like royalty. The other nautch girls were made to wait upon her. This made them very jealous.

'One day, the girls got into a squabble. They started taunting Girija bai, calling her a hoax. They challenged her to a dance competition, to which Girija bai readily agreed. They all went up to the terrace. "If you can do the Kathak twirl on the parapet of the terrace, we will admit you are the best dancer amongst all of us," they said. Without wasting a minute, Girija bai climbed on to the parapet and started twirling, round and round, her nimble feet not missing a step. And then suddenly she lost her balance and fell to her death.

'Benigopal was deeply shocked by the incident. He drove away all the girls from his home and moved elsewhere. An old police file that had chronicled the incident was discovered. Benigopal himself had written about it in detail in his diary, which the lawyer produced in court.

'The property was lying vacant for many years, and had become the home of some local goons. Then one real-estate company traced down its current owner, and renovated it into a heritage home, before it got sold off to the Roy Chowdhurys.'

They considered the story in silence.

'*Nah*, let me get going,' said Debdas Guha Roy eventually, getting up from the bench. 'Am going to Esplanade today...

thinking of paying a visit to Rajib once.'

'Who?' asked Bibhuti Bose.

'Rajib. Rajib Guha,' emphasized Debdas Guha Roy, then seeing the confused frown on Bibhuti Bose's face added, '*arrey*, I'm talking about Probhat Sanyal's employee.'

'Oh ho!' exclaimed Bibhuti Bose. 'Ronobir Kapoor!'

Debdas Guha Roy chuckled. 'I daresay, he is quite a handsome fellow! He would easily get a chance in Bengali films if he tried.'

'Umm…I somehow don't recall his last name,' said Akhil Banerjee. 'Debdas babu, are you sure he mentioned "Guha"?'

'Ah…no…not really,' Debdas Guha Roy hesitated. 'I just happened to ask him,' he said, hoping he sounded casual.

'You say you want to visit him?' asked Chandan Mukherjee, getting up. 'Why?'

'No, no…no reason as such,' replied Debdas Guha Roy hastily. '*Oi,* I am going to Esplanade anyway…so thought, why not meet him once.'

Silence followed. Debdas Guha Roy could almost hear what his friends were thinking. *But why does he want to meet Rajib? And why did he have to ask him for his last name?* He had to say something to get their minds off this.

'O Joj Saheb?'

'Yes, Debdas babu?'

'I needed your advice on a particular matter.'

'Yes, tell me.'

'The other day, the Principal of Ashutosh College had sent for me.' He recounted the whole incident, adding, 'Is there any way to find out discretely who has the poison? Without raising an alarm?'

'Hmm…let me think,' replied Akhil Banerjee.

'Principal sir is quite disturbed by this theft,' continued Debdas Guha Roy. 'But if he calls the police, there will be so much negative publicity.'

'You need Birbal or Gopal Bhaar, Debdas babu,' quipped Bibhuti Bose. 'You know all those stories from our childhood on how they would be able to identify the guilty by using unconventional wisdom? Some behaviour on the part of the guilty would invariably give him away.'

'Well...in the olden days, in the days of the Raj that is, our police used a fairly ingenious technique that served as a primitive lie detector,' said Akhil Banerjee.

'What technique is that?' asked Debdas Guha Roy.

'In those days, the British officers lived in huge bungalows in Calcutta, and typically had a few dozen servants. Petty thefts were quite common. How could one find out who among all the servants had actually stolen the watch or the wallet?

'It seems, the police officer would call all the suspects, and give them a little amount of rice grains that had earlier been washed and dried in the sun. He would then ask them to chew the rice and spit it out on the banana leaf in front of him. The one who would spit out dry grains was the culprit. Apparently, this method had a very high success rate.'

'How so, Joj Saheb?'

'It may not be foolproof, but it is not entirely unscientific either,' said Akhil Banerjee. 'You see, for most people the chewed mass will be wet with saliva. But the guilty one will be scared and as a result his mouth will have gone dry. Hence his grains will appear much drier than the others.'

'Oh ho! I see,' said Debdas Guha Roy. 'Interesting, but I doubt I can use this method with the students of the college.'

'No, no, of course not. We will have to think of some other way. Let's just hope the boy does not do anything stupid in the meantime.'

The others nodded.

'Alright sir, we'll be off,' called out Chandan Mukherjee. 'See you tomorrow.' Both, he and Bibhuti Bose, waved goodbye and made their way towards Daily Market.

'Joj Saheb, I had another question,' asked Debdas Guha Roy, when they had reached the corner of street where Akhil Banerjee would turn left towards his house and Debdas Guha Roy would have to go straight ahead.

'Yes, tell me, Debdas babu.'

'Uh...what do you think of this boy...Rajib? He seems alright, doesn't he?'

'Hmm...Debdas babu, I hope you realize one thing,' said Akhil Banerjee, thoughtfully. 'If at all there is some foul play in the death of Probhat Sanyal, then the likelihood of the guilty being Rajib is the strongest.'

'Why? Why do you say so, Joj Saheb?'

'Think about it. First, the motive. In the event of Probhat Sanyal's death, he stands to inherit the business. For a young man who has struggled all his life, this is certainly a windfall. He was well aware that Mr Sanyal's family was putting pressure on him to write a will leaving everything to them. What was the guarantee that Mr Sanyal would not succumb to the pressure? Second, opportunity. He visited Sanyal babu that day, just hours before his death. He could have easily mixed something in his food or given him the wrong medication.'

'No, no, Joj Saheb,' protested Debdas Guha Roy, shaking his head and waving his palms as if to erase the words he had just heard. 'I'm afraid you are mistaken. Rajib did not even know about the will in the first place! He only learnt of its contents when the lawyer contacted him. And besides, you heard the way he talked about his boss. He had nothing but the highest regard for the man. Why would he...?'

'Yes, true, true. But Debdas babu, we have only *his* version of the story. Also, you remember he said Probhat babu was angry with him that day, had even lost his temper and called him names. I'm afraid, but all this only helps to point the finger in Rajib's direction. He could have done something to his boss simply out of hurt...people tend to do such things. One moment they respect someone like God, and the instant he says or does something hurtful, they feel so betrayed that they cannot even think rationally anymore. Besides, the fact that Probhat babu was angry with him that day, might have scared him into thinking that the will—provided he knew of its contents—was likely to be changed.'

If Debdas Guha Roy was crestfallen, he refused to show it.

'What about intuition, Joj Saheb?' he said after some thought. 'Seeing this boy, hearing him speak about his life, about Sanyal babu...do you think he is capable of committing murder?' He shook his head vehemently. 'The boy is genuine, I tell you.'

'He might well be,' said Akhil Banerjee. 'I'm not accusing him of being a murderer. All I am saying is that, *should* there be any foul play in the death of Probhat Sanyal, then, to my mind, Rajib Guha is a very strong suspect. That is all I am saying.'

Biplab Maity Has an Idea

'Cultural nights!' announced Biplab Maity, silencing Bappa, who was in the midst of narrating a particularly frightening scene from a horror movie he had seen the night before.

Outside the clubhouse, in the Sabuj Kalyan Park, a loud cheer frightened a couple of sparrows resting peacefully on the nearby gulmohar tree. Someone had hit a six. Or so he claimed. The others argued that the penalty for hitting the ball outside the park boundary and onto the street, was a lost wicket. It was tough to recover the ball once it had crossed the limits of the park. It would have likely been flattened under an oncoming car unless a street urchin had grabbed it in time and made a run for it.

'Cultural nights?' asked Partho, after a few seconds of stunned silence.

'Yes,' said Biplab Maity. 'I announce that from now on, we dedicate at least one evening a week to some cultural activity... you know...songs, poetry, theatre...'

'We are going to see a *jatra*?' asked Soumen. 'That's a fantastic idea, Biplab da! Just last month there was a performance in Bansdroni—Bollywood Sri Krishna Leela. What a performance it was! The crowd was on its feet. *My name is Sheela, Sheela ki jawani...*' He crooned a few lines of the latest Bollywood hit.

'*Chhee, chhee.* Sheela ki jawani?' Biplab Maity sounded aghast. 'In Sri Krishna Leela?'

'No, no. They had changed the lyrics—*my name is Radha,*

I'm his favourite Gopi…'

'This is outrageous!' protested Biplab Maity. 'I am not talking about cheap street-side *jatras*! I have something more cultured, refined, educative in mind.'

He paused briefly before continuing. 'Once a week, say every Friday, we gather together to do something "cultural". *Ei* take for example, we read a story written by Robi Thakur or act out a play by Chekov…'

Encouraged by the silence in his audience, Biplab continued, 'Once in a while, we could also go for a "cultural excursion". *Ei*, just the other day, I read in the papers, there is going to be a weeklong theatre festival in Robindro Sorobor. Theatre troupes from all over India will perform the works of Shakespeare, Tolstoy, Chekov and Moliere, and, of course, our very own Robi Thakur. It would be educative to say the least, you will hear and learn so much. What do you say?'

'That's boring, Biplab da!' said Bappa, voicing the collective opinion of his friends. 'Who wants to see anything educative? I say, we go for this *jatra* performance. *Ei* Soumen, what was the name of the troupe?'

Soumen scratched his chin in an effort to remember. 'Sotyembor Opera, I think,' he said.

'Let's talk to them,' said Bappa with an air of authority. 'It's been a long time since we have had any good entertainment around here. There are only so many tree plantation drives and primary school inaugurations we can take. What do you say, guys?'

There followed a unanimous agreement. A *jatra* would be the perfect way to spend a chilly winter evening, wrapped up in shawls, munching peanuts sipping a hot cup of tea.

'No, no, no!' protested Biplab Maity. 'Don't you boys want to do something different for a change?'

They responded with vigorous head shaking.

'Maybe, we could do both—the cultural nights and the *jatra* performance,' offered Jishu, inviting stern looks from his friends.

'I am not spending club money on a *jatra*!' announced Biplab Maity with a tone of finality. 'If you want some inspiration, we can kick-start our cultural night by attending the week-long theatre festival.'

'Well, we are members of the club, too,' argued Kaltu. 'We have a say in all the activities. And we say, we want to see a *jatra*!' His friends nodded in unison.

'A Bollywood *jatra*,' emphasized Kaltu, which resulted in more enthusiastic nodding.

'Alright then, we will take a vote,' said Biplab Maity. 'All those who want to see the *jatra*, raise your hands.' All hands except Biplab Maity's own instantly shot up in the air.

'All those who want to go for the theatre festival.'

'All those who want to do both,' said Biplab Maity, in a last-minute effort to save the day.

'That's settled, then,' said Bappa. '*Ei chol.* We'll go talk to Sotyembor Opera tomorrow.'

Biplab Maity looked away. There was only so much you could do to help these boys. You can bring the horse to the water but you cannot make it drink, he thought ruefully.

'Biplab da,' said Jishu, walking over to their club president, 'Look at it this way. If we are going to the theatre festival, then we will be spending money. If we do the *jatra* in Sabuj Kalyan Park, we can actually make money by selling tickets and refreshments. If we price it right, and do enough publicity, we could have a neat sum left over even after settling the payment with the *jatra* company. What do you say?' He hoped this logic delivered in a most placatory tone would be enough to cheer their leader.

'Yes, but...'

'But what, Biplab da?'

'This is not what I had in mind.'

'Oh, come on! Let us do something fun for a change,' pleaded Bappa.

'Also, don't you think we need to ease our way into this cultural onslaught?' asked Bhombol. 'I think this is a good beginning, a very good beginning. We can start with the *jatra* and work our way up the cultural ladder...slowly, very slowly.' The others agreed.

Biplab Maity let out a long sigh. 'Alright,' he said. 'We will go meet Sotyembor Opera tomorrow.'

If he were to be entirely honest with himself, Biplab Maity had to admit, that the loud, exhilarating cheers and back thumping with 'Jiyo Biplab da!' that followed, did feel good.

This is what I do, he thought, smiling to himself. I give the boys reason to cheer.

I Have Found the Boy!

Chhaya Guha Roy stirred the curry distractedly. She reached for the spice container—a circular stainless steel vessel containing several small jars arranged neatly like petals of a flower—took a spoonful of salt and held it in mid-air. Had she put salt already? Her mind, and heart, were not in the *niramish jhol* today. Which was a pity, because, for a change, every ingredient—right down to the *hinger bori*—had been brought from the market.

She poured the salt back into the salt jar, inserted a fresh spoon into the bubbling curry, blew the vapour off the spoon and slurped the liquid. Yes, salt had already been added. And a little too much at that. Adding another spoonful would have been a disaster. She covered the vessel and lowered the flame.

Her thoughts went back to the phone call from Mr Ganguly. He was unable to make the trip to Calcutta. Something urgent had come up. He was sorry, he had said. His tone…had not been rude, thought Chhaya Guha Roy, but it lacked the 'softness' inherent in a genuine apology.

Chhaya Guha Roy, on her part, had sounded most accommodating. Of course she understood. And certainly they will wait till the Gangulys could plan another trip to Calcutta. There was absolutely no need to apologize.

When she replaced the receiver, she became aware of a heaviness in the heart. She found herself thinking, *they have made their choice. They probably want to wait and see if the negotiation will work out. If it does not, they would consider seeing Piya. That would explain why they do not want to cut off all communication with us.*

And frankly, this should not come as such a surprise. Had she not said right from the start, the Gangulys were too good, too 'hi-fi' for them. But no, her husband, Debdas Guha Roy, daydreaming about a doctor son-in-law, had paid little heed to her misgivings. He would be heartbroken. He would never say it out loud, of course, but he would be just as upset on hearing the news.

This was the last potential alliance on their list. They had seen umpteen families. They had rejected some, most had rejected them. As far as Chhaya Guha Roy was concerned, this was really the end of the road. Would Piya never get married then? The possibility had not occurred to her till now. And now that the thought—ominous as it were—formed in her mind, the probability of this being true seemed very real. She forced herself to shrug it off and consider other possibilities. Should she call her sister in Bangalore? She had mentioned a neighbour's son, Chhaya Guha Roy recalled, an IT professional working at Infosys or Wipro or one of those names one gets to hear all the time.

Having adjusted for the extra salt and having switched off the burner, she sat down on the bed. The telephone diary, replete with handwritten entries, lay open on her lap. She began thumbing through the pages when the front door opened announcing that her husband was home.

'The Gangulys had called,' she said, trying her best to sound casual.

'Who?'

'Ganguly babu. Doctor Rajshekhar Ganguly's father,' she emphasized.

'O, him.'

'They cannot come to Calcutta now. Some urgent work.' She

waited. Her husband, supporting himself with one hand on the wall, bent down to unstrap his sandals.

'I don't think they really want to see Piya,' she continued. 'If you ask me, they have already decided on someone...'

'Good!'

'*O ma!* What are you saying? How is this good? The Gangulys were our last hope. We have no other leads. You know how difficult it is to find qualified Bengali Kayastha boys!'

'I have found the boy,' her husband replied matter-of-factly.

'What? What did you say? You have found a boy?'

'No. I didn't say that,' Debdas Guha Roy shook his head. 'I didn't say I have found a boy. I said, I have found *the* boy.'

'Oh? Why didn't you say so?' asked Chhaya Guha Roy. She rushed to the kitchen to fetch a glass of water.

'Who is this boy? Where did you find him?'

Debdas Guha Roy took the glass and gulped down the water in one go. He sat himself on the armchair, wiped his mouth with the sleeve of his *panjabi* and began, 'His name is Rajib. Rajib Guha. Kayastha. Chartered Accountant.'

Chhaya Guha Roy looked up at the ceiling and briefly shut her eyes. *There was always God.*

'Handsome fellow,' continued Debdas Guha Roy. '*Ei* about 5'8". Age not more than 28, I would say.'

'Where did you meet him?' asked Chhaya Guha Roy sitting gingerly at the edge of the divan, the empty glass of water still in her hand.

'He had come to see Joj Saheb the other day...regarding a possible murder investigation. Do you know what struck me most about this boy? He understands the value of hard-earned money. He has had to struggle quite a bit in his life...orphaned at a young age, brought up by a spinster aunt—and now by God's grace, he stands to gain a huge inheritance. Good looking, polite, intelligent—there is no way Piya will not like him.'

'*Bah! Bah!*' exclaimed Chhaya Guha Roy. 'But about this murder investigation…whose murder?'

'His boss, Probhat Sanyal. Died of cardiac arrest. But Rajib feels that there could be something fishy about his death.'

'O,' Chhaya Guha Roy's face darkened. 'Is there any possibility of…trouble?'

'*Arrey*, no, no!'

'I see. And Joj Saheb? What does he think?'

'Joj Saheb? Uhh…well he thinks that Rajib is probably the murderer. But the…'

'What?! You plan to marry off your daughter to a murderer? Have you completely lost your mind?!'

'Ah Chhaya! You exaggerate. First of all, we do not even know if this is at all a case of murder. Secondly, even if it was…all Joj Saheb said was that Rajib Guha is a strong suspect, given that he is the one who stands to gain the most from his boss's death. But that does not necessarily make him the murderer, does it? Besides, if he himself was the culprit, why would he come asking for an investigation? Tell me?'

Chhaya Guha Roy considered this. 'Na, na…I don't like the sound of this at all,' she said eventually, shaking her head and throwing her hands up in the air. 'A murder suspect as my son-in-law? Is there a famine of qualified Bengali boys in the country!?'

'You only said just now how difficult it is to find a good boy.'

'Yes, but still…'

'Don't worry, Chhaya. You leave this one to me. I will take care of it, you'll see.'

'What exactly are you going to do?'

'Just leave it to me.'

Unwelcome News

Chandan Mukherjee made his way into the Daily Market. On either side of him, vegetable vendors sat on coarse jute carpets, surrounded by heaps of vegetables. This being December, the variety and quality of vegetables was definitely more appealing than the drier summer months. The cauliflowers, observed Chandan Mukherjee, looked fresh and white, and the apples, nice and red. Though a closer inspection revealed that they had been imported from other lands. He replaced the apple in the pile. Didn't apples come from Shimla earlier? How is it that we have to now eat apples from New Zealand?

Several shoppers, armed with their nylon *tholis*, jostled for space in the crowded marketplace. Ladies, Chandan Mukherjee had noticed, had a particularly tough time, holding on to the bag and clutching on to their purse at the same time. No wonder they were the easier targets of petty thieves. He immediately slid his hand into the *panjabi* pocket to ensure that his wallet was still there.

It was a pity sarees did not have pockets. All this talk one heard about how our country had become 'westernized', and how it was most noticeable in the attires of modern ladies… well, perhaps there was a practical reason to it, thought Chandan Mukherjee. In his time, he could not recall his mother having to step out of the house in order to shop for fish and vegetables. It was a man's job to do that. It was well understood. But women today, not only had to shop in market places, but they also had to work in offices, travel in trams and buses…when he saw the fairer sex in this light, Chandan Mukherjee found his stance on 'today's girls' softening. Not that he had much to worry about in that regard—he had two sons, Bubai and Tubai. Although, sooner or later, they would bring home their brides. But he would worry about that when the time came. For now, he made his way through the crowd to the fish-sellers.

'*Iye*…how much for the *katla*?' he asked.

'180 rupees a kilo, babu. 200 if you want it cut and cleaned.'

'Hmm.'

'And the *parshey*?'

'280 rupees, babu.'

'280!! Give it to me for 250.'

'Cannot do it, babu.' He shook his head and bit his tongue in a gesture of apology.

Chandan Mukherjee was tempted. There was an excellent collection of fish today. The *parshey* fish was Bubai's favourite. Should he pick some up? Bubai was home this week, after his semester exams. He probably had to starve in college…his mother was always saying how he had become even thinner. God only knows what they fed the students in the college mess! For sure he did not get to eat fish like this.

But then, something about Bubai had changed. Of late, every time he visited home, Chandan Mukherjee had found his older son to be more withdrawn, more aloof. He rarely stepped out of his home to catch up with his old *paara* friends, those boys he had grown up and played football with all his life. There were those days of school vacations when young boys in shorts would be out on the street all day, kicking about a ball, calling out to each other, slapping each other on the back, paying little heed to the growing hours, till their mothers called out to them to return home, threatening them with dire consequences if they did not obey right away. Bubai—much like the other boys—would return, his face tanned from the hot afternoon sun, his body smeared with dust, his hair a mess, legs bruised and scratched, and grinning broadly, promising his mother he would return early next time.

Life was such a play of opposites! There was a time when his mother had to plead her son to stay home, and now, seeing her son locked up in his room all day, she wished he would go out more often.

He had asked his wife, Kalpana, about Bubai's strange behaviour. Not directly, of course. But a casual question here and there. Had Bubai spoken about his hostel life? This was his final year had he said anything about his future plans? Had he liked the prawn today?

'Bubai did not even touch the prawns,' she had lamented. 'I made it with so much care—with coconut and mustard.'

'Maybe his stomach is upset,' Chandan Mukherjee had offered by way of explanation. 'Have you asked him if he is feeling alright?

'Of course, I did! He said he was feeling fine.'

'How could he be fine if he is not eating his favourite fish?!' And he would leave it at that. He did not want to alarm his wife unnecessarily. But he had not been able to help thinking if Bubai had fallen into bad company? Was he taking drugs? He could not bring himself to believe these things. Bubai was—had always been—a bright, polite, soft-spoken child. Then, why this sudden change in behaviour? Perhaps he was in love, thought Chandan Mukherjee, and immediately felt tension drain from his face. Young people in love often did the strangest things. Maybe his girlfriend did not like prawns. That wouldn't be quite as disastrous. A vegetarian girlfriend was definitely more welcome than a case of drug addiction. But then…why be so cagey? Was he afraid that his parents would not approve of his choice? Was she a non-Bengali, then? A fresh crease appeared on Chandan Mukherjee's forehead.

'O babu! Will you buy fish or not?'

Chandan Mukherjee was forced to halt that thought and address the matter at hand.

'Yes, yes,' he said hastily. '*Parshey*. Half kilo.'

Debdas Guha Roy dialled the number and waited. Four rings… five…he probably should hang up right now. Rajib had to be busy. This was Wednesday, a weekday. Perhaps, he should try an hour or so later, when it was closer to lunch time. Rajib had to be taking a break for lunch. But one never knew with the busy executives of today. Ever so often, one saw them in the office *paaras*, smartly attired, talking on the cell phone while driving a car and munching on a sandwich. One did not have time to sit for a meal any more. There was way too much to be done, and way too little time…

'Hello?' The tired voice of an elderly lady answered the phone.

'Umm…ah.' Debdas Guha Roy cleared his voiced. 'Is this Rajib Guha's number?'

There was silence on the other side.

'Hello? Is this Rajib Guha's number?' he repeated.

'Who is calling?'

'Umm…my name is Debdas Guha Roy.'

'What do you want?'

Debdas Guha Roy was taken aback. Was it possible that a boy as polite as Rajib Guha was raised by an aunt this rude?

'Can I speak to Rajib, please?' He tried again.

'He...he is not here.'

'Oh, I see.' He must have left his phone behind today, he thought. 'When will he be back?'

Silence.

Debdas Guha Roy cleared his throat again. 'I was asking... when will he...?'

'I don't know. I have no idea.'

Debdas Guha Roy thought he heard a heavy sigh on the other end of the line.

'You must be his aunt?' he asked, desperate to not let the conversation end on an abrupt note.

'Why, yes. How did you know?'

'Well, Rajib has told me all about you. How you have brought him up... He speaks very highly of you.'

Did he hear sobbing on the other end?

'Is everything alright...?'

'No. How can it be?' She sniffed.

'Why? What happened?'

'The police...'

'The police? What about them?'

'The police have taken him away.'

She wailed loudly now. 'What has he done, tell me? What could he have done?'

'Please, please calm down,' pleaded Debdas Guha Roy. 'Tell me, when did this happen?'

Nilima Guha, the aunt, took some time to gather herself. 'Last night...just after dinner. I was clearing the table when suddenly there was a loud banging on the door. Rajib went to answer it, and before I knew, two policemen grabbed him and dragged him out of the house. They did not give him time, not even to put on his slippers. Two other policemen searched the whole house.

Said they had a warrant, they waved a paper at me. What do I know of these things? I screamed—"Why are you taking him away? Why are you taking him away?" But they just wouldn't answer me.' She wailed loudly.

'I went to the police station,' she continued, regaining control. 'The inspector said Rajib was being detained for questioning... for the murder of Probhat Sanyal! Murder?! I could not believe my ears. It had to be a mistake, a terrible mistake. Rajib would never...' The remainder of her words were drowned in a howl.

'Yes, yes, I know.' Debdas Guha Roy attempted to provide consolation.

'God knows what they are doing to him.'

Debdas Guha Roy thought fast. Joj Saheb had been right. But this had to be a huge mistake. Somewhere, something was not quite right.

'Please don't worry,' he said hastily. 'I will take care of this. Rajib will be out in no time, you will see. Everything will be alright...didi,' he added.

Lab Inspector for a Day

It was amazing how the mind worked. At one moment, you could be staring at a long list of names, feeling utterly lost. How could one tell, armed with just names and past academic records, if someone was thinking of ending his life? People with suicidal tendencies did not have names starting with the letter M, for example. That would have made things much simpler. And moments later, by simply using the power of observation and inference, one could narrow it down to a single person.

Debdas Guha Roy's keen eyes had been on the students all day. He watched batch after batch of students, fiddling with chemicals—the copper carbonates and the hydrochloric acids—then measuring them, pouring them in test tubes, stirring, heating and observing the results.

The chemistry lab always reminded Debdas Guha Roy of a household kitchen. Things were always bubbling, brewing, being added in spoonfuls or heated. It could then be rightly referred to as 'the queen of physical sciences', while physics was definitely the glamorous prince. But neither could exist without the king—mathematics. And geology, Debdas Guha Roy's own subject, being a combination of all three, was surely the entire royal family in one package.

Debdas Guha Roy had devised a clever plan with the help of Kapil, the lab assistant, and Professor Bagchi, who taught inorganic chemistry. He hung around in an unassuming lab coat, smeared with stains and patches redolent of an experienced lab manager. If someone asked—and chances were very little that any student would—he would be introduced as a government official visiting for a day to check if lab safety standards were being followed. It seemed plausible enough, and Debdas Guha Roy felt confident that he would be able to carry off the part with relative ease.

A minor problem did arise from time to time, when one of the boys, mistaking him to be a new professor, insisted on asking him complicated questions. 'Sir, sir, what would happen if we added sulphuric acid to the sodium tetraborate decahydrate, instead of the hydrochloric acid?' At such times Debdas Guha Roy would acknowledge the boy with a 'Very good question. Think about it some more,' and retreat hastily to another table.

Amidst all the chaotic activity, Debdas Guha had noticed a boy—short with spiky hair and round glasses—who seemed utterly disinterested in what was being done. He would stare out of the window, absentmindedly stirring the test tube in his hand. When Professor Bagchi went about checking what the students had done, commenting on their day's work, he remarked that this boy had nothing to show. What had he been doing all morning? The boy mumbled an apology. Professor Bagchi was about to write 'Incomplete work' in his lab note book, but hesitated. He threw Debdas Guha Roy a hasty look, before writing, 'Continue in the next class'.

Kapil had noticed him, too. 'Porag Nandi' he whispered in Debdas Guha Roy's ear. His academic record showed a steady decline—from being at the top of the class to barely managing to pass the course. In an instant, all the confusion evaporated.

We have found the one, Debdas Guha Roy nodded at Kapil.

The ABCD Take up the Case

'It doesn't look good, *moshai*.' Akhil Banerjee shook his head. 'Doesn't look good at all.'

The look of concern on his face unsettled Debdas Guha Roy. 'What do you mean, Joj Saheb?' he asked timorously.

'I spoke to Prokash Dhar, the criminal lawyer,' continued Akhil Banerjee. 'This is how it stands. Probhat Sanyal had a big argument with Rajib that morning—the maid, as well as Probir babu's wife heard him speak agitatedly. Probir babu's wife swore she heard him mention the word "will" at least a couple of times. So in all likelihood, Rajib actually knew the contents of the will. Rajib might have been aware that Probhat Sanyal had called Biren earlier that morning. Rajib knows Biren is a lawyer. What if Probhat babu was considering changing his will?

'The evening of 13th December, a little after eight, Probhat babu was served dinner in his room. Sometime later, his brother Probir babu went to speak to him. According to Probir babu, they were talking about this and that, when suddenly Probhat babu clutched his chest and appeared to have trouble breathing. Probir babu, guessing his brother was having a heart attack, alerted the remaining family members. But Probhat babu collapsed almost immediately…even before they had the chance to call for a doctor or an ambulance.'

'But where is the proof that Rajib was involved?' asked Debdas Guha Roy. 'He had left the house hours earlier.'

'Yes, well, this is further bad news. It seems Probhat babu's dying words were, *Raj…Raj.*'

'That doesn't prove anything!' exclaimed Debdas Guha Roy. 'Probhat Sanyal was very fond of Rajib. In their dying moments, people want to be with the ones they love the most.'

'It could well be an explanation, Debdas babu. But think about this. Probhat Sanyal knew that Rajib was not around. What was the point of calling out his name?'

'So why do you think he did, Joj Saheb?' asked Chandan Mukherjee, unwrapping his muffler, and re-wrapping it tightly around his face so as to cover his ears.

'Well, at first his family interpreted it in much the same way—that Probhat babu was fond of Rajib and probably wanted to see him in his dying moments. But later, when they got to know about the inheritance he stood to gain, and when Probir babu's wife and maid mentioned the argument, it did seem rather suspicious. What if Probhat babu was actually accusing Rajib of some foul play?'

'But how could Rajib commit the murder? He was not in the room when Probhat Sanyal passed away!' argued Debdas Guha Roy.

'The most likely guess—and again, we haven't proved it is a murder yet—is poisoning. Rajib could have mixed something in Probhat babu's drink or his medication. It is not difficult to imagine that he might have had the opportunity…'

'No, no, no, no, *moshai*,' said Debdas Guha Roy exasperatedly. 'Somehow, I find it impossible to believe. If Rajib was indeed guilty, would he have come to us looking for help, tell me? If he is guilty in any way, why would he want anyone to dwell on the matter?'

'I have to say, that is one point that goes in Rajib's favour,' admitted Akhil Banerjee. 'In my long career in crime, I am yet to come across a single case where the guilty wants an investigation. But then...'

'What, Joj Saheb?'

Akhil Banerjee did not respond immediately.

'Debdas babu, I'm only thinking aloud here, what if Rajib did commit the murder.' He raised his hand to stop Debdas Guha Roy's verbal protest, 'And what if he suspected that Sanyal babu's family would be onto him sooner or later. Then, by coming to Biren, and saying things like he smells a rat, and that there had to be something going on, he is actually precluding himself from the list of suspects?'

Debdas Guha Roy knitted his brows in an effort to comprehend this fully.

'*Moshai*, there is one other point,' said Bibhuti Bose, speaking for the first time. 'Let us say Rajib indeed had malicious intentions and wanted to do away with his boss. But how is it that he had the poison ready with him that day? I mean, how would he know that Probhat babu was going to be angry with him or that he would call Biren Ghoshal that very day?'

'Yes, excellent point, Bibhuti babu!' agreed Debdas Guha Roy. 'What do you think, Joj Saheb?'

'Well, once it is proved that this is a case of murder, the question will naturally arise whether this is a "spur of the moment" thing or a premeditated act,' said Akhil Banerjee. 'We will need to wait and see how the facts unfold. If indeed it is death by poisoning, the likelihood is that it must be a premeditated act, which further weakens Rajib's stand.'

'Joj Saheb,' said Debdas Guha Roy, 'I was just thinking, can we not do some investigation on our own. I mean, after all, we are the All Bengali Crime Detectives. Somehow, I am finding it quite difficult to sit back and be a mere spectator.'

'I second that, Debdas babu,' said Chandan Mukherjee, supporting himself on the walking stick while getting up. 'It has been quite a while since we did some *detectivegiri*. My wife has already started taunting me, *moshai. Ki holo? Why in the house all day? No more cases to solve?* I say, this is as good an opportunity as any to exercise the brain cells before they start rusting again.'

'Hmm... I suppose we could do some sniffing around,' said Akhil Banerjee thoughtfully. 'I don't think Prokash, the lawyer, will mind. I'll keep him in the loop in case we manage to find something of significance.'

'How do you propose we go about it, Joj Saheb?' asked Debdas Guha Roy.

'I was thinking we could start by paying a visit to Rajib's aunt.'

'I was thinking the same. Shall we go today?' asked Debdas Guha Roy.

'We could. But perhaps all of us need not go. It might be unsettling for her to suddenly find four old men at her doorstep. Debdas babu, how about you and I visit her later this morning?'

'Sounds like a good idea.'

'Will you call her once and inform her that we will be there 11-ish?'

'Sure, Joj Saheb. Will do.'

Bengalis Cannot Be Vegetarian

'Come, eat,' called out Kalpana Mukherjee to her sons.

A second later the sound of flip-flops filled the otherwise quiet house. Tubai came down the stairs and occupied his usual chair. His mother sprinkled water on his stainless-steel plate, and drained it off. Tubai took a spoonful of rice and poured it on his plate.

'Wait, wait, I'm giving!' said Kalpana Mukherjee in an exasperated tone, snatching the serving spoon from her younger son. 'Where is Dada?'

Tubai shrugged in response.

'Maybe he hasn't heard me call out for lunch,' said his mother, pouring *daal* into the little well Tubai had dug out in the pile of steamed rice. She put spoonfuls of vegetables and fritters along the perimeter of the plate, and the fish curry in a bowl.

'Wonder what is taking him so long,' she said, glancing up the stairs. 'Go call him.'

Tubai pursed his lips in mild irritation. He sucked *daal* off his fingers, tapped off the extra rice on his plate and pushed his chair behind to get up.

'Oh there he is,' said Kalpana Mukherjee. 'What took you so long? The rice was beginning to get cold.'

Bubai sat down silently. Kalpana Mukherjee saw from the

corner of her eye—while putting an extra couple of fish in a bowl—how unlike his younger brother—Bubai had not immediately begun gorging on the food. Instead, she noticed with caution, he had touched the rim of his plate and briefly closed his eyes, as if praying in silence. She pretended not to have seen this, averting her gaze as soon as Bubai opened his eyes. She noticed how he ate—slowly, almost with reverence—unlike her younger son, who ate like he had a train to catch and was running desperately late.

She pulled a chair and sat down. These little quirks had begun to bother her. No one in their family ever prayed before a meal. They all sat at the table and ate, like normal people. She knew Christians did that—thanked God for the meal, and the good life in general—she had seen it in a movie once. Had her son changed his faith, then? Was that the reason he was so secretive these days? Who knew, perhaps he had a photo of Jesus Christ hanging in his room, which is why he never allowed anyone to enter while he was there.

There was a perfectly good explanation for all this, she thought. All his life, Bubai had attended Don Bosco School in Park Circus. He had prayed to Jesus, looked at statues of Christ, read passages from The Holy Bible during school prayers and had Fathers for teachers. It was not altogether difficult to imagine then, that while getting an excellent education, he had been unconsciously influenced by these factors.

These things happened all the time. There was Madhusudan Dutta, the great Bengali poet and the author of one of her favourite literary pieces—*Meghnad Bodh Kabyo*, or *The Saga of Meghnad's Killing*. The poet had changed his faith and converted to Christianity. Changed his name too, to *Michael*. Poets for centuries had glorified the righteous King Rama, but it took a genius like Michael Madhusudhan Dutta to exalt the bravery and the tragic death of a hero in the enemy camp. How excited she had been when Tubai, her younger son, was being taught this very piece at school. She had spent hours rereading the lines to her son, explaining the difficult metre of the poem, writing out explanatory notes to all the allegory. And in the end, when the answer sheets were returned from school, she was aghast to see several question marks beside the answer to the *Meghnad Bodh Kabyo* question. For instead of writing "The above lines have been taken from *Meghnad Bodh Kabyo* written by Michael Madhusudan Dutta.", her son had written "The above lines have been taken from *Meghnad Bodh Kabyo* written by Michael Jackson."

It had been an honest mistake, she knew. A momentary lapse of concentration…But she had been unable to swallow the sheer humiliation of it all.

Had Bubai changed his name, too? From Shyamal Mukherjee to…to…Samuel Mukherjee, perhaps? She sighed. If only her husband had invested some time in reading to their sons from the Bhagavad Geeta. It was not Bubai's fault at all, she saw that clearly now—if the only holy book one had read all throughout the growing years was The Bible, then it was quite natural to assume that the Bible was the best world religion had had to offer. There was nothing wrong in reading The Bible or learning more about other religions. But she would encourage her son—gently, casually—to look into the books written by Thakur Sri Ramkrishna, perhaps. Or, at the very least, watch a few episodes of The Ramayon. These days there were a dozen spiritual channels on television. Sages and saints gave discourses, some of them not entirely boring to listen to. Something had to be…

'Ma,' said Bubai interrupting her planning. 'My *poitey* is almost in tatters. Could you get me a new one before I leave for college?'

Kalpana Mukherjee heaved a huge sigh of relief. If her son

was still concerned about the condition of his sacred thread, the symbol of his high Brahmin caste, then certainly Samuel Mukherjee was no longer a cause for concern. She pushed the bowl of fish curry towards Bubai.

'What is this?'

'Fish. *Parshey.* It's full of eggs, just the way you love it.'

'I'm not having this.'

'Why?! You won't get this in the hostel. Try it. You'll love it.'

'I don't want to. Give me some more *daal*.'

He said it in a tone of finality that suggested to Kalpana Mukherjee that it was pointless to argue. She sighed deeply and poured more *daal* onto her son's plate. Her younger son who was sitting with his plate empty, except for the pile of fish cartilage, asked, 'Can I have Dada's share, then?'

Kalpana Mukherjee reluctantly pushed the bowl towards Tubai, who immediately put morsels of the succulent fish in his mouth, pulling out the harder cartilages between his lips, much like magicians pull out ribbons from the hidden corners of their mouth. She waited till her younger son had finished and left the table. Some matters were best discussed in private.

The other day her husband had been trying to tell her something. Not directly, of course, but beating around the bush as was typical of men, who found such topics 'uncomfortable' and hoped that the need to talk about them would never occur in their lives.

'*Iye*,' he had started, 'I was just saying…have you spoken to Bubai, lately?'

'About what?'

'Na, nothing as such. I bought *parshey* fish today.'

'What about Bubai?'

'The fish are full of eggs, see? There was prawn too, but I thought…'

'You were saying something about Bubai?'

'Huh?! Oh...yes. He seems to be a little *iye* these days.'

'*Iye*?'

'You know...'

'You mean...withdrawn?'

Her husband nodded.

'Yes, I noticed.'

'Do you think maybe...he has an *iye-tiye*?' Here the addition of the rhyming '*tiye*' alarmed Kalpana Mukherjee. It could only mean one thing.

'You mean...?'

Her husband had shrugged, keeping his eyes on the bag of vegetables at all times. 'He's a young man now...maybe...'

'Do you think she is someone he met in college?' She had to be direct. This was no time for ambiguity.

'Possibly. If you ask me...' Here he had had to stop. The maid had just entered the kitchen.

Kalpana Mukherjee ordered the maid to take out the vegetables from the *tholi* and indicated 'to the living room' to her husband, who followed reluctantly.

'You were saying?'

'Na, it's just a thought.'

'Tell me.' They spoke in hushed tones.

'I was thinking...maybe she's a non-Bengali. I'm not sure, of course,' he hastened, seeing a shadow of alarm cross over his wife's face. 'It's just a thought that occurred,' he added.

'Why would you think so?'

'Well...you know how he has been avoiding fish and mutton lately? You remember how much he used to love Golbari's mutton or biriyani from Shiraj? So I was thinking...Marwaris are vegetarian...'

'Marwari?! You mean our son is bringing home a Marwari?'

'*Arrey* na, na…it could just as well be a South Indian…'

'Madrasi?!'

'Uff! I don't know! All I am saying is…' And just then Tubai had walked in to the room, switched on the television set and plopped onto the sofa, as if completely oblivious to the presence of his parents right next to him. This conversation would have to continue at another time.

Well, now is as good a time as any other, thought Kalpana Mukherjee as she heard the door of Tubai's room slam shut. She turned to face her older son, who had stood up with an empty plate in hand.

'Sit,' she ordered.

'Ma, please…I don't want to eat fish.'

'That's alright. I am not asking you to.'

'Then?'

'We need to talk.'

'About what?'

'About your career.'

Tubai sat down reluctantly. 'What about it?'

'*Na*. your father was just saying…this is your final year. have you decided what to do? Go for an MBA or an M.Tech, or look for a job?'

'Please ask him not to worry about all this.'

'But…have you thought of something?'

'Ma, I'll think about it when the time comes.'

An uncomfortable silence followed.

'Can I go now?' asked Bubai.

'Yes…no, wait.'

'What now?'

'Is there something you want to tell us, *baba*?'

Bubai shrugged. 'No. Not really.'

'I am your mother, *sona*. Is there anything at all that we need to know?'

'Not that I can think of.'

Kalpana Mukherjee tried another approach.

'Is she a Madrasi?'

'Who?'

'You know what I am talking about, Bubai. Just tell me, is she non-Bengali?'

'I have no idea what you are talking about!'

'I'm talking about your friend.' Here she used the feminine gender to stress her point.

Bubai looked at his mother inquiringly.

'What are you driving at, Ma?'

'You know very well. Just answer my question. Don't I at least have the right to know who my son has decided to bring home?'

'Ma! I'm not bringing anyone home!'

'Then why won't you eat fish anymore?'

'Huh?! How did you connect not eating fish to having a…a… girlfriend?!'

'What else could it be? Your father was saying…'

'What?!'

'He said maybe Bubai is now friends with a Madrasi girl. They are strict vegetarians, aren't they?'

'Ma, please! There is no Madrasi girl…'

'She could be Marwari, too…'

'Marwari?'

'Your father was saying…'

'Ma, I am not involved with any girl. No Madrasi, Marawari, Punjabi, Gujarati…'

'Look, sona, there is nothing wrong in all this. All I am saying is, right now is the time for you to study, build your career. When it is time for marriage, Baba and I will find someone really nice for you. And if you do not approve of our choice, and want to marry a non-Bengali girl, it will be perfectly fine with us. Trust me, you will not find such progressive mind-set in people of our generation. So don't think of marriage right now. When the time comes…'

'Ma, I am not thinking of getting married! I do not even have a girlfriend. Why won't you believe me?'

'Then why have you changed so much, tell me? You don't talk to us, you stay locked in your room, you don't even go out to meet your friends. You don't eat fish anymore. What has happened, *baba*? Is there something else. Are you…are you taking drugs?' Her eyes were moist, her voice thick with anxiety.

'Uff!' Bubai rolled his eyes and got up from his seat.

'Tell Ma, na?' pleaded his mom.

'Can't you think of a better, a more obvious reason?'

Kalpana Mukherjee's expression changed from anxiety to that of puzzlement. She shook her head in response.

Bubai let out a sigh before answering. 'I lock my room so that no one can disturb me when I meditate. I don't go out to meet my *paara* friends because frankly, I don't enjoy their company anymore. They only want to go to pubs and drink and waste time talking about mundane things…'

Kalpana Mukherjee beamed at her son. How could she even doubt this gem of a boy?! She couldn't wait to speak to her husband. Girlfriend, drugs…and all the ridiculous ideas he had come up with! But there was one other thing that puzzled her.

'But…why won't you eat fish, *baba*?'

'I don't eat fish because,' he paused briefly before dropping the bomb, 'I have become vegetarian. *Holo?* Does that satisfy you?'

By the time the words had sunk in, Bubai was up the flight of stairs and back in his room.

For a few seconds, Kalpana Mukherjee sat in stunned silence, unable to make sense of what she had just been told. She struggled to find words to articulate the incongruousness of the current situation.

'But…but…you are a Bengali,' were the only words that eventually tumbled out of her mouth.

Nilima Guha

Akhil Banerjee's Mark IV ambassador sped across Sukanto Setu, then turned right to enter into Kasba. It meandered through the narrow lanes, stopping only once, to ask for directions from a pedestrian, who took one look at the address scribbled on the piece of paper held out by Debdas Guha Roy and waved in the general direction ahead. Minutes later, the white and gray building of Abasan Housing had been spotted. Akhil Banerjee and Debdas Guha Roy climbed up the two flights of stairs to find themselves in front of a door that had the words 'R. Guha, N. Guha' painted on a wooden nameplate.

Debdas Guha Roy pressed the doorbell. Sounds of various locks and latches being turned and pulled was followed by a cautious opening of the door. A safety latch, Akhil Banerjee noticed, was still in place.

'Who is it?'

'It is us, didi,' replied Debdas Guha Roy. 'I had called you earlier today. Debdas Guha Roy. And this is my friend, Mr Banerjee.' He had been forewarned not to mention the judge's past profession right at the onset.

'Oh yes, of course,' she said, still sounding unsure.

'*Iye*—can we come in? Just for a few minutes? We may be able to help Rajib,' said Akhil Banerjee.

The door opened and they stepped into the living room. A strong citrus smell hit their nostrils. The room was small, modestly furnished with a sofa—the dark brown upholstery of which had given way in several places to reveal the innards of foam and spring, a couple of cane chairs and a table. The television set rested atop a glass showcase, which housed, among other things, miniature clay statues of Gods and photographs of a young Nilima Guha with a small boy on the terrace or by the sea-side.

Nilima Guha was a short statured, frail looking lady, probably in her late fifties. There was a certain similarity of features between the aunt and her nephew, the same longish face, the prominent jaw line, the pale skin colour. Her eyes though, looked tired, as if she hadn't slept in days.

'Tea?' she asked, once the visitors had settled down on the sofa.

'No, thank you,' replied Akhil Banerjee. 'Ah...what is this smell?'

'Oh this?' said Nilima Guha waving her hand in a way that included her entire house. 'It's a perfumed candle. Bought one yesterday from a sales girl. There have been a lot of them lately—young boys and girls who go from door to door selling everything from washing powders to cosmetics to even car loans. And they will come at the oddest hour, right when I'm about to take a bath, or have managed to doze off a little in the afternoon.'

The visitors nodded politely.

'Didi,' said Debdas Guha Roy, after a surreptitious eye signal from Akhil Banerjee, 'We are not sure how much we can help, but my friend here is a retired High Court judge. He is on our side,' he added hastily. 'Rajib had come to see him—to see us—right after the death of Probhat Sanyal. He suspected there could be some foul play in his boss's death.'

'Oh he did? Did he? He never told me anything though,' said Nilima Guha, looking doubtful.

'Well...I have arranged for Prokash Dhar to represent Rajib.

He is a top criminal lawyer. Rajib is in good hands,' assured Akhil Banerjee.

Nilima Guha nodded slowly as if taking time to comprehend.

'Could you tell us what happened that day, December 13th, the day Probhat Sanyal died?' asked Akhil Banerjee.

'Well, Rajib returned late…said he had gone to see a movie after work…'

'Did Rajib say anything about his day? Did he look upset, enraged, or excited?'

Nilima Guha shook her head thoughtfully. 'Although…' she stopped.

Debdas Guha Roy coaxed her to continue.

'Well…it's probably nothing,' she said after some thought. 'But…normally, I make him a cup of tea as soon as he comes home. That day he went straight to his room, so I brought him his tea there. The next day, when I went into his room, the cup was still full. He hadn't even touched it.'

'Hmm…I see. How did you find out about the news?'

'We had just sat down to dinner, when the phone came. Someone from his office… Manohar babu, I think. Rajib took the phone and went out into the balcony. I could not hear what they spoke about but I could see he was terribly upset. Twice I called out to him, his dinner was getting cold. Eventually, he came into the room looking disturbed. I asked him what was the matter. Sir has passed away, he said. He got ready and left immediately.

'He returned very late in the night, then went to the burning ghat at Keoratala early next day. Poor boy…he was grief-stricken. He had never known a father, you know. Orphaned at a very early age. Probhat babu was like a guardian to him. He was extremely fond of his boss, worshipped him, you could say.'

'The arrest,' said Akhil Banerjee, 'it came almost a week after Probhat Sanyal's death, am I right?'

'Yes, on the 18th, to be exact. Two days ago.' Nilima Ghosh shook her head. 'Worst day of my life, you could say. Rajib came home from work, very tired as usual. I made him a cup of tea. The doorbell sounded. I thought it must be the bank salesman. He had come two or three days previously, and had started talking about a complicated savings scheme. It had sounded promising, I have to confess, though I understand very little of financial matters. I had asked him to come in the evening one day, when Rajib was around.' She paused briefly. 'It turned out to be the police. Four policemen with pistols and batons. I almost fainted. They barged into the room, grabbed Rajib and pulled him out of this chair, like that.' She mimicked. 'Before I could even understand what was going on, Rajib was dragged down the stairs and shoved into a police van. He did not even have the time to put on his sandals.' Her eyes welled up and she dabbed them quickly with the lose end of her sari. 'They have made a mistake, a huge mistake, dada.'

A torrent of tears came flowing out of her eyes. They gave her time to gather herself.

'Do you have any reason to believe that the relationship between Rajib and Probhat babu was strained of late?'

She thought carefully before shaking her head.

'Did Rajib mention any squabbles with his boss?'

She shook her head again, now beginning to look worried. 'Why are you asking these questions, dada? Was there any trouble at office?'

'No, no, didi,' replied Debdas Guha Roy reassuringly. 'Joj Saheb is just trying to get a clearer picture, that's all.'

'Can we see his room once?' asked Akhil Banerjee.

'Yes, yes.'

Nilima Guha led them into a small bedroom, as sparsely furnished as the rest of the apartment. A single 'camp bed' lay alongside a wall on which pillows and blankets had been dumped. Other furniture in the room included a desk, a chair and an *aalna*—the old-fashioned clothes' rack still found in many homes in Calcutta. The green walls had plaster peeling off in places. A large crack had appeared on the ceiling. The only thing that seemed glaringly out-of-place was a bulbous music system beside the bed. A single window offered a view of the adjoining rooftop, with its TV antennae, a satellite dish, and a clothesline on which washed laundry swayed in the gentle breeze.

Akhil Banerjee glanced quickly through the books and papers lying on the desk.

The door bell sounded, and a sudden anxious look returned on Nilima Guha's face.

'Shall I go check?' asked Debdas Guha Roy.

He opened the door to find a tall, young boy, perhaps in his late teens.

The boy looked at Debdas Guha Roy quizzically, then asked, 'Is Kakima there?'

'She's inside,' replied Debdas Guha Roy.

'Kakima, do you need something from the market?' yelled the boy.

Nilima Guha hurried out of Rajib's room.

'No, *baba*,' she replied lovingly. 'Not much cooking these days.'

'Er…any news of Rajib da?' he asked in a lowered voice.

She shook her head in response. 'We have a good lawyer. Rest everything is in God's hands.'

The boy nodded. 'Let me know if you need anything,' he said, before turning away to leave.

'Who is he?' asked Debdas Guha Roy.

'Oh him? Sumon. He lives downstairs. Loves Rajib like an older brother. Poor boy…even he is heartbroken.'

A few further questions followed but they did not seem to yield much result.

'We should get going,' said Akhil Banerjee presently.

'Will you help Rajib?' asked Nilima Guha, anxiousness returning in her voice.

'We want to. As I mentioned earlier, Prokash is the best criminal lawyer I know. If Rajib is innocent—and I am sure he is—Prokash will get him out in no time.'

'Oh, alright, if you say so,' she sounded unsure.

'Didi, there is one other thing,' said Debdas Guha Roy, when they had stepped out of the door.

'Yes?'

'Just one word of advice…please don't take it otherwise. You stay alone in this house most of the time, I do not think it is wise for you to entertain sales boys and girls, especially those who want to sell you things like candles and room fresheners.'

'Why is that, dada?'

'Haven't you seen in the papers? There was a case not too long ago. A young man went door to door selling an insect repellent or something like that. In one apartment, there was an elderly lady living all alone. The salesman offered to demonstrate the effectiveness of his product. He came inside the apartment and apparently sprayed something from a can right onto the lady's face. She became unconscious. The man looted everything—cash, jewelry—and fled.'

'Yes, I remember the story,' said Nilima Guha. 'Normally, I do not entertain them. But there was this young girl—quite nice to look at, and in desperate need of money.' She paused.

'I could not turn her away. Showed me a bag full of perfumed candles and incense sticks that she needed to sell by the end of the day. She studies in a girl's college in the city and works in her spare time to make ends meet. I suppose, she reminded me of myself, when Rajib was a child. I would take up every odd job that came my way so that his fees could be paid and books and stationary could be bought.'

The gentlemen nodded their comprehension.

'Alright, then, we should get going,' said Debdas Guha Roy folding his hands in namaskar. 'You have my number, didi. Do call me if you need anything.'

'Thank you, dada.'

Once inside the car, Akhil Banerjee remarked, 'What is it, Debdas babu?'

'Huh? Sorry, did you say something, Joj Saheb?'

'You look lost in thought. What seems to be the matter?'

'*Arrey,* no, no, Joj Saheb,' replied Debdas Guha Roy, easing his face into a smile. 'I was just wondering...never mind, it's not important.'

*

Nilima Guha shut the door, replaced all the locks and latches and walked absent-mindedly to Rajib's room. She sat on the camp-bed, going through the conversation she had just had with the retired Judge and Mr Guha Roy. They seemed nice enough, and were probably willing to help. That had to mean Rajib was innocent. But then...what about the rift he mentioned between Probhat babu and Rajib? Did Rajib harbour a resentment towards his boss, but took care not to show it? She shook her head—it seemed utterly impossible. Besides Probhat babu loved Rajib dearly—left him a large inheritance. A fresh crease appeared on her forehead. Was that why they suspected him? If he stands to gain by Probhat babu's death, then he must be the killer…is that what they are thinking? It was ridiculous! Rajib would never even dream of such a thing. But then…what was in the packet she had discovered while cleaning Rajib's room the day before? A whitish powder in a transparent white packet, the opening of which had been tied with a rubber band? She had found it, while changing the sheets of Rajib's bed, buried deeply under the pile of blankets. She thought of asking Sumon as to what it could be, but something had told her she needed to keep it a secret. Maybe Rajib was doing drugs—she shook her head and mentally cursed herself for even thinking such thoughts. It was impossible! In any case, it was best not to draw attention to this discovery.

It was a good thing she had discovered it before the police came raiding her house a second time—throwing the clothes out of the *aalna*, rummaging through the papers, pulling out the bed sheet. She was glad she had not mentioned it to the visitors today.

The Problem of Love: Can Never Be Fully Hidden, nor Fully Expressed

Poltu took a long hard look at the mirror. He narrowed his brows, clenched his jaws, turned this way and that, flexed his golf-ball sized biceps, and let his shoulders droop. It was hopeless, he decided. Nothing he did ever yielded any result.

He had been applying cheap gel on his hair, aiming for the Shah Rukh Khan look, but it only made his hair stick out like a porcupine. He had been secretly working out with a couple of bricks stolen from a nearby construction site—bicep curls and shoulder presses, till his arms ached. But his muscles, if it were possible, proved to be shyer than Poltu himself. He had been wearing dark glasses to up the cool factor, but that only invited snide comments from his friends, Bappa and Bhombol, who had questioned aloud the need for the accessory in the failing light of early winter evenings. He eventually had to abandon the sunglasses when, on one occasion, he had bumped into a lamp post, unable to see what was directly in front of him. This had resulted in a rather unsightly bump on his forehead, inviting further unwelcome comments, and raucous laughter accompanied by finger-pointing from his 'friends' for days. He was finally left alone when attention was shifted to Jishu, who skid on a banana peel, setting off a whole sequence of events best suited for a slow-motion scene in a movie: Jishu had landed backwards on a vegetable cart, making the vegetables fly every which way. A ripe tomato had landed on the white shawl of Chandan Mukherjee, who at that precise moment had been negotiating the price of ladies' fingers with the vendor. Fuming and frothing, Chandan Mukherjee had chased Jishu down the road, shouting expletives and waving his walking stick in a menacing way, while Jishu clutching his behind, face contorted in agony, had just about managed to hobble away to safety. This was epic! And even though Poltu had joined in on the laughter and the finger pointing that had followed, he had secretly felt grateful to Jishu.

There were times when Poltu was forced to question the need to invest more time and energy on self-improvement. What was the point? He would wonder. Piya, self engrossed as she was in her own little world, would never look at him anyway. She probably thought she was too good for him. After all, she had a college education *and* a job. What did Poltu have? Not even a certificate from High School.

'*Ei* Poltu! Are you there?' hollered Bhombol from the street outside.

'Coming, coming,' he replied, putting on a shirt and buttoning it in haste. He tried one last time to correct the tuft of hair sticking out from the last generous dose of hair gel, but eventually gave up.

Bappa and Bhombol were waiting on the other side of the street, under the shade of a neem tree. Bappa had on a black leather jacket, making him look all puffed up and heroic. This was not good news. It definitely made Poltu look under-dressed in his white and brown striped T-shirt. Bhombol, he noticed, still had his blue sweater on from the day before. Except that today, he was wearing it inside-out. He had been meaning to ask Bhombol about this for a while. But it would have to wait. For now, Poltu made a mental note to make sure Bhombol sat between Bappa and himself on the Sabuj Kalyan Park boundary wall. That way he would be able to create some distance between himself and the uber-cool Bappa. Though sitting next to the pudgy Bhombol, made Poltu look scrawnier than usual, it was a risk he was willing to take.

'What took you so long?' asked Bhombol.

'Oh, nothing.'

'What's that I smell?' asked Bappa, sniffing the air. 'Are you wearing perfume?!'

'*Arrey*, no, no!' replied Poltu, brushing his sleeves as if in an effort to get the smell off him.

'Then what's that smell?' asked Bappa.

'Uhh…it's probably the incense stick my mother uses. Come, come, let's go.'

They walked silently towards Sabuj Kalyan Park. There was still some light outside, and Poltu considered pulling out his dark glasses from the back pocket of his figure-hugging denims—but resisted the thought. Bappa and Bhombol on his either side, were bound to ruin the effect.

Once at the Sabuj Kalyan Park, they hoisted themselves on the boundary wall. And waited. For Poltu, this had been the routine for the past year or so, ever since he had been hopelessly smitten by Piya Guha Roy, the most beautiful lady of Golf Garden, Golf Green, Jodhpur Park area and who happened to reside in Haripada Das Lane, just a stone's throw from Poltu's shanty. He would wait there, for hours it would seem, to catch a glimpse of his love—when she got off the auto-rickshaw or the bus, and walked towards her home gracefully, clutching a file over her breasts, adjusting her dupatta or checking her watch—her long, black hair tied in a high ponytail, swinging behind her head. It was the best thirty seconds of Poltu's day.

'There she comes! Check her out,' said Bappa in hushed tones, his voice thick with glee.

'Who?' asked Bhombol, scanning the street in both directions.

'Who else?' replied Bappa. 'Mrs Poltu.'

'What??' Poltu looked scandalized. 'What rubbish are you saying?' He looked desperately at Bhombol for support, and realized—seeing his friend's bulging eyes and half-open mouth—that none would be forthcoming.

'Come, come, Poltu,' said Bappa, slapping his back, 'How long did you think you were going to hide your secret crush from us?'

Poltu blushed, blinked, fumbled for words. 'Ba...ba...ba...'

'*Arrey,* what *baa baa black sheep* have you started?' laughed Bappa. 'Tell us clearly, do you *lobh* her or not?'

Poltu stared blankly in response, not daring to turn his head to catch a glimpse of Piya, who, he knew from experience, would disappear behind the bend in another five seconds.

'Is this true, Poltu?' asked Bhombol, finally regaining his voice. Poltu could not decide whether his best friend sounded more shocked or hurt. In either case, cornered as he was, Poltu decided he'd rather make a formal confession to his trusted ally, Bhombol, than to the scheming Bappa. Still turned towards Bhombol, he lowered his eyes and nodded. He distinctly heard Bhombol let out a gasp seconds before Bappa lauded the confession by clapping loudly, singing aloud a couple of lines from a romantic Hindi number...something about a bee chasing nectar in a garden full of flowers.

Poltu felt exposed, naked. His ears hurt, his cheeks burnt. He wanted to disappear in the folds of the earth forever.

'It's alright, Potol,' said Bappa, jumping off the wall, and quite obviously enjoying Poltu's embarrassment. 'We are your friends. You can trust us. The question is, what is the next step?'

'Wha...what next step?'

'This is not the way to woo a girl, Potol,' replied Bappa, with an air of someone deft in the art of wooing girls. 'You need a different approach, a proper game plan.'

'I...I...have a plan,' stammered Poltu, suddenly aware of how fast he was breathing.

'What? What is the plan, tell me? You have been sitting here, on this boundary wall, waiting to catch a glimpse of her, for at least six months now? Or was it longer? What progress have you made, huh? Six months ago, you were on this wall enduring mosquito bites. Today, you are still on this wall, enduring mosquito bites. You continue like this, and very soon Piya Guha Roy will be married off to someone else. She will be off to her in-laws' before your very eyes. And what will you be doing? Sitting on this wall and enduring mosquito bites!'

The highlights of his life thus laid out before him, Poltu could only respond with a gape.

Bappa went on and on about how this was no good, and how he needed to be a man. But even though the words fell on Poltu's ears, his mind was elsewhere. A profound realization had hit him. Thanks to his friend Bappa, he saw it clearly now. He was the textbook example, or at least the celluloid example, of the ultimate tragic hero. The poor, uneducated, unemployed, yet impossibly good-looking boy, who had made the mistake of giving his heart to a woman way out of his league. The beautiful, educated, rich Piya Guha Roy, had held his fragile heart in her hands, crushed it between her fingers before feeding it to the dogs. O the agonies of lost love... What would Poltu do the day Piya, dressed in a bright red Banarasi sari, *chandan* on her cheeks, red vermillion on her forehead, left this neighbourhood for good? He would gulp an entire bottle of poison. No pain could be more than what he would be otherwise going through. Or he could hang himself from the ceiling. When the news reached Piya, would she even bother to shed a tear for this nameless, faceless secret lover.

'*Ei* Poltu!' called out Bappa, forcing him to stop. 'So what is your plan?'

Poltu sighed. 'Poison seems faster than hanging myself,' he replied. 'Hanging seems complicated. What if the rope snaps, or the roof collapses, the knot…'

'*Arrey, dur, dur!* What are you saying?' shot back Bappa. 'Are you thinking of ending your life?!'

'What else is there to do?'

'Idiot!' replied Bappa. 'You think you can commit suicide that easily?'

Nope, thought Poltu, looking even more deflated than before. He would probably fail at that too.

'Be a man, Poltu!' said Bappa. 'Go tell her you *lobh* her!'

What? Talk to Piya?! Of all the ridiculous ideas Bappa had had so far, this had had to be the dumbest! Poltu responded with vigorous head shaking.

'Why not? What have you got to lose?' asked Bappa incredulously. 'What's the big deal about talking to a girl anyway? At the most, she will slap you hard.'

If this was supposed to be Bappa's way of boosting his confidence, it sure wasn't working, thought Poltu.

'But I'll tell you something,' said Bappa, lowering his voice. 'Secretly she will admire your guts.'

Poltu was not convinced. 'I can't do it,' he said simply.

'Okay, if you can't do it, I will,' offered Bappa.

'No, no, no, you cannot talk to her!' forbade Poltu, now jumping off the wall, and shaking his index finger vigorously to emphasize his point. Bappa was a notorious womanizer—it was well known. There was hardly a girl in the neighbourhood, below a certain age and social status, whom Bappa hadn't spoken to. Even Poltu's own sister, he feared, was smitten by his charms. She would stammer and blush impossibly every time Bappa came home, Poltu had noticed. Who is to say Bappa would not manage to entice Piya, too?

'Hmm...okay, then write to her. A beautiful *lobh* letter. I can go give it to her,' said Bappa.

'No, you will not.' said Poltu, looking alarmed.

'Okay fine!' said Bappa, throwing his hands up in the air in surrender. 'Then, you go give it to her yourself.' He smirked.

'Why me? Bhombol can,' said Poltu. He looked at his friend. Bhombol was someone Poltu could definitely trust with the job. He was loyal, hugely overweight, and most importantly, as awkward in front of girls as Poltu himself.

'Or you could do something else,' offered Bhombol, hastily. There *had* to be a way out of this mess. Surely, the price of being a best friend could be paid with another currency.

'Like what?' asked Bappa.

'You could follow her around,' said Bhombol.

'What? Why would he want to do that?' asked Bappa.

'Uh...umm...I saw it in a movie once,' said Bhombol. He had to think fast. 'This boy was in *lobh* with this rich girl. She would not notice him at all. So he followed her around. The girl took notice of this. At first, she felt threatened, angry even. But then she started enjoying it. She liked the idea of being stalked. Then one day, she did not see the boy—he was not at the bus-stop, not in front of her college where he usually stood at the end of the day. She was very upset. The boy did not turn up the next day either, and the next, and the next. She became anxious and started asking the people around, "Have you seen this boy? Have you seen this boy?" Then someone told her, "He has had an accident." A bus had run over him. She ran to the hospital, teary-eyed. There he lay in his death-bed, bandaged beyond recognition, blood oozing out of his body. The girl cried her heart out. Begged the doctor to fix him. She said she would pay for his entire treatment. She came to see him every day at the hospital. Brought him flowers and gifts, sang songs. Then slowly but surely, he recovered. Walked straight out of the hospital to the marriage *mandap*, where his beloved awaited him. They got married then and there.' He stopped. A spell had been cast on his audience. 'So, what do you say?' he asked.

Poltu thought about it for a moment. It did not sound too bad an idea. For the most part, it would be the girl who would do the talking and the singing, while he would silently follow her around, at first, and later, be rendered mute on account of the bandaged face.

'Alright,' he said finally. 'I will do it.'

A Reunion

Bibhuti Bose spent much of the afternoon of Christmas eve at Abani Mohan's house in Behala, thinking of plausible excuses.

He could speak the truth—that he did not really enjoy coming to these reunions anymore, and there was only so much nostalgia that you could seek comfort in, at this age. Or he could mention another engagement and slip away just this once.

A neglected harmonium surfaced from some hidden corner of the house. Stripped of its floral cover, it revealed a thin layer of cobwebs that Abani Mohan dusted away and blew hard at, before inviting Sushobhon Das to take over. Sushobhon's mild protests were shot down by the group, who reminded him of various college concerts where he was a star performer, singing songs written by Kobi Nozrul or Rojonikanto, and an occasional errant number—a film song by Hemonto or Kishore Kumar—much to the delight of the audience. Sushobhon reminded the gathering that there was no dearth of talent in their batch. Had anyone been able to forget Abani Mohan's acting, in the Bengali interpretation of *King Lear*? No one had, much to Abani Mohan's delight. The reminiscence continued for a while.

Bibhuti Bose stayed through the first couple of songs, then mentioned a doctor's appointment and showed himself out. Abani Mohan walked up to the gate with him.

'Was really nice catching up with you after so many years, Bibhuti,' he said, voice thick with sincerity.

'Same here, Abani, same here.'

'Let's meet again soon, one of these days? Maybe at your place?'

'Sure, sure. Why not?'

'Alright then. See you next Friday.'

'Alright. *Choli.*' Bibhuti Bose raised his right hand to indicate he was off.

'And *iye...*' started Abani Mohan.

Bibhuti Bose turned.

'I was just saying...if you need any help from me in solving this murder case...(hehe)...you know... since I'm in the *paara.*'

'Sure, sure,' replied Bibhuti Bose. 'No problem.' He waved a final goodbye and crossed the street.

He walked up to a *paan* shop and placed an order of '*mishti-pata* with *Baba zarda*' and waited. The sun had set at least half an hour ago and there was a distinct chill in the air. He shivered slightly, in spite of the warm woollen sweater. It was reckless of him not to bring the muffler and the monkey cap, but then, he had not really expected the reunion to stretch till the evening hours.

The betel-leaf—now smeared and sprinkled with his favourite ingredients—in his mouth, he made his way towards the bus-stop. An uneasiness, a botheration seemed to bubble inside him, yet he could not quite put a finger on its cause. Now, alone with his thoughts, he reflected on the day. Most, if not all, of his friends were *doing* things after retirement. Not necessarily big things that kept them gainfully employed, though there was Suprotim Bose, who was hired as a consultant to a big MNC right after retiring from his previous job, and obviously looked like he could not get enough of the good life. But there were others, like Abhijit Ghotok or Shoibal Dhar, who were attached to NGOs and religious organizations, volunteering in their spare time, and from the looks of it, thoroughly enjoying their activities.

Yet, what could Bibhuti Bose do? Even if he had the inclination, how could he go about volunteering in one of these places? Could he simply walk into Ram Krishna Mission for example and say, 'I am a retired executive from BOC India Ltd, and would like to join your organization in the capacity of a volunteer.' *Surely not*, he thought. They would ask him a dozen questions. About who he really was, and where he came from and why was he interested in the organization. Had he attended their discourses on the Vedanta? Which of Swamiji's books had he read? Was he a registered member of the organization? Would he like to become one?

The truth was that Bibhuti Bose had never been a religious person. That was not to say that he did not believe in God. He had never questioned God's existence. But had never really been *curious* about him. Or her, whatever the case might be. It was just one of those things where you had more questions than answers, he believed, and left it at that.

As a child he had seen his mother light incense sticks at the altar and read verses from a prayer book. Unlike his sisters, he was never asked to join in. The closest he had come to praying was when, on his way to the matriculation examination hall, he had stood before a poster of a religious movie, where the heroine was dressed as a Goddess. He was surprised about being able to recall that incident vividly…now, after so many years…right down to the amused expressions of his friends, some of whom had the traditional *tilak* on their foreheads or a flower from the morning prayers tucked away in their shirt pocket.

He knew that people after a certain age felt a natural pull towards religion and rituals. He had wondered if it would be the same with him. Would he, one fine day, suddenly find himself thinking about God and pondering over existential questions? He seriously doubted it. It was just not his thing, he had decided.

Of late, his wife, Joyoti Bose, had been telling him to read works of spiritual masters before going to bed. It was important to go to sleep with a peaceful mind, she would say. It was true that sleep did not come easily to Bibhuti Bose. And when it did, it was plagued with unpleasant dreams that woke him up often. For a while, he did try it out. But on no occasion was he able to get past page two. No sooner had he read a few paragraphs, than the book slipped off his hands and he was off to a dream world. Not a bad way at all to fall asleep…it was definitely better than taking soporifics…but it spoke volumes about the interest such books held for him.

Which brought him back to the question that had been gnawing at him for a while now. If not religion, then what? With what was he going to occupy the rest of his life? He could continue doing what he was doing—eat, sleep, watch TV, play bridge—but none of this seemed to fill the void he had been experiencing of late. And he had absolutely no idea what he was going to do about it… Maybe he was thinking too much, he told himself. Maybe, all men experience this from time to time—and learn to live with it. Maybe, it was simply the fear of death—the idea that you only had so many more years to live and that you were not going to be able to do all those things you had wanted to. From now on, it was only an eternal wait for the body to wither away, till one day you'd breathe out and forget to breathe in again.

Hence, if there was one thing Bibhuti Bose particularly hated being asked, it was, 'What are you doing these days?' If truth be told, he was doing nothing. Nothing of any significance, that is. But today he had come prepared. As soon as the inevitable was asked of him, he had replied with an air of gravity, 'I'm investigating a murder.' The hush that befell the room can only be described as 'awe'.

'Murder?! Whose murder?' asked Ashit Ranjan, his tone laced with a sliver of mockery.

'A businessman. *Ei toh*, lived not too far away from here.'

'Who are you talking about, Bibhuti?' asked Abani Mohan. 'If there was a murder in this *paara*, I would have heard of it, I'm sure.'

'His name was Sanyal. Probhat Sanyal. Lived in James Long Sarani.'

'Sanyal…Sanyal…' reflected Abani Mohan. 'Are you talking about the tea importer?'

'Yes, exactly!' exclaimed Bibhuti Bose. 'Did you know him?'

'Umm… Can't say I knew him well. *Ei toh*, lived in house number 23, just around the corner there. We had met only last year, in a function—can't remember what it was—oh yes, it was a wedding of one of our neighbours' daughter. We got talking about this and that…and he mentioned his business. I mentioned my fondness for fine Darjeeling tea. So the following day, he had a packet of the finest blended tea sent home to me. Later, I went to his house to thank him personally. After that, I ran into him a few times on the street, and he would always ask me if I wanted more of the tea. But I would politely refuse…you know—it is an obligation, since he refuses to take money.'

He paused before continuing.

'But you say he was murdered? I thought he died of cardiac arrest?'

'Yes, well…it is a bit complicated. What was originally thought of death by natural cause, is now being investigated for murder.'

'But…I don't understand,' said Abhoy Kanti. 'You said, *you* were investigating it? But you are not the police?!'

'No,' replied Bibhuti Bose, by now thoroughly enjoying the sensation he had created. 'But I am a private detective.'

If it was possible, the eyebrows rose higher and the mouths opened wider.

'*Bolish ki?* What are you saying?' asked Suprotim Bose incredulously.

'Not a professional detective,' Bibhuti Bose clarified hastily. 'But we have this group. It includes the retired High Court Judge, Akhil Banerjee. We call ourselves The All Bengali Crime Detectives. We have solved a couple of cases here and there and have been mentioned in the papers, too.'

'My, my!' exclaimed Abani Mohan, slapping Bibhuti Bose's back. '*Ta,* why didn't you tell us this before?'

Bibhuti Bose shrugged and tried his best to look modest.

'*Arrey*, what are you saying?' cried Abani Mohan. 'This means we have a minor celebrity amongst us.'

Questions had followed, about the nature of his detective work, the cases he had solved. For those few minutes, Bibhuti Bose felt, his friends would do anything to be in his shoes. It was a nice feeling, indeed.

Now, lost in thoughts, Bibhuti Bose had not realized how far he had walked. He stopped to look back. Had he crossed the bus stop already? He found himself in the middle of a pavement, lined on one side with makeshift stalls that sold last minute Christmas toys and gifts. A cake shop had a variety of cakes for the *borodin*, the winter solstice, with creamy Santa faces smiling at you. Up until a few years ago, Bibhuti Bose had regularly visited the cake shop in New Market—Nahoum's—during this time of the year. No one in Calcutta, he believed, made the traditional Christmas plum cake like them, rich with dry fruits, that made people from all faiths queue up at the shop throughout December.

He walked on, now even more unsure of where the road led, his mind still lingering on memories of a past Christmas. What a place New Market used to be! All lit up with colourful lights, smelling of cakes and dry fruits, with carol singers doing their rounds, singing songs about the birth of a Saint in Israel. Yet, when only a couple of years ago Bibhuti Bose had taken his three year old grand-daughter on a tour of the area, he had been crestfallen at the lackluster state of what once used to be *the* shopping market for Calcuttans. So much of the city had changed. And so fast, too. Would today's shoppers, who were used to swanky malls and multiplexes, ever know the pleasure of shopping at stores, where the owner actually knew you by name, and was never too busy to offer you a seat and lemonade, and talk about how things were, and how things used to be.

Bibhuti Bose found himself in a quieter part of the street now, lined on both sides by residential homes. Voices of people, and an occasional honk of the mini-bus or jingling of the bells of a tram, carried faintly from the distance. He stood there for a while, wondering whether he should retrace his steps...when the sound of voices singing carols reached his ears. It was a soft, melodious song, the words of which he could not quite catch—but a song he was certain he had heard his daughter sing as a child. He walked towards the source of the music, feeling more drawn to the melodious strains with every step.

A couple of bends later, he found himself in front of a small church decorated with lights. A group of young boys huddled around a Christmas tree with song books in their hands. A gentleman accompanied the choir on the keyboard. Bibhuti Bose closed his eyes and allowed the notes to fall on his ears. He stood there for a long time, soaking in the music, swaying his head slightly to the rhythm, the sweet innocence of the children's voices drenching him in an overwhelming feeling of peace and hope.

He was not sure of how long he stood there, listening to songs on the birth of Jesus Christ. He finally opened his eyes when the singing had stopped. He approached the choir as the boys were stuffing the song books in their saddle bags. The gentleman on the keyboard was asking them to form groups, touching his index finger to his lips to indicate that the children should do so in silence.

'Can we help you?' asked an elderly nun in a gray habit, as she smiled at Bibhuti Bose, exposing her yellow teeth. Her face was heavily wrinkled, and few strands of white hair peeped from under the white and gray cornette.

'Uh…I just wanted to say…I really enjoyed the singing.'

'Thank you.' The nun smiled at him warmly.

'Who are these children?'

'Orphans,' she said simply. 'From Meghalaya and Nagaland, mostly. Their families were taken away in the recent earthquake, but now the sweet Lord has found them a new home.'

'Hmm…I see…'

'Would you like to see some of the things our children have made?' she asked, touching Bibhuti Bose gently on the arm and leading him to a table nearby. There were books and rosary beads, handmade candles of every colour and size, little square cakes wrapped in cellophane. Bibhuti Bose picked up a thing or two then placed them back. In the end, he bought a couple of cakes and a cap similar to the kind Nepalis wear, even though it was a tad too colourful for his age. At least, his head would be protected from dew that evening.

'God bless you, my son!' said the nun as Bibhuti Bose placed a few crisp notes in her palm.

He put the cap on and walked away, munching on the plum

cake, feeling light and happy.

*

'*Babba!* What a *jompesh* cap you have on?!' remarked Chandan Mukherjee, as he broke away a piece of the cake that Bibhuti Bose held in his palm.

'Hehe!' laughed Bibhuti Bose. 'Yes, true! *Jompesh* cap for *jompesh* winters!'

'Mmm...nice cake,' said Chandan Mukherjee, helping himself to another piece.

'Yes, but not as good as Nahoum's. Do you remember the shop in New Market?'

'Yes, of course! Who can forget Nahoum's? But I tell you... come winters, I would much rather indulge in *moya* from Joynogor, or *payesh* made with *patali gur*, or *nolen gurer sondesh*. These English cakes are no match for our traditional Bengali sweets, *moshai,* whatever you say.'

'Yes. Maybe you are right.'

Chandan Mukherjkee finished his cake, brushed the crumbs off his sweater and got up, taking the support of his walking stick. 'I say, let's walk a few rounds,' he said. 'I've been having trouble for the past few days, *moshai*.' He rubbed his tummy to indicate the region of discomfort. 'Winters are usually worse. Even isabgol is not working.'

'Hmm...I hear you, Chandan babu. In this weather, it's a tough pitch to bat on, *moshai*,' agreed Bibhuti Bose.

'*Arrey*, I was very much in form up until three days ago,' replied Chandan Mukherjee. 'Was scoring reasonably well, you could say. But suddenly these past few days...'

'Clean bowled for a duck?'

'*Iye*...retired hurt, you could say.'

They walked on in silence for a while, enjoying the incessant chirping of birds.

'Chandan babu,' said Bibuti Bose, 'There was something I wanted to discuss with you.'

'Tell me.'

'Yesterday, I had gone to a friend's place in Behala. Abani Mohan. We studied together in college.'

'Oh? The reunion?'

'Yes, yes. Well…anyway, Abani Mohan's house is not too far from that of Sanyal babu's. I mentioned that we were investigating Probhat Sanyal's death, by way of conversation. And it turned out that Abani knew Sanyal babu. He had met him a few times in the *paara*. So, I was thinking, why don't we—you and I…'

'*Arrey*, Joj Saheb!' called out Chandan Mukherjee, interrupting Bibhuti Bose. 'You are late today! We beat you for the first time, I believe,' he smiled jovially.

Akhil Banerjee smiled as he walked towards the duo. 'I was tempted to stay just a few minutes longer inside the *lep*. I see both of you have not allowed the dip in the temperature to disrupt the morning ritual. Good, good. Where is Debdas babu?'

'He is not here yet,' replied Chandan Mukherjee.

'Hmm…did he update you about our visit to Rajib's house?'

'No, Joj Saheb. What happened? Did you meet his aunt?'

'Yes, we met Nilima Debi,' nodded Akhil Banerjee as they continued to walk. He recounted the conversation of visit, adding, 'I'm afraid we did not find any new information. The lady was not aware of any rift between Probhat babu and her nephew. But other than that, whatever she told us is what we knew already.'

'Joj Saheb,' said Bibhuti Bose. 'I was just about to suggest something to Chandan babu. Don't you think we should visit the scene of crime once? It is quite possible that we find something that will indicate whether Rajib is guilty or not.'

'Rajib is innocent!' The pronouncement made them all look back. Debdas Guha Roy was a few paces behind them. 'After meeting Nilima Debi, I'm even more convinced of it,' he continued talking as he walked up to the group. 'Such a simple family—no airs, no pretentiousness. More often than not, these are exactly the kind of people who become victims of circumstances, I tell you.'

'Yes, Debdas babu, but the question is, how do we prove Rajib's innocence?' asked Akhil Banerjee.

'Like I was saying,' said Bibhuti Bose, 'I feel we ought to visit the Sanyal house once. Talk to the family members, snoop around a bit. Who knows what we might discover?'

'I do not think that is advisable, Bibhuti babu,' said Akhil Banerjee. 'This being a murder investigation, I don't think the police will look too kindly upon a bunch of old men questioning suspects, snooping around, where they have no business to be. You never know…it just might make things worse for Rajib.'

Bibhuti Bose looked deflated. 'So we just sit in the sidelines and watch? Tsk! This is no fun, *moshai*.'

They walked on in silence till they reached Ramu's tea shop in the corner of Sabuj Kalyan Park. Ramu took out four earthen teacups, lined them on the ledge in front, and began pouring the steaming tea from his kettle.

Young boys in cricket garb had begun to assemble at the park. The handle of a cricket bat was being used to hammer the stumps in to the ground. Fielding positions were being taken. References were being made to a tournament that was currently being played with a few neighbouring clubs. Sabuj Kalyan had won the last match against Udayan Songho by twenty-three runs. If they beat Forward Club in the next match, they had a good chance of making it to the finals this year.

'*Ei* Partho!' called out Chandan Mukherjee, gulping down his tea and throwing his empty earthen cup into the dustbin nearby, 'How much did you score in the last match?'

'83 not out, kaku!'

Chandan Mukherjee pursed his lips, shook his head and murmured, 'Youth!'

Poltu Has a New Routine

It was on a Wednesday morning that Poltu finally decided to embark on his stalking project.

It was not a particularly extraordinary day. The sun had come up a little before six, but had chosen to remain hidden behind a mass of gray clouds before finally allowing its weak rays to fall on Poltu's already sweaty back. He had been up very early that day, with a feeling that bordered on nervous excitement and dread. Today is the day! He thought to himself as he jumped off the bed. Clutching the two red bricks, he started with bicep curls followed by other weight-training exercises he had seen the young men at the Trim and Fit gym do.

For the past few days he had debated with himself about which day would ensure an auspicious start. Friday and Saturday, by virtue of their cosmic connections with certain unfavourable planets, had been ruled out right away. Sunday had the distinct disadvantage of being a holiday. If at all Piya went out on a Sunday, it would be with her family or friends.

Monday seemed…too soon, somehow.

By late Monday afternoon, Poltu had made up his mind that the following day being Tuesday—which in Bengali literally *spelt* auspicious—would mark the beginning of the next phase of his love life. Gone were the days of sitting atop the boundary wall of Sabuj Kalyan Park and enduring unending mosquito bites. He was no longer a passive participant in this romance. No longer in the extras of a football team, only allowed to watch the game from the sidelines. He was now a man of action, carving out the very destiny he had dared to dream for himself.

But come Tuesday morning, Poltu woke up to find that the brave thoughts of the previous day—temporary residents in the dwelling of his mind—had packed up and left without so much as a *Ta Ta*. And in their place, his familiar companions, self-doubt and worry, had arrived with bag and baggage and had comfortably settled in. The rest of Tuesday then, was lost in further analysis and brooding, by the end of which Poltu was forced to acknowledge the wisdom in Bappa's words.

Today was Wednesday.

Poltu finished his last repetition, showered and put on his best shirt, a gray sweater, a pair of denims, a muffler round his neck. He debated whether to put the sunglasses on right away, but eventually, pushed it inside his back pocket. He called out a hasty goodbye and stepped out of the house before his sister or mother had the chance to ask him any inconvenient question.

Once at the bus stop, he felt the few rupee notes in his pocket to reassure himself. There were a bunch of people waiting when he had arrived—a lady accompanying a small boy; a couple of middle-aged men, one with an attaché case and another with a side-bag and a tiffin-carrier, office goers most likely; and an elderly gentleman in white *panjabi* pajama with a brown shawl wrapped around him. Two young girls clutching cloth bags and decorated folders also arrived. Poltu craned his neck to see if he could catch sight of Piya, conscious of a nervous tingling excitement growing within him with every passing second.

It was close to 9 a.m., and there was still no sign of Piya. Some unwelcome thoughts crossed his mind. *What if Piya was not going out today? Or what if she was late and chose to take a taxi?* Poltu would not be able to afford one with the few rupee notes he was carrying. Would he have to go hungry all day? His stomach gave out a low growl in response. He cursed himself for not having eaten something before leaving home. He had been so anxious to not miss Piya that breakfast had completely skipped his mind.

'O bhai, where do you want to go?'

Poltu was too engrossed in his thoughts to realize that the question was directed at him.

'O bhai?' Someone tapped lightly on his shoulder. Poltu turned around to see *Panjabi* pajama-brown shawl smiling benignly at him. 'Where do you want to go?' he repeated his question.

Poltu hesitated. He had no idea where he was supposed to be going. And he could not say 'nowhere' either, for that would sound rude to the kindly gentleman so obviously interested in helping him out.

'Golpark.' he said simply and looked away, hoping that was the end of the conversation.

'O bhai.' There was the tap again. 'The bus for Golpark was here only a minute ago. Why did you not take it? You must be new in the city? *Ishh…*' exclaimed the gentleman, his voice full of regret. 'You could've at least *asked* someone.'

Poltu shrugged and looked away.

'It's alright, it's alright. Don't be upset. Buses to Golpark are frequent. I will tell you when the next one comes. Don't worry.'

Poltu threw him a nod and a half smile.

'*Ta*, what do you plan to do in the city? Are you here to study or look for a job?'

This interrogation was getting more unsettling by the minute. Should he abruptly turn around and leave? Maybe Piya was not even coming today.

'I have a nephew...about your age,' the man continued, unperturbed. 'He came from my native village in Midnapur. Smart boy, very bright. He did some computer course in the city, and now he is doing a good job. Earning 12,000 rupees a month. Are you doing a computer course, too?'

Poltu mumbled a vague reply, hoping this career counseling session would end soon.

'These days, there is no job unless you learn computers.' Apparently the counseling had just started. 'Earlier, you had to fill out so many forms, so many papers when you went to the bank. Now, it is simple.' His frail fingers did a dance in mid-air to mimic typing on a keyboard.

Poltu was not sure how much more of this he could take. He was about to turn around and leave, when suddenly from the corner of his eye he caught a glimpse of a beautiful girl in a white salwar kameez and yellow dupatta. His heart stopped. Piya was approaching.

The older gentleman's voice floated vaguely into his ears. 'You should talk to my nephew...come over to my house. I live right here,' he pointed some distance away.

Poltu fixed his eyes on Piya. It was difficult to not want to stare. She was walking hurriedly, checking her watch, an anxious expression on her face.

'He works in a big office in Esplanade. He can give you good advice.'

'Yes, yes, sure,' nodded Poltu hastily, his anxious eyes fixed on Piya.

Piya must have spotted an approaching bus, thought Poltu. She had quickened her pace. Arriving at the stop just as a bus came to a halt, she clutched her handbag with one hand, pulled the dupatta that had begun to slide off her slender shoulders and climbed on to the bus. Before Poltu had time to react, a whole bunch of people materialized from nowhere and jostled to get into the same bus as Piya's.

'O bhai, that is not the bus to Golpark,' called out the elderly man, as Poltu got ready to board. The man had caught Poltu's collar from behind and held on to it with surprising strength. 'He is new in the city! He is new in the city!' announced the man, pointing at Poltu. Like he was alarming the curious onlookers—*He is a pickpocket, he is a pickpocket*! 'Wants to go to Golpark, he is getting on to a bus for Park Street!'

Poltu struggled to free himself even as others around him started to give out logistical advice. 'Bus number so and so goes to Golpark.' Or 'Take an auto from here to Jadavpur, then take bus number…'

Poltu looked desperately as the last passenger boarded the bus.

'I don't want to go to Golpark!' He yelled, a trifle too loudly than was needed perhaps. The elderly gentleman backed off a little, giving Poltu just enough time to free himself and scamper on to the bus that had started to roll. He heaved a huge sigh of relief. Piya, he noticed, had found a seat near the window. Poltu made his way through the standing passengers, finding a spot close behind her. He had a good vantage point. He would notice the instant she got off her seat.

Had she seen the embarrassing spectacle a minute ago? There was no time to reflect on that. Right now, Poltu was in the same bus as Piya. This was the closest he had ever been to her. It was practically a date! He felt a thrill he had never experienced before.

The romance was finally taking off.

*

'*O moshai*? Are you at home?' The question was redundant. Bibhuti

Bose had already heard Chandan Mukherjee say a 'Hello' on the other end of the line.

'Yes, tell me, Bibhuti babu.'

'I have come up with a plan.'

'Plan? For what?'

'For visiting the Sanyal house.'

'*Iye*...but Joj Saheb said...'

'Yes, yes I know what Joj Saheb said. Trust me, we won't get into any trouble. I have thought this through.'

'Oh...kkay. What exactly is the plan?'

'I will tell you when we meet. First tell me, are you coming or not?'

'When?

'Tomorrow morning at 10.30.'

'O...alright,' Chandan Mukherjee sounded doubtful. 'But don't you think we ought to inform Joj Saheb and Debdas babu once?'

'*Arrey,* no, no. There is no need. I want to do this discreetly. If we end up finding anything significant, we can always tell them.'

'Hmm...okay.'

'10.30 tomorrow. Alright?'

'Alright. See you then.'

A Letter for Biplab Maity, President, Sabuj Kalyan (Youth) Association

Dr Bishwanath Nandi, MD, FRCOG (London, UK), OB/GYN
Dr (Mrs) D. Nandi, MD, OB/GYN
Clinic Open: Tue, Thu (5.30 p.m.-8.30 p.m.)
By appointment ONLY
Beware of Dogs

Debdas Guha Roy read the engraved letters on a granite nameplate on the outer wall of a huge three-storeyed house on Harish Mukherjee Road. He debated whether to sound the doorbell, but the warning of the canine inhabitant made him decide otherwise.

'Yes, babu?' A uniformed guard appeared and looked inquiringly at Debdas Guha Roy.

'Uh…*iye*…is doctor babu in?'

The guard shook his head. 'Tuesdays and Thursdays only,' he said rapping on the nameplate with his baton. 'Write your name on the register over here and bring Madam on appointment day. Collect token when you arrive. First come, first served.'

Most of the doctors' patients would be ladies, hence the assumption on the part of the guard—that a 'madam' had to be involved—was perhaps not entirely unjustified.

'Hmm…okay,' said Debdas Guha Roy and walked away.

Behind him he could hear the guard mutter in Hindi under his breath. '*Kya waqt barbaad karney aa jatey hain log.*' Really? thought Debdas Guha Roy to himself. And what would have the guard done otherwise in those precious twenty seconds? Smoked a bidi, listened to another Bollywood number on the radio? People are always complaining about how their time gets wasted by others—one gets to hear it all the time. On the streets, in coffee shops, on buses—people are always saying, 'So and so came to see me today and wasted so much of my time.' As far as Debdas Guha Roy was concerned, time was being wasted anyway. What difference did it make *how* it was being done?

He crossed the street to a tea and snacks shop adjacent to the historic Gurudwara. An old sardar ji asked him in clear Bengali, 'What would you like, babu?'

'One tea,' said Debdas Guha Roy and settled down on the bench adjacent to the shop. As he sipped the fragrant masala tea, Debdas Guha Roy could not help but marvel at the beauty of his city. The beauty may not be apparent to all, what with its worn down buildings and congested streets, its traffic jams and its humidity. But as someone who has lived here most of his life, Debdas Guha Roy could discern another layer of beauty beneath—of friendship, kinship, acceptance and tolerance, of warmth, generosity and goodwill that was lurking in every corner, waiting for a foreigner, like this sardar ji, to land on her streets only to steal his heart forever.

The iron gates of Dr Nandi's house opened with a clamour and Porag Nandi stepped out. Debdas Guha finished his tea in a gulp and hastened after him.

*

When circumstances are bad, you either get really angry or you curse the world in general and your fate in particular. But when circumstances are downright hopeless, you can only smile and wonder at God's cruel sense of humour.

The latter was Biplab Maity's current state of mind.

Earlier in the day, an envelope had arrived by post. A neatly written letter in Bengali, addressed to Biplab Maity, President, Sabuj Kalyan (Youth) Association. It contained the following words:

'Sotyembor Opera regrets to inform that due to an unavoidable circumstance, they will not be available to perform at Sabuj Kalyan Park on the 15th of January. Please find enclosed the cheque of the advance amount. Our sincere apologies...'

Today was the 7th of January. Exactly a week away from the performance.

Posters had been put up, tickets had been sold, Chatterjee Decorators and Sri Bishnu Lighting had been paid an advance, the construction of the stage was halfway through; Monginis, Jolojog and other small time egg-roll and vegetable chop owners had paid the club handsome amounts to secure a spot in the refreshments stand. The air therefore, was rife with heightened expectations.

It was then—not an entirely unjustified behaviour on the part of Biplab Maity—that, fuming and frothing, he arrived at the doorstep of Kartick babu, manager of Sotyembor Opera, and demanded an explanation. What exactly was this 'unavoidable circumstance'? he had demanded. One could understand if one or two members of the troupe had fallen ill or had to go attend a marriage somewhere in the country. But shouldn't a professional troupe have a contingency plan for such situations?

It was not just about the money, asserted Biplab Maity, when Kartick babu's feeble response was that he had returned the cheque. It was a question of ethics! And integrity! And professionalism! These words—potent with the power to awaken even a dead man's conscience—fell in this case, on deaf ears. Kartick babu's efforts to placate Biplab Maity, had seemed insincere, to say the least. He did not seem to be able to offer any plausible reason for this sudden change of plans, except that it was 'regretful' and 'unavoidable'.

After having ranted for half an hour, and threatening Sotyembor Opera with legal action—which Biplab Maity noticed, had a mildly unsettling effect on the manager—he returned to the Sabuj Kalyan clubhouse to introspect.

It was one of those unnaturally cold January evenings. Biplab Maity shut all the windows tight, switched on a light bulb, hoisted himself on the dust-layered desk. Light from the bright halogen lamps put up outside for the badminton tournament, filtered through the windows and formed narrow streaks on the clubhouse floor. Sounds of the shuttle cork getting rhythmically whacked by rackets reached his ears.

Crossing his legs on the table and supporting his chin on his interlocked fingers, he reflected on the current situation. Should he cancel the performance and refund all the money? It would be an utter shame! For once, Sabuj Kalyan Club looked like they were actually going to bring some cash into the coffers. He could try contacting another *jatra* company. But this being the peak season, it was unlikely one would be available at such short notice.

It would be a huge loss of face. What would Sudhir Bagchi, President of Milonee Club say when he met him next? *What, Biplab? Didn't I hear there was going to be a* jatra *performance in your club? Was it a mime? Could not hear a single dialogue?*

What was one more insult in the face of an ever-present tirade? He sighed, took out his cell-phone and called Partho's number.

Sleuthing: The ABCD Way

Bibhuti Bose and Chandan Mukherjee got off the taxi in front of Abani Mohan's house. The latter was standing at the gate and waved enthusiastically at the duo as their taxi rolled to a stop.

'Come, come, Bibhuti,' he said smiling broadly. 'Let's get started. I have been unable to sleep last night. This is so exciting.' He couldn't keep his hands still.

Bibhuti Bose, one leg out of the taxi, hesitated.

'*Ki holo*?' asked Abani Mohan, impatiently.

'I'm just thinking, why don't you hop in? We could take the taxi right up to the Sanyal house. Then there will be no need to walk.'

'*Arrey*, no, no, Bibhuti!' protested Abani Mohan. 'It's only a short walk from here. Will hardly take ten minutes.'

'Ten minutes!' exclaimed Bibhuti Bose.

'*Moshai*, you're off to do *detectivegiri*.' piped in Chandan Mukherjee, 'and you are getting intimidated at the prospect of a little physical exercise? Let's get off here. *Cholun, cholun.*' He slid sideways on the seat getting closer to Bibhuti Bose, a gesture that forced the latter to climb out of the taxi.

'Besides,' added Abani Mohan, 'It would look terribly suspicious if we said we are from this *paara*, and yet we are seen getting out of a taxi.'

'This is my friend, Chandan babu, and this is Abani Mohan. We were in college together.' Bibhuti Bose concluded the introductions as the taxi sped away.

'*Iye*...what is the plan exactly?' asked Chandan Mukherjee. 'I'm a bit *iye* about this whole thing. What exactly am I supposed to do?'

'Relax, Chandan babu,' said Bibhuti Bose, 'You just follow my lead.'

'Do I have any dialogues?'

'You can make your own dialogues...improvise, be spontaneous.'

'I'd rather not say anything. Can I just stay silent?'

'Yes, yes, sure. Whatever is comfortable.'

Abani Mohan, who was a few paces ahead, turned around the bend. Bibhuti Bose increased his pace, stepped on a lose tile on the pavement, and let out an expletive remark. He turned back to alert Chandan Mukherjee, who was a few steps behind. Pointing to the tile he said, 'Look out, *moshai*. There is a loose character there.'

Chandan Mukherjee raised a hand in thank you.

'By the way, who are we again?' he asked as they neared the Sanyal house.

'We are from the *Behala Senior Citizens Welfare Committee*,' replied Abani Mohan.

'O,' Chandan Mukherjee looked unimpressed. 'What exactly do we do, *moshai*?'

'We go about bothering senior citizens,' replied Bibhuti Bose.

'This is all a bit *iye*... Should we perhaps rehearse it a bit?'

'There is no need to rehearse. We will play it by the ear. Come, come, it will be fun,' assured Abani Mohan.

'Our Abani is quite an actor, I must tell you, Chandan babu,' said Bibhuti Bose, by way of assurance. 'You should have seen him in our college days...'

Soon they stood in front of of 23/1/B, James Long Sarani.

It was a small two-storey house, built right on the edge of the road. There were a couple of large windows, barred by iron grills on the front facade, which looked out onto the street. A few pots of petunia had been placed along the front perimeter.

Abani Mohan rang the doorbell and waited. It was a quiet street this time of the day, except for the few boys playing cricket a little distance away. An expensive looking car came to a halt behind the makeshift cricket stumps. The person behind the wheels scowled at the boys for blocking the street. One of the boys gestured that there was enough space for the car to pass, dismantling of the 'stumps' was not required. This only angered the driver more. He gesticulated angrily pointing at the stumps then spreading his arms to indicate the expanse of his car. The boys gave in. They removed the tower of bricks from the middle of the road and stood in reverent attention on the sidewalk as the driver, a contemptuous look still on his face, sped away.

Play resumed with the replacing of bricks, but soon had to be halted again when an ambassador car came behind and honked. The boys began to dismantle the stumps, but the driver behind the wheels gestured them to stop. He would attempt to maneuver the wheels so as to be able to pass in the space available. For his kindness, he was awarded with big 'thank you' waves and broad smiles. This gentleman has not forgotten what it was like to be a kid, thought Bibhuti Bose.

'Try again,' said Bibhuti bose. 'Someone has to be inside. I can hear the television.'

Abani Mohan rang the doorbell again.

'O kaku!' called out one of the boys, 'the bell doesn't work, try knocking hard on the door.'

Abani Mohan did as told. Moments later, sound of flip-flops were heard approaching.

'What do you want?' The young lady in her early twenties regarded the trio with suspicion.

'We are from the Behala Senior Citizens' Welfare Committee, *didibhai,'* began Abani Mohan. 'I live in this *paara*, just a few blocks away…'

'We are not giving *chanda* for Saraswati Pujo this year,' she replied curtly. 'We have had a death in the family.'

'*Arrey,* no, no.' called out Bibhuti Bose hastily, as she was about to close the door on their faces. 'We are not here to collect *chanda*.'

'Then?'

'*Iye*…we do this social service from time to time,' said Abani Mohan. 'We go to different houses where elderly people live, and sit with them for a while, give them company, talk about the old times. Makes them feel good,' he paused before continuing. The young girl still had a questioning look on her face. 'Is there any senior citizen in this house?'

She hesitated, just a little, giving Abani Mohan the time to pipe in, 'Like an elderly uncle or a grandfather, perhaps?'

'There is Dadu, my grandfather, but he is hard of hearing,' she replied. 'I don't think there is much use in talking to him…'

'Don't worry, don't worry,' assured Bibhuti Bose, 'We will just sit with him a little while. He will enjoy our company, I'm sure.'

She threw them an apprising glance and perhaps decided the gentlemen looked harmless enough. Holding the door open, she ushered them in.

'*Ta*, what is your name, ma?' asked Chandan Mukherjee, once they were inside.

'Rumi,' she said simply.

'Nice, nice.'

They found themselves in a living area, with sofas, chairs

and a television cabinet. Sounds of running water and clanging of utensils from a corner—a little distance away—suggested the kitchen was nearby.

'Dadu's room is this way.' She led them to a room on the left and pushed open the door.

An elderly man in a *lungi* and a dark brown sweater was seated on a divan. He had no teeth and his face was heavily wrinkled. A few frail strands of white hair clung to his otherwise bare scalp. His glassy eyes did not look away from the television set, when the visitors walked in.

His grand-daughter switched off the television without any warning. Mr Sanyal continued to stare at the television set, a vacant look in his eyes, a sliver of smile on his lips.

'Dadu?' she called out. 'DADU?'

He seemed to realize at last that he had company. He stared at the girl and then at the other three visitors, and blinked.

'Huh?'

'These gentlemen here have come to see you.'

'Huh?'

She repeated, louder this time. 'It's not good to watch so much TV,' she went on. 'Talk to these gentlemen for a while, okay?' She motioned the three of them to sit, indicating the vacant space on the divan and the arm chair.

She closed the door behind her. The visitors glanced about the room and each selected a place to settle down.

Bibhuti Bose cleared his throat. 'We are just here for a bit of *adda*,' he began. 'Sir, do you enjoy watching television?'

The old Mr Sanyal looked at him blankly. 'Ration?'

'No, no. Not ration. Vision, vision. Television.'

He shook his head in response. 'These days nobody uses a ration card to buy anything. I had a ration card. I could buy rice, and *daal*, even kerosene oil. God knows where they have hidden my ration card. Can't see it anymore.' The three of them nodded politely.

'Everyone shops at supermarkets these days,' volunteered Abani Mohan after a few moments of silence. 'Salaries have increased manifold, *moshai*. Now-a-days, no one wants to step into a dirty bazaar and haggle with the vendors for every single item.'

Mr Sanyal nodded slowly, but his eyes bore a blank look, like a child who was pretending to understand but was not getting a word.

'Do you watch cricket, *moshai*?' Bibhuti Bose tried again.

Mr Sanyal raised his head sharply as if to ask 'What?'

'Cricket. CRICKET. Do you watch cricket?'

'Ticket? Which ticket?'

'Not ticket. Cricket.' He pretended to hit a ball with an invisible bat.

'I once traveled without ticket.' His eyes glowed suddenly with mischief. He bit his tongue and cupped his mouth as if to suppress a smile. 'But don't tell anyone.' He waved his palm, smiling broadly to reveal his toothless gums.

'No, no, we won't,' they assured him.

'You are not from the police are you?' asked Mr Sanyal, a sudden look of serious concern on his face.

They shook their heads.

'We are your friends,' said Abani Mohan, who was sitting next to Mr Sanyal on the divan. 'You can trust us.' He added.

'O.' Mr Sanyal was lost in thought. 'The police were here, though. Yesterday, I think. Or was it last week? They were here, asking questions…'

'Why?' asked Bibhuti Bose, leaning forward with interest.

'Huh?'

'Why were the police here, Mr Sanyal?'

Mr Sanyal pursed his lips and shook his head slowly, as if to say, 'I don't know.'

A long awkward silence followed.

'We were asking you about cricket. Did you watch Sachin's century?' Chandan Mukherjee tried.

'*Kochuri*?' The older Sanyal's eyes lit up. '*Ei*, do you remember Dwarik's *hinger kochuri*?' His voice was hushed and he used the informal pronoun while addressing the visitors, as if he had known them for long. 'Piping hot puffed *puris* with mild asafetida flavour, served with potato curry in a *bhaar*, an earthen pot…' The description triggered the memory of the last time the sacred dish had touched their taste buds.

'*Moshai*, while studying in college, we used to frequent this shop in Esplanade—Anadi's Cabin,' said Chandan Mukherjee. 'Best Moghlai paratha in the whole of Calcutta. Guaranteed! *Ta*, one day, some four of us went there together.

'Girish asks the waiter, "*Ei* how much for a paratha?"

'The boy replies, "Six *anaas*, babu."

'"And how much for the potato curry?"

'"Potato curry is free, babu."

'So Girish says, "Okay, get us four bowls of potato curry then."'

'*Khabey?* Will you try some?' asked Mr Sanyal suddenly, when the laughter had died down.

The visitors exchanged looks.

Mr Sanyal's trembling hands reached for a switch near his divan. He pressed it as hard as he could. Minutes later, the young lady who had shown them in, entered. 'What do you want?' she asked in a tone hardly solicitous.

'*Ei,* Rumi, get us some *hinger kochuri*,' ordered Mr Sanyal, then immediately looked away, almost as if he knew the audacity of this demand.

'DADU!'

'What? Can't you see my friends are here?' he replied, still not daring to look at his granddaughter. 'Are you not going to feed them something? Go, get some, quick. You'll find them in the shop around the corner. Here, I have the money. You'll find five rupees in that drawer.' He pointed.

'*Hinger kochuri* for five rupees?' asked Rumi in an incredulous tone.

'Yes. Get about fifteen or twenty. That should be enough,' replied old Mr Sanyal.

'That must have been the price during Siraj-ud-Daula's time, Dadu!' mocked Rumi.

'Ah!' Mr Sanyal looked irritated. 'Just go bring some. I'll give you whatever it'll cost.'

'I won't,' she said sternly. 'You are not allowed outside food. You know that, Dadu.'

'It's not for me. It's for…'

But she had turned and left.

Mr Sanyal sat glumly, muttering under his breath. Chandan Mukherjee shifted uncomfortably. He looked at Bibhuti Bose enquiringly.

'So, Sanyal babu,' resumed Abani Mohan, clearing his throat. 'Where were you traveling without a ticket?' resumed Abani Mohan.

Mr Sanyal continued to stare at the floor, all the while grumbling to himself. Abani Mohan repeated his question.

'To north Bengal,' came the reply, presently.

'To visit Probhat babu?' asked Chandan Mukherjee before he could help himself. Bibhuti Bose and Abani Mohan shot him warning looks. Thankfully though, the old Mr Sanyal seemed to not have heard him.

'The Senior Regional Manager of my bank was at Jalpaiguri then,' continued Mr Sanyal, in his quivering voice. 'He sent a telegram: "Urgent. Come immediately." Immediately, it had said. I packed my bag and went straight to Sealdah station. But they would not give me a ticket. *The train is full*, they said. *Not a single seat is available.* I climbed on to it, nonetheless. It was overcrowded. Not a place to sit. I kept avoiding the ticket checker by hiding in the bathroom for much of the time.

'Early in the morning…it was maybe 5 or 5.30, the train halted. I looked out of the window. The first rays of light had just touched the earth. We were in the middle of nowhere, surrounded by a dense forest. The eerie silence of the surroundings was only disturbed by the rhythmic snoring of a few fellow passengers. I climbed out of the train and started making my way through the trees—the cool, gentle morning breeze providing a much needed relief after having spent the whole night in the toilet.

'I do not know how long I walked or even where I was going. The chirping of the birds and the cool breeze on my face egged me on. Suddenly, in the distance, a structure came into view. It was hidden amidst the tall trees and the dense shrubs. Curious, I walked cautiously towards it. As I came nearer, I realized, it was a small temple—a Kali temple, I presumed, from the similarity in its architecture to the Dakshineshwar Temple. Tinkling of bells suggested that there was someone inside, a priest perhaps. Who could be worshipping Ma Kali here in this deep dense forest in the middle of nowhere?'

He paused. The question hung in the air for a while. The visitors exchanged looks, unsure if the story would continue any further.

'The priest gestured me to come inside,' started Mr Sanyal. 'I was at once impressed by his presence. His skin was fair, so fair!

You could mistake him for a white. *Tok-tokay rong*, as we would say. He had a long flowing gray beard. After I had done my genuflections to the Divine Mother, I sat on the temple ground with this man. We talked for a long time…an hour, maybe even longer. He asked me who I was, where I was going. He spoke the refined tongue of Calcutta Bengalis, his every utterance chiseled with wisdom. I realized immediately this was no ordinary man.'

There was a pause.

'Can you guess who he was?'

The others shook their heads.

'Netaji!' exclaimed Mr Sanyal. 'He was none other than our very own Netaji!'

'Ah! Dadu! Again that story!' Rumi stood at the door, looking disapprovingly at her grandfather.

'You don't believe me, but it's true, I tell you. I met Netaji!'

'If we were to believe all your tales, then you have met Netaji at least a dozen times, in a dozen different locations.' She did not wait for a response. Turning to the visitors she said, 'You may leave now. It's time for Dadu to have his lunch.' Her manner was curt, not leaving much scope for the visitors to say anything to the contrary. They stood up obediently.

'*Iye*…Which way is the bathroom?' asked Bibhuti Bose.

Rumi pointed to the door on her left. Bibhuti Bose excused himself.

Once inside, he noticed that the bathroom had another door. It was a common bath in between two rooms, he guessed. Having finished his business there, he cautiously unlatched the second door and peeped in. It was, like he had guessed, a second bedroom, neatly furnished but unoccupied. He stepped into the room. The main entrance to this room, the one through the living room, was closed but not latched. The room was sparsely but elegantly furnished. It had a large bed placed against a wall, a large intricately designed teak wood almirah, a low glass table, the base of which was a truncated tea shrub, a desk and an arm chair. This had to be Probhat Sanyal's room, he thought.

Bibhuti Bose allowed his eyes to take in as much as they could. There was a large window on the wall opposite to the bed. This must be the window outside which Probhat Sanyal saw the ghost! He parted the curtains slightly to get a peek of the quiet street outside. There were a couple of Bengali novels lying on the desk. He tugged at the drawer but it was locked. He noticed a waste paper basket under the desk and peered into it. It had been emptied.

It was frustrating…to have come this close to the crime scene and not have found a single clue. He pulled at the almirah door. It opened easily with a slight creaking sound. Shirts and trousers hung from hangers. A few towels were neatly folded and stacked one on top of the other.

Voices from the living room reached his ears. An unknown male voice, mentioned 'Probhat babu'. Bibhuti Bose moved closer to the door and placed his ears against it.

'We raided Rajib Guha's house once again, based on a tip from an anonymous caller,' the male voice continued. 'But it proved to be a false alarm, I'm afraid. We could not find what we were looking for.'

'What were you looking for, Inspector babu?' asked a middle-aged female voice.

'For proof, naturally. Some kind of incriminating evidence that Rajib Guha was involved in the murder of Probhat babu. The caller distinctly said, what we were looking for is in his room.'

'But is it not obvious that he is guilty?' asked the female voice. 'I thought the case against him was very clear.'

'It is not that simple, Mrs Sanyal,' replied the male voice. 'We need to find out *how* he committed the murder. What weapon did he use? He was not present at the scene of crime? Unless we find the means employed by him to carry out the murder, I'm afraid, we do not have a case against him. Just being a beneficiary, does not automatically make him a murderer. Do you see what I am saying, madam?'

Bibhuti Bose had become so engrossed in the conversation that he had not realized the voices had come closer. Even as his brain comprehended what was about to happen, the male voice said, 'I'd like to see Probhat babu's room once more.'

Porag Nandi

'Porag!' called out Debdas Guha Roy.

The young boy turned, scanned the street, then seeing Debdas Guha Roy waving at him, knitted his eyebrows.

'Do you remember me?' asked Debdas Guha Roy, walking up to the boy, smiling affectionately.

'Yess…but…how do you know my name?' He looked nervously at Debdas Guha Roy and gulped several times.

'Never mind that. Uh…if you have some time, can we just sit by the tea stall there and talk for a few minutes?'

Porag hesitated.

'Don't worry. Everything is fine,' said Debdas Guha Roy reassuringly.

'Okay.'

Debdas Guha Roy had gone through this conversation over his head several times in the last couple of days. He would start off by saying that life was a gift of God, and nothing justified ending it. Exams, marks, relationships were just temporary events, that came and went. He had two children of his own. He understood how young boys and girls felt at this age. Everyone went through a crisis at some time or the other, and in those dark moments, life did seem unbearable. But the truth was that the dark clouds never lasted long. It was only a matter of time before the winds of change blew them away.

But right now, seeing this 18-year-old scrawny kid with his

round-rimmed spectacles and his unkempt hair, staring at him for guidance, Debdas Guha Roy found himself fumbling for the right words.

'Would you like a cup of tea?' he asked presently. And before the boy could shake his head, he called out to the Sardar ji to send two more cups their way.

'The other day…when I was at your lab,' started Debdas Guha Roy. 'I noticed you had not done any work. Are you having difficulty understanding the lesson?'

The boy looked away.

'You probably think it is none of my business,' said Debdas Guha Roy. 'And you are right. But, you know, I'm not really a lab inspector. I went there…to your lab…on the request of Professor Bagchi, to see how students were doing—were they really learning chemistry, were they enjoying the subject? We are all worried about you, Porag.'

That touched a chord somewhere. Porag looked up. 'Worried about me? But I'm a nobody. Professor Bagchi does not even know my name. If I stopped coming to college one day, no one would even take note.'

Lack of self-worth, noted Debdas Guha Roy. Tell-tale signs of someone attempting to end his life.

'Ah! That's what *you* think! But that's not the truth, Porag. Everyone knows you, everyone is concerned about you. Professor Bagchi, Kapil, even the Principal.'

'Principal sir? Why?'

'Because, you are a good kid. I saw your academic records—you did very well in your Xth, then XIIth, you were at the top of the class in the first year. What is happening now? Are you unable to follow the lessons?'

Porag stared at his feet.

'It is not a big deal,' said Debdas Guha Roy. 'If you don't understand something, you only have to ask your professors for help. They will explain. Again and again, if required. Professor Bagchi is a very good friend of mine, I know that he is passionate about his subject, and wants all his students to learn. You have no reason to be afraid of him.'

Silence.

'Do you have friends in college?'

No, he shook his head.

'Then make some! Go and talk to a few boys in the class. Take their help. Go take some tuition. There is always a way out.'

'I don't think it's going to work. I will continue to disappoint, no matter what.'

'Why? Why do you say that?'

Porag took a while to answer, speaking softly, almost to himself. 'My parents are doctors. Gold medallists, both of them. It was almost a foregone conclusion that I'll be a doctor, too. But I had no interest in medical science. I sat for the Joint Entrance exams. Twice. Did not get a good rank. In the end, Baba said, "At least take up Pure Science in college, do a BSc. What are we going to tell our friends?"'

Porag Nandi took a sip from his cup. 'So I did. But I really do not like chemistry.'

'So, you don't like chemistry. That's not a crime! You have only one more year to go, then you are free to do whatever you like...study management, or whatever.'

'You don't understand, sir. I hate every second inside those labs. My heart is elsewhere.'

'Sure, sure. But Porag… Life is a beautiful gift from God, to be lived, enjoyed and celebrated. And nothing justifies ending it. Exams, marks, relationships are just temporary events, that come and go. I have two children of my own…I know what it's like. You are young, you have so much to offer to this world. There is no reason to want to end your life…'

'End my life?! Do you think I'm about to end my life? Is this what it's all about?' Porag looked shocked.

'Yes…uh…aren't you contemplating…suic…?'

'What are you saying, sir?! Why should I?' Porag had stood up from the bench. 'Not at all!'

'Oh.'

'What is this really about?' demanded Porag.

Debdas Guha Roy was unsure of how to respond. In the end, he thought it was best to come clean.

'Uh…there were some chemicals missing from the lab. Dangerous chemicals. Professor Bagchi, Principal sir, Kapil—they all thought someone was trying to end his life. So they called me to observe the students, to see if I could pinpoint someone who might be disturbed.'

'But why you?'

'I'm a det…' started Debdas Guha Roy. But the term, he feared, would sound ridiculous to this young man. 'I'm a psychologist,' he finished.

'Oh, I see.'

'Are you sure, you did not steal any chemical from the lab?'

'No, of course not. What chemicals were they?'

'Arsenic oxide.'

Porag Nandi let out a low whistle.

'We all thought it must be you—you know, since you don't show any interest in studies and your grades have fallen steadily.'

Porag considered this. Then shook his head, 'I don't know what to say. It is true, I have lost interest in chemistry. But suicide? The thought had not even crossed my mind. It's not that I have lost interest in studies or do not want a good career. In fact, I am thinking of changing my stream. I will make a fresh application this year. I don't mind losing another year if it means I will be able to study a subject closer to my heart. I have good marks in my XIIth, I don't think it will be a problem to get admission. Since I have already made this decision, I feel free, sir. And chemistry is becoming even less bearable. Hence, my lack of interest in the subject.'

'Oh. Good. Very good,' said Debdas Guha Roy, thoughtfully. 'Is there anyone else in your class who you think might be depressed or upset over some reason?'

The boy shook his head. 'I have no idea. I hardly talk to anyone in college.'

'Hmm, I see. *Ta*...what subject are you applying for?'

'Geology,' came the prompt answer.

Debdas Guha Roy's face lit up. Finally, after thirty years of teaching, he had found a boy who wanted to study his subject for the sheer love of it.

'I've always been fascinated with rocks and their compositions, about how earth was formed, what is happening underneath,' Porag continued. 'I think one of the biggest contributions of scientists in our times will be towards environmental studies—climate change, how it used to be in the past, how it might be in the future. There is a serious lack of this kind of approach in India. Imagine how many lives would be saved if the government acted on the advice of geologists—don't build houses there, that area is prone to floods or don't blast those rocks with dynamite, it might cause landslides. But no. No intelligent kid in this country will want to study geology. *Arrey,* when the very house you live in is going to be washed away, what good is your medical or engineering degree, tell me?'

Debdas Guha Roy listened in rapt attention. His chest swelled with pride. It was difficult to argue against the excellent points this boy had raised. But he felt compelled to add, 'Porag, how do you know you will enjoy this new subject? I have been a professor of geology for over thirty years. Trust me, the students in my class could not care less what was in the ground beneath their feet. One of my best students, Subhrojit Dutta, First Class First in Geology Honours—what does he do after graduation? Enrolls for Chartered Accountancy!

'One thing I will tell you, if you take my advice, that is: everything looks attractive from afar. While I understand your passion for the subject, the reality is that things will not be so exciting in the classroom. And then, you might find something else which looks exciting, challenging, worth exploring. And then again, the mind will say: who needs to study geology? It's boring. Here, let me study physics, it is far more exciting to know the workings of the sub-atomic particles.

'Do you know how many engineering and medical students—the ones who had dreamt of nothing else all their lives—end up hating their subject by the time they are into their second year of studies? Mind is a slippery substance, my friend. It always looks for an exit option. If not this, then that. If not that, then something else. Complete what you have started, then go to the next. Why go from failure to failure? Go from success to success.'

Porag Nandi did not respond.

'Anyway, I can only give advice,' said Debdas Guha Roy getting up. 'It's your life, you will know what to do with it. At least I am glad that my deductions, which brought me to you, have turned out wrong.

'All the best!'

Clues from the Crime Scene

Poltu drowned his third cup of tea and glanced—perhaps for the hundredth time—at the entrance of 'Success Language Training Institute'. It was only midday, according to the wall-clock at Horo Gouri Mishtanna Bhandar, the local sweet shop, which had more or less become his home over the past week. There were still at least four more hours to kill. Every second in this shop seemed to stretch to an hour.

Today was his fifth day of stalking. And Poltu could claim, with a certain degree of assuredness, that he was quite good at it. He had followed Piya step for step. If she had turned right, so had he. If she had quickened her pace, so had he. If she had gotten off the bus at an unscheduled stop, so had he. If she had stopped to admire a dress, so had he. At times he felt Piya knew that she was being followed. Once while on her way back home she had stopped abruptly and turned to look back, but Poltu had managed to duck behind a pedestrian just in time.

He tapped his fingers on the wooden table. He was beginning to get hungry. He debated whether to have a samosa, then decided against it, in spite of his tummy's not-so-silent protests. He had discovered another shop down the street that sold a full plate of rice and egg curry for the price of two samosas here. Poltu decided to wait just a little longer. At times Piya did come out during lunch, usually with another lady friend. They went to an expensive-looking coffee shop. Poltu would stand outside and watch her nibble her lunch and sip her coffee. It was the best forty minutes of his day!

Of late he had been wondering though—in the long hours in between 10 and 5, when Piya was at the institute—about the futility of this stalking exercise. If Bhombol was to be believed, then Piya must have noticed him many times, but was careful not to show. Poltu was not as convinced. How would Piya notice him, if all the while he was taking care not be seen? There was some inherent fallacy in this plan. And on the face of it, was not much different from his earlier program of sitting on the boundary wall, simply waiting for Piya to come home. Though this had more action, he had to admit.

There was that one time when Piya's eyes had rested on him briefly. But, it was the worst moment ever and he prayed that she forgets all about it. He had followed her right into what he thought was a shop of some kind, but realized, once inside, that it was a cyber cafe, with rows of computers, and people sitting in front of them, typing away frantically. The owner of the place had stepped forward and asked Poltu a number of personal questions. Was it his first time there, how long did he plan to surf, what plan would he like to opt for? Poltu had stared blankly at him in response. A few others, he noticed with increasing trepidation, had stopped typing and were staring at him. Piya too had turned to look at him briefly. Poltu panicked. He did the only thing any guy in his situation would do. Turned around and walked right out, without having uttered a single word.

He had felt like an idiot. But what else could he have done? Opened his mouth to broadcast his ignorance?

12.15. Poltu glanced around the sweet shop. He noticed a familiar face at the table in the corner—a young man, about his age. He was sure he had seen him somewhere. Poltu threw him an unsure smile when their eyes accidentally met, but the man looked away.

The waiter came around and asked for the third time if there was anything else he wanted. His tone had begun to sound less and less polite. Poltu shook his head and got off the chair. He walked aimlessly on the sidewalk for a while, pacing up and down, glancing over his shoulders to check if Piya was at the gate. Unless he found a way to speak to her, to make an impression, Poltu failed to see how this plan was helping his cause anyway.

Truth was, and Poltu had perhaps known this right from the start, that he had never really had a shot with Piya—what with her expensive education and her 'cultured' upbringing. He would never even have the courage to speak to her. Or to any girl for that matter. He was not like Bappa, who, if rumours were to be believed, had been slapped a few too many times by young ladies. This failed to deter him, though. Indeed, he looked like he enjoyed it all the more. Poltu was different. If Piya even glanced at him contemptuously, it would be reason enough for him to end his life.

Perhaps Biplab da's suggestion to hold a cultural meet once every week, was not so bad after all. Maybe Poltu could learn a few things—names of books and authors, for example—after all, what would he talk to Piya about, in the extremely unlikely event that a conversation between the two took place? Besides, the cultural meets might have helped boost his confidence. If he could recite a line or two of poetry or say a few rehearsed dialogues in front of four or five people…then, maybe, just maybe, he could say a few smart things to Piya to impress her.

There had to be a way to get Piya to notice him, which did not involve him being embarrassed or ridiculed or run over by a bus. There was that event coming up in the *paara*—Bollywood

Ram Leela by Sotyembor Opera. Perhaps he could be the volunteer behind the ticket counter. That way Piya would be forced to speak to him. And he could even ask her a question or two without arousing suspicion.

'How many tickets?'

'Two please.'

'Chair or floor?'

'Chair, please.'

'Yes, of course. That'll be twenty-four rupees, please.'

'Here's thirty. Keep the change.'

Or maybe, he could be the usher. Go around with a flashlight, directing people to their seats. He would make sure Piya got the best seat possible, and would sneakily put a 'Reserved' sign on the chair next to hers. And when everyone had settled down, and the performance had started, he would quietly go and occupy that chair. And watch the whole show with her. Side by side. Could life possibly get any better?

Maybe it could. If one was fantasizing, why not fantasize about something big? I mean, *really* big! What if…Poltu could be the hero in the performance? Lord Sri Ram, Prince of Ayodhya! He pictured himself, standing tall with a bow, raining arrows on the enemy, humiliating Lanka's demons, surrounded by the monkeys (Partho, Soumen, Jishu, Bappa, Kaltu) who worshipped at his feet, getting a hero's welcome back home after rescuing his wife Sita from the clutches of the evil King Rabon. What an impression he would create on Piya! She might just rush to meet him after the show, to congratulate him, ask him his name, and if he was free for dinner the next day.

With a smile on his lips and that happy thought still in his mind, Poltu made his way towards Badshah canteen. It did not look like Piya was going to go out for lunch today. His tummy growled a last thank you, in anticipation of the rice and egg curry meal.

*

Bibhuti Bose dared not breathe.

Barely managing to fit his body behind the array of shirts inside Probhat Sanyal's teak-wood almirah, he felt a nervous excitement that he had never experienced before. There was a very strong, sweet, unidentifiable odour. The closet felt cramped and suffocating. But Bibhuti Bose could hardly complain. Here he was, hiding right in the murder scene, eavesdropping on a conversation which he presumed was between a police officer and Probir Sanyal's wife. It just did not get any better than this in a detective's life! Already he was finding it difficult to suppress the smile. What would his friends say when he recounted this adventure?

'At the time of death, Probhat babu was here, on the bed, am I right?' the male voice was asking.

Mrs Probir Sanyal probably nodded her reply.

'And where were you?' asked the male voice again.

'I was here, near the door,' she replied.

'And your husband, Probir babu?'

'He was standing near the bed, very close to Dada.'

'And you?' asked the male voice of a second person.

'I was not in the room when...when Jethu collapsed,' replied Rumi.

'Where were you?'

'Upstairs. Studying.'

'And...what did Probhat babu have for dinner that night?'

'Uh...I don't recall.' replied Mrs Probir Sanyal. 'Komola would know.'

'Komola? Your maid?'

'Yes. *Ei* Komola!' she called out. 'Come here one minute. Inspector babu wants to have a word with you.'

In the moments that followed, Bibhuti Bose tensed up even more, as sounds of drawers being tugged were heard. Did he hear footsteps nearing the almirah?

He let out an imperceptible sigh of relief, when Komola walked in asking, 'What, Inspector babu?'

'Did you clean Probhat babu's plate that night?'

'Uh...yes. I suppose I did.'

'What was his dinner?'

'Ah...lentils, *alu-posto*, cauliflower, two rotis...'

'And he ate it all?'

'Uh...no, no...he had hardly touched his food. When did he even get the time? *Ei toh,* I brought in his meal around 8.30 as usual—about the time when Boudi's TV serial started—and by 8.45 everything was over.'

'Hmm... So you cleared the plates right then?'

There was a slight pause.

'Umm...I can't remember...maybe right then, or maybe after Dadababu's body was removed? Oh yes, I remember...it was much after. The body was taken to the living room, relatives had started gathering, everyone was sobbing, we were all so upset. Boudi asked me to get a fresh pair of clothes for Dadababu from the almirah, and when I came to get them, I realized that the plates had not been cleared yet.'

'Hmm...so that's when you...?'

'Yes, I cleared the plate.'

'Hmm...What did you do with the food?'

Silence. The Inspector repeated his question.

'I...I must have left it on the kitchen counter. I can't recall.'

'Did you leave it on the counter, or did you eat it yourself? Think carefully. It is not a crime to eat leftover food,' said the Inspector. 'But what you did with the food could be crucial evidence in this case.'

'I may have eaten it...only a little bit,' she added quickly. 'No one in the house was in the mood to eat, naturally. I was also so upset. Dadababu was such a wonderful human being. I could almost hear his voice imploring me to have my dinner. *Komola, there is a lot of work that needs to be done now. If you stay hungry, you will not be of much help to Boudi,* he seemed to tell me.'

'Now think carefully,' said the Inspector. 'Did you feel any stomach cramps or nausea or any discomfort of any sort after you ate? Maybe not immediately, but a few hours later, maybe even the next day?'

Komola took some time to respond, but eventually she said, 'I don't recall any such thing. Those two days there was so much to do, if I had felt ill, I would have surely found it difficult.'

'Hmm...I see. That rules out the option of poisoning his food.'

'What about his lunch, Inspector babu?' asked Rumi. 'Rajib was here that morning. Is it not possible that he mixed something in Jethu's lunch and the poison had a delayed effect?'

'Rajib had left before lunch was served. If he had somehow entered the kitchen and mixed something in the food, every one of you would have been affected,' said the Inspector.

'Oh yes, that is right,' said Rumi.

'Komola, you said you heard the argument between Rajib Guha and Mr Sanyal?' asked the Inspector.

'I was still cooking when I heard the raised voices in Dadababu's room. Both Boudi and I rushed out of the kitchen. A little later, he left...Rajib babu, I mean.'

'Hmm... It's a pity we did not get a post-mortem done.

Poisoning would have surely showed up.'

'The doctor…?' asked Rumi.

'He had not noticed anything special. But of course, he was not trying to, either. If you presume it is death due to cardiac failure, you don't go about looking for clues to see if it was murder. I somehow cannot help but think that what we are looking for is right here, right in this room.' He tapped the teak almirah twice with his baton, almost making Bibhuti Bose's heart stop. 'Well anyway, we are doing the best we can, I assure you. But unless we have a watertight case, it'll be very, very difficult. Rajib has a very good lawyer on his side.'

Bappa Has News for Poltu

'Ei Poltu! Where have you been?' hollered Bappa from across the street. 'I went to your house. Your sister said you have been out all day.'

Poltu crossed the street hurriedly. 'Yes, I've been out. Why? What's the matter?'

'I've got urgent news for you.'

'What?'

Bappa looked this way and that, brought his face closer to Poltu's, lowered his voice and said, 'You have competition.'

Poltu stared back blankly. 'What do you mean?'

'You've got competition, Poltu. There is someone else after your girl.'

'WHAT??! Who is it?'

'Kumar from the next *paara*.'

'Kumar?'

'You know the boy…tall, dark, hair up to his shoulders like a girl…from Milonee Club,' he added the last nail in the coffin.

'Oh *that* Kumar!' exclaimed Poltu. 'Ma Kali! I have seen him several times on the street and at the tea shop when I'm following Piya. I even offered him my seat on the bus, once. That backstabber!' cursed Poltu.

Bappa nodded gravely. 'He has been seen speaking to her. It seems once he pretended his watch had stopped, and asked her the time, to which she replied *4.30*.'

There was a sharp intake of breath. 'The scoundrel!' fumed Poltu. 'How do you know all this, Bappa?'

'I have my sources,' he said simply.

'What sources?'

'But I'll tell you this, Poltu,' said Bappa, ignoring Poltu's question and poking his chest with his index finger, 'Piya stays in our *paara*. She is *our* girl. There is no way a boy from Milonee Club is taking her away.'

Poltu nodded briskly, 'Yes, you are right. She is ours. I mean... she is mine. I have to step things up. I'll go and ask her the time tomorrow. I don't care if she replies or not. I'm not going to lose out to Kumar from...from...Milonee Club.' He uttered the name like it was the most despicable word he had ever spoken.

'That's the spirit, Poltu!' exclaimed Bappa. 'But let us think this through. Why do you want to ask her the time? Just because Kumar did so? What is that going to help you achieve?'

'Yeah, you are right, Bappa,' Poltu nodded briskly. 'I need to ask her something else...like...like...which bus goes to Bhowanipur, for example. Or...or...do you have change for a 100 rupee note? Something like that. You know, casual conversation that does not arouse too much suspicion. What do you say?'

Bappa stared back at him. He then slapped his friend on the back and said, 'Sure, Potol. You go home now and think of some more questions to ask. Let me do what I have to do.'

'What? What do you have to do?'

'I need to find out more about Kumar. What is he like, what does he do, what is his plan, what are his strengths and what are his weaknesses? Unless you know who you are up against—there is no way you can thwart your enemy. *Choli,* I'm off.'

'Bappa...' Poltu's voice quivered unexpectedly.

'What?'

'You are a good friend.'

Bappa shrugged like it was nothing.

'No, I mean it, you really are, Bappa,' carried on Poltu. 'I mean who in our *paara* would do this for me? Tell me?' He threw himself on Bappa in an unexpected embrace.

'*Holo, holo,* enough already,' said Bappa. That boy simply did not know when to stop.

Bappa freed himself from Poltu, raised a hand in a goodbye and was off, the smile still on his lips.

As far as he could remember, he had never done anything selfless for another person. This would be a first. He felt something swell up inside of him. It was a very good feeling.

*

Rumi closed the door behind the inspector. From the corner of her eye, she caught a glimpse of the gentlemen—the senior citizen volunteers or whatever they called themselves—across the street. Weren't there supposed to be three of them? She thought she saw only two. They were a strange lot, she caught herself thinking, going about door to door, asking if there were old people who needed company. It was a nice gesture, she had to admit. Dadu, she was sure, would have appreciated it more if his senses were still functional. God knows what a hard time he must have given these poor fellows.

'O! I did not realize you were still here?' Rumi was taken aback at the sudden sight of Bibhuti Bose in front of her.

'Uh…I was in the washroom.'

'O, okay. Your friends have left, though,' she added.

'Yes, well…I have to be going, too. Thank you for letting us talk to your grandfather. I hope he enjoyed our company.'

Her stance softened. 'I should be the one thanking you. You

know, Dadu does not really interact with people much. Stays in his room all day watching TV. I'm sure it was a welcome change for him. He was quite a storyteller in his younger days.'

'Hmm...some of that has stayed on, I suppose,' smiled Bibhuti Bose.

'It's a pity he can hardly hear these days, and his memory is all muddled up. He must have given you a very hard time.'

'*Arrey*, no, no...we quite enjoyed it, *didibhai*. After all, we are also fast approaching his stage, are we not? I did not mean you, of course...you are still in your prime. But me and my friends. Very soon, we too will be left only with our memories which would eventually refuse to co-operate.'

Rumi smiled politely. 'I must apologize,' she said holding the door open for Bibhuti Bose, 'I could not even make you all a cup of tea.'

'Please don't worry, *didibhai*,' replied Bibhuti Bose.

'It's just that my *jethu*...he passed away quite suddenly. Things are a bit chaotic now.'

'I'm very sorry about Probhat babu's death. Please accept my condolences.'

'Thank you.'

'*Choli*,' waved Bibhuti Bose and let himself out.

Rumi closed the door and went back into the living room. She hand-dusted the sofa and rearranged the cushions. A sudden crease appeared on her brow.

How did the gentleman know her uncle's name?

A Meeting with Prokash Dhar

'*Ki moshai*?' asked Chandan Mukherjee. 'Where had you been? You said you were going to the washroom, then vanished?'

Bibhuti Bose held up his palm, gesturing Chandan Mukherjee to stop. He walked away from the Sanyal house, beckoning his confused friends to follow him quickly. He did not stop till he had crossed the block of houses on James Long Sarani and taken a left at the main road. He waited till his breath was back to normal, then said, trying hard to suppress a glee, 'You are never going to believe what I just did!'

*

Retired High Court Judge Akhil Banerjee found himself in the office of the eminent criminal lawyer, Prokash Dhar. He was seated in a high-backed leather chair normally reserved for clients, and had been served a cup of tea by the office *chapraasi*. 'Sir' will join him in a moment, he was informed.

Prokash Dhar's office, on the third floor of an 'office building' in Dharmatola, was plushly furnished, reflective of the lawyer's thriving business.

'So sorry to have kept you waiting, sir,' he apologized hurriedly. 'Call from an overseas client,' he offered by way of explanation.

'It's alright, it's alright,' assured Akhil Banerjee. 'Tell me, what seems to be the matter?'

Prokash Dhar took his time to respond. He stared at his

desk, and stroked his forehead. Not a good sign, thought Akhil Banerjee.

'Sir...there has been a development.' He paused. 'Yesterday... at about noon, I got a call. Probhat Sanyal's niece is seriously ill, she has been rushed to the hospital. Doctors suspect arsenic poisoning. I went to the hospital immediately.

'It seems, Rumi, Probhat babu's niece, had earlier in the day visited her uncle's old office. There she helped herself to a cup of tea. There was no sugar in the kitchen shelf, so she inadvertently took some from a bottle labelled "Sugar" from one of the employee's desks. According to Manohar babu, the senior accountant in Probhat babu's firm who brought Rumi to the hospital, it is common practice for all the employees to keep their preferred brand of tea bags in their cubicles. Most even keep a supply of sugar cubes or sachets of powdered sugar, milk powder and an electric kettle with them, so they don't have to walk all the way to the pantry to fix themselves a cup of tea.'

'Let me guess,' said Akhil Banerjee. 'She poured herself some white powder, thinking it to be sugar, and it turned out to be arsenic oxide?'

Prokash Dhar nodded gravely.

'And...the desk happened to belong to Rajib Guha?' finished Akhil Banerjee.

'Yes, I'm afraid so.'

'Hmm... Interesting.'

'This would have been my fiftieth win in a row,' the lawyer shook his head. 'As long as we were not able to determine the cause of death, as anything other than heart failure not brought about by an external agent, we could argue "reasonable doubt". But now...'

'Yes, I see that. But Prokash, there is still no proof that Probhat babu was given arsenic, is there? I mean, when did Rajib even get a chance? He was not present at the time the death occurred.'

'Arsenic oxide, if mixed with food or drink in smaller quantities, over a long period of time, has a cumulative effect. It is well known that Rajib used to regularly give Probhat babu his medications and even fixed his drinks. He could have been doing this for a while. The poison might have crossed the threshold that day, and proved fatal. The only thing that can save us now is the fact that the body was cremated even before a post-mortem could be done. Arsenic poisoning would have surely shown up in the post-mortem.'

'Or it may not have shown up, in which case it would have been easy to prove Rajib's innocence,' said Akhil Banerjee.

'I see, sir, that you still believe in Rajib's innocence,' Prokash Dhar smiled wryly.

'It is impossible to put in your 100 per cent to defend a client unless you truly believe he is innocent, isn't it?' smiled Akhil Banerjee.

'Yes, perhaps. But the circumstantial evidence in this case is now too strong, sir. Rajib stood to gain a lot by the death of his boss, he had had an argument with Probhat babu—perhaps there was some tension brewing underneath for quite some time—and now with the arsenic angle...he even had the opportunity of bringing about the death slowly without arousing any suspicion. A violent death would have immediately pointed fingers at him. But this was well thought out, calculated, not a heat-of-the-moment act, which is another factor that will go against him.'

'Hmm... How's Probhat babu's niece—I'm sorry, what was her name again?'

'Rumi.'

'Yes, Rumi. How is she doing now?'

'Better. It was good that she got medical attention immediately. Ingesting a spoonful of arsenic at one go could prove to be lethal. She is extremely lucky to have made it, I must say.'

Bappa and Poltu Do Some Sleuthing

At the time when the All Bengali Crime Detectives were racking their brains on how to uncover the mystery shrouding the death of Probhat Sanyal, Bappa and Poltu were engaged in doing detective work of a different kind. Taking care to cover themselves well (the winter season was excellent for putting on extra layers of clothing without arousing suspicion, they realized), they stealthily made their way towards the Milonee clubhouse, where, if Bappa's 'sources' were to be believed, there was going to be a 'very urgent meeting'.

'Kumar must be there at the Milonee Club this evening,' Bappa informed Poltu. 'Their President, Sudhir Bagchi, has called an important meeting. Let's go early and find a place to hide.'

'But…but…is this really necessary?' asked Poltu.

Bappa looked exasperated. 'Everything is necessary, Poltu! Everything is necessary! If we have to beat Kumar in this game, we need to find out everything we can about him.'

There was no arguing with that logic. Poltu wrapped himself well, and despite Bappa's silent snigger, put on his dark glasses. If they were going to do some snooping around, he wanted to look his part.

Milonee's clubhouse was a two-storey high building right in the middle of a row of residential homes. As they neared the clubhouse, Bappa touched Poltu's arm lightly, cautioning him to slow down. If two Sabuj Kalyan boys were spotted near the Milonee den, there could be trouble. The last thing they wanted was to draw attention to themselves. Bappa gestured Poltu to follow him. He took a left turn, a little before the clubhouse came into full view. It was a dark, narrow alley sandwiched between two tall buildings, with barely enough space for one person to pass. Bappa hushed Poltu's 'why did you come here?', and signaled him to follow.

'But this is taking us away from their clubhouse,' protested Poltu.

Bappa ignored the observation. 'This way,' he said, as they took a serpentine route through an even dingier alley, lined on either side by ramshackle structures that passed off as homes. Poltu tried to keep up with Bappa, barely avoiding a cat that sprinted, it seemed, right off his ankles with an angry 'meow'.

'This way,' said Bappa, as he turned abruptly to his right and disappeared in the dark.

Poltu stood dazed. 'Bappa?' he called out as loudly as he dared.

'I'm here,' came the reply. 'Come up the stairs.'

'What stairs?'

'To your right. Just start climbing.'

Poltu spread his arms about and groped in the dark. He took off his glasses, and thrust them in his back pocket. His eyes slowly got used to the dim light. He could barely make out the first step. He stepped on it gingerly.

'Come up. It's just one flight. You'll know when you reach the landing,' assured Bappa.

Poltu continued to walk up the steps slowly, feeling the wall on his right as he went up. Sounds of a soap-opera being played on the television came through the wall. The smell of burnt charcoal suggested a hot dinner was being cooked nearby. Poltu's stomach gave an involuntary growl. He lingered a second or two, taking in a deep breath, filling his lungs with the aroma of potato curry and hot puffed rotis.

'What's taking you so long?' whispered Bappa.

Light from the lamp post on the street filtered through a window, giving Bappa's silhouette, standing tall with hands on his hips, the appearance of a superhero. Poltu couldn't help but feel a tinge of pride. Bappa was *his* friend!

'Where are we?' he asked as he reached the landing.

'Come this way,' replied Bappa.

He unlatched a door to his left and pushed it open. The cold sting of the January night hit their faces. Poltu followed Bappa out of the door. He found himself on an open terrace. Clothes lines, now bare except for pegs that sat like tiny birds, zigzagged all across.

'Why are we here?' asked Poltu.

Bappa ignored the question and walked straight ahead, lifting the rows of nylon cord over his head till he reached the very edge.

'Ma Kali!' exclaimed Poltu. Through the grilled window that lay open, barely five feet from where he stood, Poltu could clearly see the first floor room of Milonee clubhouse. Sudhir Bagchi, President of Milonee Club, was seated on a chair. A few of their boys were seated in a half circle on the floor. Bappa nudged Poltu as Kumar walked in with a friend.

The meeting was about to begin.

Debdas Guha Roy Remembers!

'What is it, Joj Saheb? Something serious?' asked Debdas Guha Roy.

Akhil Banerjee stood up and began pacing the length of his living room. He rubbed his palm over his chin in an effort to put his thoughts together.

'I met Prokash this afternoon,' he began. 'But let's wait for everyone to come. Have you informed Bibhuti babu?'

'Yes, yes,' replied Chandan Mukherjee. 'He must be on his way.'

'Prokash? The lawyer?' asked Debdas Guha Roy.

Akhil Banerjee nodded. 'It seems Probhat Sanyal's niece had to be hospitalized following...'

'Who? Rumi?' asked Chandan Mukherjee. 'What happened?'

Akhil Banerjee threw him a surprised look.

'*Arrey, ei toh,* Bibhuti babu is here!' called out Chandan Mukherjee. '*Babba*! You can't seem to get enough of that *jompesh* cap, *moshai*!' he patted the seat next to him to usher him to sit down.

'How do you know her name?' asked Akhil Banerjee.

'Whose name?' asked Bibhuti Bose.

'*Na,* I was asking Chandan babu. How do you know Probhat babu's niece's name?'

'It's a long story,' piped in Bibhuti Bose, winking both his eyes at Chandan Mukherjee. 'But Joj Saheb…please continue. You were saying she is hospitalized?'

'Ah yes…a very unfortunate incident.' Akhil Banerjee narrated what he had heard earlier that day.

'So…Rajib had arsenic oxide in his sugar pot?'

'Yes, so it seems,' said Akhil Banerjee shaking his head. 'I cannot believe how he fooled us all so convincingly. As Prokash was saying, as long as we could not figure out *how* the murder took place, Rajib was safe. But now with this arsenic angle—he could have added minute amounts in Probhat babu's food and drink over a period of time, till finally even a little dose proved fatal. That way, nobody even suspects anything. I must say, he almost got away with it.'

'But…but…why keep the poison on his desk?' asked Bibhuti Bose. 'In full public view, I mean?'

'Why not? Who would think of checking the contents of a sugar pot?' said Akhil Banerjee.

'*Tchah!* Such a young girl,' Bibhuti Bose shook his head. 'And to think we met her only yesterday.'

'Bibhuti babu, what am I missing here?' asked Akhil Banerjee. 'How did you…?'

'Oh my God!' exclaimed Debdas Guha Roy, jumping off his seat.

'What?!'

'It all fits in! It all fits in!' he said excitedly, palms on his temples, a look of horror on his face. 'You remember, Joj Saheb, the day we went to visit Rajib's aunt, Nilima Guha?'

Akhil Banerjee nodded.

'You remember a young man came to see her to find out if she needed him to go to the market? Sumit or something, the name was…'

'Sumon,' replied Akhil Banerjee. 'Go on.'

'Yes, Sumon, Sumon,' repeated Debdas Guha Roy, still arranging his thoughts. 'Ever since that day, I have been thinking…where have I seen this boy? Where have I seen him? Now I remember. The day I went to the laboratory at Ashutosh College, he was there! He is a student there and I bet it was he who pinched the packet of arsenic oxide and passed it on to Rajib!'

There followed a few minutes of stunned silence.

'Hmm…everything does fit in perfectly,' Akhil Banerjee spoke slowly. 'We'll have to inform the police of this Sumon. I'm sure they can get the truth out of him quite easily.'

'How Rajib fooled us with that cock-and-bull story of how much he loved is boss, how he was like a father to him…' Bibhuti Bose shook his head. '*Tchah!*'

'Nothing is bigger than money in this world, Bibhuti babu,' said Chandan Mukherjee. 'That is the unfortunate truth!'

'So what about Rumi? How serious is it?' asked Chandan Mukherjee.

'Looks like she's out of danger,' said Akhil Banerjee. 'She is fortunate to have received medical attention right away.'

'It's an open and shut case,' said Debdas Guha Roy. 'I will go over to Ashutosh College today itself and inform the principal.' He sighed. 'All along, we were thinking that the arsenic oxide was stolen to commit suicide. But no,' he shook his head, 'It was stolen for murder!'

Akhil Banerjee nodded in response but his mind was elsewhere. His brows were knitted, and his eyes were not focussed on anything in particular.

'The question still remains,' he said, 'who or what was outside Probhat Sanyal's window? And how did Chandan babu and Bibhuti babu come to know Probhat babu's niece?

'Suppose we begin with the second question. Bibhuti babu?'

A Discovery

From what Poltu could make out, through the iron bars and foliage that partly blocked his view of the room inside Milonee clubhouse, Kumar was clearly distracted. He seemed to be whispering to the boy next to him. They suppressed giggles. They gesticulated—shrugged their shoulders, bobbed their heads, chopped the air in front. Clearly, this conversation was more exciting than the altercation that took place between Sudhir Bagchi and a taxi driver that morning.

What were they talking about? Were they discussing Poltu? Of how Kumar had seen Poltu following Piya and how Piya never paid any attention to him? Of how Poltu had not spoken to Piya even once, but he, Kumar, had had the courage to walk up to her and ask the time?

Sudhir Bagchi's voice carried well in the still night. But his narration interested Poltu little. He inched closer to the wall and strained his ears in the hope of eavesdropping on Kumar's conversation. He reached for the nearby branch and pushed it down to get a clearer view.

'Don't do that!' warned Bappa, as he crouched behind the low boundary wall. 'If they see us, we'll be minced meat!'

Poltu paid little heed. He had to listen to what Kumar and his friend were talking about. But he just wasn't close enough. Taking support of the branch, he climbed nimbly on to the boundary wall. Then, grasping the branch with both hands he lowered his body. He now lay flat like a lizard, his face—camouflaged by leaves—barely a foot away from the window.

He distinctly heard Kumar say the words 'Sabuj Kalyan'. So it was true! They were talking about Poltu! He glided an inch closer, his eyes and ears fully glued to the scene in front. He felt like a tiger, a Royal Bengal tiger, crouched, still, yet fully alert, ready to pounce on the prey ahead.

'Poltu, what are you doing? Come back!' whispered Bappa, as loudly as he dared. But the sense of urgency in his voice was drowned by the startling revelation by Kumar's friend.

'They had planned a Bollywood Ramayon,' the friend was saying.

Kumar sniggered in response. The friend continued, 'I told Sudhir da, you leave it to me. Our magic show will not suffer because of Sabuj Kalyan's *jatra*! I will take care of it. But it will cost a bit of money.'

'What did you do?' asked Kumar.

'What else?' he smiled slyly. 'Same thing as we did last year during Durga Pujo.'

'You mean…called the police, the journalists?'

'No, no! A *jatra* does not attract the attention of media! I had to keep it subtle.'

Poltu's nose was now almost touching the iron bars on Milonee club's window.

'I simply went to the office of Sotyembor Opera…that's the *jatra* company those guys hired. And the manager there was only too happy to…'

Poltu found himself staring at the wall and realized that somehow his body had been lowered. Was the branch giving in to his weight? That was hardly possible. He was as thin as a…

The remainder of that analogy was drowned in a horrific scream as Poltu made a nose-dive to the ground below, still desperately holding on to the tip of the branch for dear life. Bappa, who had already sprinted down the flight of stairs to reach the bottom, barely had enough time to look up at the stunned faces on the Milonee window. He picked up a screaming and howling Poltu and dragged him away as fast as he could.

Behind them they could hear the war cry of Milonee boys darting down the stairs.

'CATCH THOSE RASCALS! BREAK THEIR BONES! NOT ONE OF THEM SHOULD ESCAPE!'

For the Honour of the Club

Perhaps, what his wife said often was true, thought Debdas Guha Roy. He was simply not a good judge of character. He trusted easily, too easily in fact, always giving the other person—regardless of how questionable his actions were—the benefit of doubt.

Debdas Guha Roy did not necessarily see this as a fault. If we were to accuse, point fingers, bring to task every human failing (and there were far too many), as a community it would be impossible to survive. What was the point in being a human without...without...humanness, that quality which helped forgive undesirable words and actions of others? Words that were uttered, perhaps when for a fleeting moment the ego had taken hold and pushed all humility and good sense to the background. Or actions—harsh and inexplicable—done out of sheer ignorance. As human beings we were mercifully endowed with some degree of compassion that allowed us to forgive and move on. Otherwise, one's entire life could be spent in anger and regret.

There were people, Debdas Guha Roy knew, who found it impossible to let go, holding on to a grudge like their lives depended on it, visiting and revisiting an event in their memory that had occurred in some remote past. You just could not help these people. No logic, no consolation worked. There was an aunt in his family, who had had a row—seemingly minor at that point—with her daughter-in-law. And till this day, in spite of the best efforts of her son and his wife, she had not been able to get over it.

How does a transient event gain so much importance that your family—your own kith and kin—seem worthless in comparison? With time, Debdas Guha Roy had come to accept that this aunt, like many others, found 'comfort' in this tension. It was like saying, if his aunt could suddenly find in herself the compassion to forgive and be happy, she would be miserable.

Right at this moment though, standing at the edge of his terrace, with a warm shawl draped over his shoulders, a monkey-cap pulled over his ears, fingers wrapped around a hot cup of tea resting on the parapet, watching the grey mist slowly cover the scenery before his eyes—the canopy of trees, the abandoned antennae on roof-tops, pots of white and yellow chrysanthemums—Debdas Guha Roy was finding it impossibly hard to forgive himself. He had been misled by his perception. In his firm belief that he had found the ideal son-in-law in Rajib Guha, he had lost all sense of objectivity, choosing to disregard glaring evidence of the latter's guilt that now stared him in the eye. And in the process he had let his family down once again.

Even though, rightfully, no one else was to blame for this situation, somehow Debdas Guha Roy had the feeling of being grievously wronged. He had been fooled by the innocent looks of Rajib Guha and his winding tale of hardship and struggle. He had wanted to believe Rajib so badly, wanted to believe that boys like him—boys who had a strong character, who were polite, gentle and who knew the value of hard-earned money—still existed. But alas!

With a long sigh, he picked up his cup of tea and finished the remaining liquid in one gulp.

'Baba? Are you there on the terrace?' His younger daughter,

Diya's voice called out from the landing on the stairs.

'Yes. What is it?'

'There is a call for you. Kapil Rudra. From Ashutosh College.'

*

'What did you just say?!' Biplab Maity thundered.

Bappa remained silent. It was one of those rhetorical questions.

Biplab Maity looked away. His mind raced, his temples throbbed, and in spite of the winter evening chill, cold beads of sweat trickled down his side-brows.

He started to pace the floor of the Sabuj Kalyan clubhouse, muttering to himself, 'This was all Milonee's doing! This was all Milonee's doing!' His bulging, murderous eyes met Partho's when the latter asked, 'Are we not going to do anything about this? Are we going to take this lying low, Biplab da?'

'I say we beat the crap out of them!' said Jishu. 'Let's all take *daandas* and attack them tonight!'

'No, no, Jishu!' said Bumba. 'We can't just attack like that... without reason...the police...'

'What do you mean "without reason"?! Didn't you just hear what Bappa said? They deliberately sabotaged our Durga Pujo last year, and now this!'

'Yes, I know,' said Bumba, trying to sound calm. 'But what proof do we have? And even if we have proof, this is no reason to go about beating people. In the end, we will be the one behind bars while Milonees have their last laugh. Again.'

'Then what do we do, Biplab da?' asked Jishu. 'Are we going to keep silent and let them get away with this?'

Biplab Maity shook his head—it was a slow shake, which somehow made it all the more frightening. He might have failed at a lot of things—he might have failed a few too many tests in higher mathematics and he might have failed to make his feelings known to Surochita Purokayastha, First Year, History Honours. But Biplab Maity would never be able to forgive himself if he took this lying low.

'Call all our boys!' he said. 'We will have a *jatra* at Sabuj Kalyan Park in exactly five days!' He pointed sharply to the floor to emphasize.

'But…this is a peak season for *jatra* companies. None will be available so close to the date, Biplab da,' said Partho.

'We do not need any *jatra* company to perform,' said Biplab Maity, his tone laced with bitterness.

The boys exchanged looks. None dared to ask the obvious.

'Here…Partho, you will be Ram,' came the reply soon enough.

'Me?!'

'Yes, you. And Bappa…'

'Biplab da, I can't act. I don't know the dialogues…' protested Partho.

'This is no time to argue,' shot back Biplab Maity. 'If you boys care even two hoots about your club, you will do this without hesitation.' His loyalty thus questioned, Partho remained silent.

'Bappa, you can be Hanuman. You can also double up as the playback singer. Since this is Bollywood Ramayon…'

'*Arrey,* no no Biplab da,' Bappa gave a nervous laugh. 'I can't sing…'

'Shut up! Don't lie! I've heard you croon every time the *paara* girls pass by. Do you think I'm blind and deaf?'

Biplab Maity continued. 'Who else is there? Oh yes, Bhombol… well…with his kind of physique, he can only be Kumbhokorno. And Kaltu—we can save on the make-up if he agrees to be Jambuban. Jishu, you can be Bhorot…'

The casting continued for a while. Every whimper, whine,

vexation was shot down by Biplab Maity with a tone of finality. 'This is no time to doubt your talents!' he declared. Doubts were for the weak, the insecure, the unconfident—all of which were in abundant supply among the boys of Sabuj Kalyan Club, he knew. 'But, the less we pay attention to our weaknesses the more we focus on our strengths,' he asserted.

'This is not a ridiculous idea, regardless of what Bappa has been constantly saying, to embarrass ourselves in front of a large audience. This is the time to show, once and for all, that the scheming, sabotaging Milonee Club cannot get away with everything and anything! There are times in a man's life when one needs to throw caution to the wind, and stand up for what is right. This is the time to show the world'—which in this case, thankfully, was limited to the residents of Golf Garden—'what you are really made of! This is what separates men from the boys!'

Their testosterone levels thus challenged, the boys decided to remain silent for the rest of the meeting. When all the major characters from the epic had been assigned to the members of Sabuj Kalyan Club, there remained only one question: who was going to play Sita?

Bibhuti Bose Has an Insight

Life was unusually complicated at times, reflected Chandan Mukherjee. Especially, when there was absolutely no reason to be so.

There was this case of Rajib Guha—a handsome, smart, educated boy who had everything going for him. Sooner or later, he would have been given the entire responsibility of the company. It certainly seemed like his boss, the late Probhat Sanyal, had been grooming him all these years just for that very role. But no! Rajib had to plan a murder and ruin everything for himself!

Then, there was the case of his older son, Bubai. Who would have thought that after getting the opportunity to study Computer Science in IIT—which assured him of a promising career, not just in India, but abroad as well—he would take a complete U-turn, throw his education down the drain by suddenly developing a keen interest in social work! This meditation he practised all the time locked in his room, had shown him what life was really all about, it seemed. Not that there was anything wrong with contemplation on God and the meaning of life per se, Chandan Mukherjee was quick to admit to himself. But there was a time and age for everything. Gods can wait, employers do not!

You could not help but wonder if even the brightest of brains had the habit of temporarily going into hibernation. Or perhaps, if a popular Bengali saying were to be believed, maybe the likes of his son and Rajib Guha were in fact possessed by some mischievous spirit. It had been impossible to reason with Bubai, who it would seem, had become determined to ruin his own life! It was like he had been brainwashed by someone. Even when such obvious truths had been pointed out to him, Bubai's response was shocking. Brainwash was a good thing, he had said. It was good to wash the brain sometimes to remove the clutter of the past, just like it was hygienic to take a bath every day to wash away the dirt. *How do you even talk to these kids?!*

Chandan Mukherjee was a perfectly reasonable father. If Bubai had the slightest feeling of stress because of academic pressures, he would be the first person to encourage his son to do some *pranayam* or practice meditation for a few minutes. There were a dozen channels on television that touted the health benefits associated with these ancient Indian practices. Not that he himself had tried any of these—and if truth be told, he tended to take the tall claims of its practitioners with a pinch of salt—but he saw absolutely no harm in Bubai indulging in those if he believed it could help him. But not appearing for campus recruitment, throwing away a perfectly enviable career? That was certainly not normal behaviour! If anything, it was downright irresponsible!

Bubai had pointed to the large framed photograph of Swami Vivekananda hung on the wall and demanded of his father, 'Why do you have Swamiji's photo on the wall? Do you not believe in his teachings? What was Swamiji's dream? To see the youth of India participate in building this nation…and for that, small sacrifices like career are necessary.'

Small sacrifices? Small sacrifices?! Doing social work, where there were no pressures to perform, nothing to prove, no deadlines to meet—was escapism, not a 'sacrifice'. Sacrifice was what had been done for him and his brother, by his parents! Did Bubai even know or remember what had been done for him?

When Bubai had not responded, Chandan Mukherjee had added in a softer tone, 'I'm not saying that you should not work for your country and all. But all this—this social work and building the nation—can wait a few more years, can it not? All I'm saying is, now is the time to establish yourself. Give yourself four or five years. Once you are settled, then no one is going to stop you from doing all this.'

It is not that he had not considered it, Bubai had replied. But having thought things through, he had come to the conclusion that the choice had to be made right now, before he became a 'corporate rat' ensconced in a world of cut-throat competition—a gigantic labyrinth which had no exits, a whirlpool that sucked a bit of you every day, a resort which promised unimaginable luxuries but no time to enjoy any of them.

It had taken Chandan Mukherjee some time to shake away the image of a cruel corporate amusement park, and before he could respond, Bubai had added, 'I have some good ideas, Baba. And I have a good education that I could use to make a real difference. Most students study engineering for the degree, not the knowledge. And few implement that knowledge in their future careers. Is that not an utter waste of four years in the country's most premier institute?'

While Chandan Mukherjee fully appreciated the sentiment behind this reasoning, he failed to understand why *his* son, of all people, should be the one to go about doing things differently! The arguments had continued well into the night. Bubai's mind seemed to have been made up.

'What exactly is this mediation you do? And where did you learn it?'

'Baba, you should come with me,' replied Bubai most unexpectedly. 'See, every time you get stressed, you smoke.

Have you noticed? That's harmful, not just to you, but also for the people around you, for the environment. If you learn some *pranayam* and meditation, you could…'

At this point Chandan Mukherjee had to stop his son with vigorous shaking of the head accompanied by frantic hand-waving. 'Leave me out of this. All this spirituality–*tirituality* is not for me!' He had protested. He did as much as was required, gave flowers to Ma Kali and chanted some shlokas that had been taught by his father. For a family man, that much was enough. Otherwise, one had to renounce everything and live in a cave, something his son was fast heading towards, he feared.

Bubai was determined to make him see otherwise, and had gone on to say that times had changed, and that unlike olden times, meditation was now no longer a luxury to be practised by a few. Nothing was more important than a happy, relaxed and peaceful mind—and no amount of bank balance was going to guarantee that. He had spoken passionately for hours, but much of it had escaped his father.

How had he described meditation? *It was, simply waiting… for absolutely nothing.*

Now, sitting on his toilet seat for the past half an hour or so, Chandan Mukherjee mused if that could as well be the definition of constipation.

*

'NO, NO, NO, NO, NO…NOOOOOO!!'

That was Poltu's horrified response. 'How could you even think, Biplab da?'

'It was easy,' replied Biplab Maity in a calm voice. 'We simply ruled out the men.'

Poltu stared at him blankly. To his horror, he realized a

lump had formed in his throat, and unwelcome tears had begun queueing up behind the pupil. He blinked quickly, sniffed and looked away. 'You shouldn't say that, Biplab da,' he said, his voice now almost a whisper.

'What did you say, Poltu? Couldn't hear.'

Poltu did not reply.

'Poltu,' said his best friend Bhombol, in a placatory tone, 'You are the best looking amongst all of us. Take a look around. Who else could play Sita here?'

Poltu allowed his eyes to rest on the lot surrounding him. He saw messy hair, buck teeth, blotchy and pockmarked skin, thick sideburns, and in one case, a shaggy moustache. He had to agree with Bhombol. Even with an arm on a sling, he *was* the prettiest by far. A faint smile appeared on his lips.

'Just do this for us. For the club,' said an unusually kind Partho. 'We've all agreed to our parts, haven't we? But without Sita, this play cannot happen. It's pointless. She is the main character. She is the one for whom Ram has to go through all the headache! If there is no Sita, there is no Ramayon!'

Yes, nodded Poltu, he *was* the best looking by far!

'So, you'll do it!' Bhombol slapped his friend on the back. Others did the same with varied degrees of enthusiasm. One, probably Soumen or Jishu—Poltu couldn't be sure—even roughed up his hair. Poltu had to step back. Now they had gone too far.

'Alright, I'll do it,' said Poltu, patting his hair back into place. 'But there is one problem.' He pointed to his broken arm. How were they going to justify a Sita with a sling?

'That's easy,' said Biplab Maity. 'You can double up as Jotayu. The giant bird had one wing clipped off during the kidnapping scene, no?'

'What?! Have you gone mad, Biplab da?' asked Poltu, horror

now back again in his life. The question though, was a rhetorical one, the insanity of their Club President now a foregone conclusion.

'Alright, now back to rehearsals,' announced Biplab Maity, clapping his hands. 'We have less than five days to go!'

'But...but...but,' called out Poltu. 'How am I going to save myself from being kidnapped while I'm busy getting kidnapped myself?'

*

The room was dark. Very dark. Bibhuti Bose could not see what was in front of him. He stretched out his arms but could not feel the wall. He felt claustrophobic.

What was he doing in this dark room? He had no idea. There had to be a way out. He could hear muffled voices in the distance. But even though he strained his ears he could not make out what was being said. Should he call out to them? Ask for help? Something told him that would not be wise. He felt safer in the dark room somehow. But he was beginning to feel thirsty, and was starting to get a headache from the odour—that strong, sweet, floral scent. Was it rose or jasmine? It was thick and seemed to be engulfing him in an invisible cloud. He felt giddy and nauseous. He was finding it difficult to breathe. He gasped for fresh air.

Bibhuti Bose woke up with a start. He rubbed his palms on his face in an effort to shake the sleep away. With the dream still fresh in his mind, he climbed out of the bed, and reached for the cordless receiver on the side table.

Akhil Banerjee answered after four rings.

The Complete Picture

'Before I start,' said Akhil Banerjee, getting up from his seat to face the gathering, 'I'd like to ask a question or two to Probir babu.'

The Sanyal's living room was crowded. Extra chairs and stools had to be brought in from other rooms to accommodate all those who had gathered. There was Biren Ghoshal, Bibhuti Bose, Chandan Mukherjee, Debdas Guha Roy, Dr Gupta, Inspector Bakshi, Prokash Dhar, Probir Sanyal, his wife and daughter, Manohar babu and Nilima Guha.

'In the days preceding his death, did Probhat babu complain of headaches or nausea?'

Both Probhat Sanyal and his wife shook their heads.

'Any stomach cramps? Indigestion?'

'No, not that we know of.'

'How would you describe Probhat babu's general health in the final days?'

'Normal, I would say,' shrugged Probir Sanyal.

'Doctor Gupta, let me ask you, did you find anything particularly different about Probhat babu during your routine check-ups?'

'No, nothing in particular. Except...well...after getting discharged from the hospital he had stopped drinking completely. It probably served as some kind of a wake-up call. He had got rid of all the liquor bottles and even admitted more than once that he was feeling much better,' replied Dr Gupta.

'That is why his passing away seemed all the more sudden and suspicious,' concluded Probir Sanyal.

'Right. I have one other question. For you, Nilima Debi. When is Rajib's birthday?'

'Huh?! Rajib's birthday? October 13th. Why?'

Akhil Banerjee nodded. 'I will come to it shortly.'

'Alright, let us quickly recap the events leading up to this day. In early November, my friend here, Biren, was admitted to Kothari. He was sharing the room with Probhat Sanyal, who narrated to him an incident that had occurred—some twenty years ago—when Probhat Sanyal was the manager at a tea estate in Kurseong. One night while returning from the club in an inebriated state, Probhat babu ran his jeep over a local of the area. Following this accident, he began to see the dead man's ghost outside the window of his bungalow. Panic-stricken, he left Kurseong to come settle down in Calcutta with his brother, Probir babu, and his family. Up until now, Probhat babu had shared this story with only one other person in his life—Rajib Guha, an employee at his firm, with whom Probhat babu shared a special bond.

'One evening in October, Probhat babu was in his room in this very house, when suddenly he heard a rap on the window. On removing the curtains, he saw the ghost of Kurseong standing right outside. He panicked, called Rajib, who came to calm him down. For a month, there is no further development. Then again, in mid November, the incident is repeated. This time, Rajib insists on taking him to a doctor. A hospitalization follows.

'After Probhat babu is discharged from the hospital, again, for almost a month, there is no news. Then one day, Biren gets a call from him—on Tuesday, December 13th. Probhat babu invites him over to his house. Biren comes the following Saturday to learn that Probhat babu had passed away on Tuesday evening itself, the very day that he had called Biren. A couple of days later, Biren is visited by Rajib. Like Biren, Rajib too thinks there is something suspicious about Mr Sanyal's death.

'Meanwhile, doubts regarding the nature of Probhat babu's death have cropped up amongst members of the Sanyal family as well. Upon learning that Rajib has come to gain a large inheritance, and that, on the morning of December 13th, was overheard to have had a heated argument with his boss, Probir babu casts serious aspersions on Rajib. Is it possible that the latter, fully aware of his inheritance, got scared that his boss would now exclude him from the will because of a fallout? Is he desperate enough to kill? And if so, how did he do it? Probir babu has also claimed that his brother called out to Rajib in his dying moments. Was he merely calling out to Rajib as a father would in his deathbed? Or was he in fact alerting Probir babu of something Rajib might have done?

'Upon learning that Rajib has been arrested by the police, Debdas babu and I visit his aunt, Nilima Debi. We do not really learn anything new…except…well…there was something, only the significance of it became clearer much later. So I will leave that for now.

'Now, if it is in fact a case of murder, all fingers point to Rajib. But the real baffling question here was: how did he do it? Rajib was not present at the time of death, he had left hours earlier. With the dead body not available, one could not test for poisoning. And even if it was poisoning, then when and how did he administer it?

'As we all know now, a plastic bottle labelled "Sugar" was discovered on Rajib's work-desk recently, which when tested, turned out to be poisonous arsenic oxide. We have to thank Probhat babu's niece, Rumi, for making the discovery (he looked at Rumi, smiled and nodded) even if it was made under a potentially fatal circumstance. Rumi, who had gone to visit her late uncle's office one afternoon and had decided to make herself some tea, had made the mistake of stirring in some of the poison thinking it to be sugar. She had to be hospitalized immediately. Thanks to Manohar babu's prompt action Rumi's life was saved.

'One question that naturally arises is how Rajib managed to procure the poison? It is not something that is readily available commercially.'

Akhil Banerjee paused. He allowed his eyes to meet those of the audience listening to him in rapt attention.

'Now, here I would like to fill in everyone with another seemingly unrelated incident. A few weeks ago, about a week after Probhat babu's death, Debdas babu got a call from the principal of his former college. There had been some thefts from the chemistry lab which was of concern to the authorities. Test tubes and some generally harmless chemicals had often gone missing from there. But this time a toxic chemical, arsenic oxide, was missing, raising the concern that perhaps one of the students was contemplating suicide.

'Debdas babu was not able to offer any advice up front, but only recently it occurred to him that one of the students he had seen at the college's chemistry lab during his recent visit was Sumon, a young fellow whom we met briefly during our visit to Rajib's place. Sumon lived in Rajib's apartment building, one floor below, and according to Nilima Debi, was extremely fond of Rajib. Did Rajib then get Sumon to steal arsenic oxide from the college lab?'

'He must have,' said Inspector Bakshi. 'Now everything fits

in like a glove. He had the motive, the opportunity and now, even the means!'

'True. But the question I asked myself was: if Rajib had indeed used arsenic oxide as a means to poison his boss, then did he do it that very day with a large dose, mixing it perhaps with his food?

'It would seem impossible. Rajib had left long before the dinner had even been cooked. So this possibility is immediately ruled out. Besides, Probhat babu did not get a chance to have his dinner that night. His food was in fact, consumed by the maid Komola, who as we see now is hale and hearty.'

Akhil Banerjee allowed the pronouncement to sink in, then continued, 'But there could be one other way the poison could be administered—slowly without arousing suspicion. But this would not be a heat of the moment act. It would be a well-thought-out, cold-blooded murder.

'You see, tiny amounts of arsenic oxide can be used over a long period of time to slowly poison someone. The symptoms are usually not alarming—headaches, stomach aches, nausea. Hence, it is one of those poisons that can go undetected very easily. In fact, for this very reason, in the medieval times, this was the most common means of murder amongst royalty. So the question is: did Rajib use arsenic oxide to slowly poison his boss, little by little every day, until one day that tiny dose became too much? It would have been easy enough for him, given that he often mixed his boss' drinks or gave him his medication.

'But, as both Probir babu and Dr Gupta have just confirmed, Probhat babu did not show any signs of arsenic poisoning in the days leading up to his death. In fact, if anything, he was in much better health than normal. That can only mean that Probhat babu's death, if at all a murder, was not a result of arsenic poisoning.

'And yet, a large quantity of the toxic substance was found on Rajib's desk.'

No one spoke. All eyes rested on Akhil Banerjee.

'This is where the case becomes interesting and intriguing. What was Rajib doing with the poison?' Akhil Banerjee paused. 'Was he planning something sinister...or was he being framed for a murder that NEVER happened?' His keen eyes met everyone else's.

'Now, one can see immediately that there are people in this room for whom a murder would be very convenient indeed. If Rajib is found guilty, then he does not inherit...'

'What are you suggesting, Mr Banerjee?!' thundered Probir Sanyal. 'That I...that I...'

'Relax, Mr Sanyal,' said Akhil Banerjee. 'I am just talking about the various possibilities. That is all. Anyway, let us move on to the events that occurred following Mr Sanyal's death. Some days ago, Bibhuti babu, along with Chandan babu paid a visit to this house under the pretext of doing community service.'

'O ma!' exclaimed Komola, the maid. 'That is why I have been thinking from that time...where have I seen these gentlemen before?'

'I recognized them the moment they walked in,' said Rumi, a sly smile on the corner of her lips. 'I was waiting to see when that would be revealed.'

'Hmm...well...you must forgive us, *didibhai*,' said Akhil Banerjee. 'I should have introduced ourselves at the beginning. We, that is the four of us, are what you could call "*shokher* detective"—investigating and solving a crime is our hobby.'

'Do you think that is a valid justification?' she shot back. 'Your friends had barged into our private homes, pretending to be social workers! That is not a casual visit Mr Banerjee. That is called "trespassing". You, of all people, should know that trespassing is a punishable offense!'

Akhil Banerjee smiled. 'I'm happy to see you take such keen interest in the law, Ms Sanyal. By the way, what is it that you study?'

Rumi did not respond.

'Never mind,' said Akhil Banerjee, waving his hand, 'We will come to that soon, I am sure. But before we level charges against anyone, please allow me to finish. So, in spite of my discouragement, Bibhuti babu and Chandan babu had to pay a visit to the so-called "crime scene".

'As a result of that visit, new light was shed on the case, and finally all the pieces of the puzzle started to come together. Without going in to too much detail about how this was discovered, let me just say that we primarily learnt two things: one, an anonymous call had been made to the police, informing them that the "murder weapon" was hidden in Rajib's room. And two: Probhat babu, it was discovered, had a fascination for perfumed candles, something he did not keep on his table for decoration as normal people would, but hid in the almirah, behind a layer of clothing. This discovery by Bibhuti babu puzzled me terribly.

'Now, I have already made it clear that the chances for this being a murder are slim—I'm not saying it's impossible, but it's rather slim. And here, the informer is talking about a "murder weapon" being concealed in the suspect's room.

'Inspector, let me ask you—this anonymous caller, was it a man or a woman?'

'A woman.'

'Hmm...just as I had suspected. And now, Nilima Debi, I will request you to look around the room and see if you can identify any of the faces. Maybe someone you had seen elsewhere, in a different situation?'

Nilima Guha allowed her eyes to rest on the faces briefly till she gasped. 'That's her!' she said pointing to Rumi. 'That's the girl who came to sell perfumed candles to my house...except...I think she had glasses on.'

Akhil Banerjee nodded. 'Very good. Just as I had thought. Rumi here had dressed up as a girl from a poor family, going from door to door to sell perfumed candles to meet her educational expenses.' He looked at Rumi briefly. She glared at him but did not protest.

'That is impossible!' said Probir Sanyal. 'Why would she do such a thing?'

'I'm coming to that. First, would you please describe to us what exactly Rumi did the day she came to your house?' he asked Nilima Guha.

Nilima Guha took a while to answer. She stared at Rumi open-mouthed, as if unable to swallow what had just been revealed.

'She came that day...I think a day or two after Rajib was taken away,' she spoke slowly. 'I was terribly upset, did not want to see anybody. She said she had been out in the sun all morning selling her stuff. She still had a lot of rounds to do, her bag was full of candles that needed to be sold that day. She asked if she could sit for a little while? I took pity on her, she reminded me of myself. Anyway, I asked her to come in, offered her a glass of water. She said I looked worried, was anything the matter? I did not tell her what was weighing on my mind, but I was glad to have a little company, to be honest. She talked about her life, how hard it had been for her and her mother ever since her father had passed away. She said it was her dream to live in a house like ours! Our tiny two-bedroom place was her dream home! She asked me a lot of questions about the house—how many rooms there were, how much was the rent, did we go through a broker? I told her she could take a look around if she wanted, there was nothing much to see anyway. She went to my room, then to Rajib's room.

'I said I would like to buy some candles. She was very happy, placed many of them before me, helped me choose some. And then she left.'

'Alright. Now, according to what Bibhuti babu overh…er… discovered, the police received an anonymous call informing them that the murder weapon was concealed in the suspect's room. Following this, the police raided Rajib's house once again, am I right?'

Inspector nodded. 'But we did not find anything.'

'Perhaps, Nilima Debi can help us here?' he coaxed.

Nilima Guha did not respond. She stared at the floor.

'My Rajib is innocent,' she said aloud. 'That is all I have to say.'

'That is exactly what we are trying to prove here. And unless you cooperate, I'm afraid it will be very difficult.'

Nilima Guha hesitated, then spoke slowly. 'I discovered it while cleaning Rajib's room. It was tucked away in the folds of the blanket.'

'This was after Rumi's visit, am I right?'

She nodded. 'That evening, in fact.' She hesitated and looked anxiously at Akhil Banerjee. 'I…I thought maybe Rajib was taking drugs or something. I got scared. What if the police are right and I am wrong? Maybe Rajib was into things I was not even aware of. Maybe he was taking drugs and needed the money desperately. What if he really killed…' she broke off.

'So what did you do?'

'I threw it away. It was a good thing I got rid of it immediately. The police came that very evening to ransack the house. Searched every room, pulled out the covers of the beds, threw all the clothes from the almirah on the floor.'

'Hmm…so even though Rumi was successful in planting the murder weapon in Rajib's room, her plan failed. She…'

'Oh? Really!' exclaimed Rumi, with a contemptuous tilt of the head. 'While you are narrating this fantastic tale, let me ask you an obvious question. Where on earth did I get a packet of arsenic oxide? This is not exactly something that the *moodi'r dokan*, the local grocer, would keep!'

'Uh…who said it was a packet?' asked Akhil Banerjee. 'And perhaps, I should ask you again. What exactly do you study Ms Sanyal? And in which college?'

Akhil Banerjee broke the silence that ensued with, 'Very well, I will tell everyone. What we broadly know as Ashutosh College, is really three different colleges in one premise. The early morning section, from 6 a.m. to about 11 a.m. called Jogomaya Debi, is for ladies' only; the day section, called Ashutosh College, starts from noon onwards, and is co-ed except for lab-based subjects like physics, chemistry, zoology etc., which are for boys only, and there is an evening section, Charu Chandra, which I believe, is for commerce students. Students of Jogomaya and Ashutosh share the same lab facilities, but at different times—the ladies in the first half of the day and the boys in the latter half.

'When the principal of Asutosh College called Debdas babu to clandestinely investigate the theft of chemicals, he made the mistake of assuming it was one of his boys from the day section. Perhaps, the possibility that it could be a girl from the morning section seemed highly unlikely to him. Besides, the theft was noted right after the boys had finished their lab work.

'But, as it turns out, our Rumi here, is in fact a Chemistry Honours student in the morning college. So, I think it would be fairly easy for her to pinch the poison, would it not?'

'But tell me this, Joj Saheb,' said Inspector Bakshi, clearing his throat. 'Arsenic oxide was found in Rajib's room (by Nilima Debi) and he had the means to acquire it through his friend Sumon. Then how are you ruling him out altogether?'

'Good point, Inspector. I must say, it would have been impossible to completely prove Rajib's innocence, had it not been for a tiny mistake on the part of whoever was trying to frame him.'

'The pot of sugar?!' exclaimed the Inspector.

'Exactly!' replied Akhil Banerjee. 'But before I explain what really happened, let us try to understand what Rumi was trying to establish here. She was trying to prove that her uncle's death was not due to natural causes, and that Rajib Guha was the killer. Now, based on the facts presented to the police, it was becoming extremely difficult to prove both the above points. First, Rajib was not even present at the time of death. And second, what was the means he used to carry out the murder?

'The only possible way would be by slowly poisoning Sanyal babu with arsenic. So what does Rumi do? She steals a packet from her lab, visits Rajib's house, plants the packet and calls the police. If everything goes right, the police will raid Rajib's house, discover the hidden packet and conclude the obvious. Now the problem was that it did not go as planned. The police found nothing. They had no other lead, so the case would have been closed soon.

'So now, Rumi makes a desperate last-minute attempt to convict Rajib. She steals another packet, pours it in a bottle labelled "Sugar" and carries it with her to Probhat babu's office. She makes herself a cup of tea. When she reacts violently after a couple of sips, complaining of nausea and severe cramps, Manohar babu rushes to her aid. She shows him the bottle of sugar claiming to have picked it up from a random employee's desk, which as luck would have it, turns out to be Rajib's. She is taken to the hospital where clinical tests confirm traces of arsenic in her system. So now it becomes glaringly obvious that Rajib was up to something.

'But, what Rumi could not have forecast was that the instant the second packet was stolen, the college informed Debdas babu. So while the police are now convinced they have got their man, we were suddenly asking the question, why would Sumon steal again, when Probhat babu was already dead and Rajib was in a police lock-up? And why and how did the poison surface at Rajib's work desk, when Rajib was not going to the office for so many days?!'

'I'm not so sure, Joj Saheb,' said Manohar babu, shaking his head. 'How do you know that Rajib did not have the arsenic bottle with him from before? Maybe, when he acquired the first packet of arsenic, he poured out some and kept it in his office. Just in case. And maybe, the thefts at the college are not related to this case at all.'

'Inspector, let me ask you,' said Akhil Banerjee turning to the Inspector Bakshi. 'When you searched Rajib's office the first time after his arrest, did you find any bottle labelled "Sugar"? I'm sure your men would have made a complete list of things found.'

'No, we did not find any such bottle,' replied the Inspector. 'In fact, I was furious with the incompetence of my men, when I discovered that such an important clue had not been listed.'

'There you go, Manohar babu,' said Akhil Banerjee. 'There was no such bottle on Rajib's desk to begin with. And I will tell you one more thing. The college, concerned about chemical theft, had installed security cameras in the lab. I'm sure you can guess what showed up?'

'I don't understand. It does not make any sense,' said Nilima Guha. 'Why would she want to do such a thing? Why does she hate Rajib so much?'

'Would you like to answer that?' Akhil Banerjee asked Rumi.

Rumi looked away.

'Very well. I will tell you what I think happened. And then perhaps Rumi can correct me if I'm wrong.'

He paused before continuing.

'For some reason, Probhat babu was disturbed on the morning of December 13th. Now, my theory is this: He first saw what he claims to be a "phantom" on the evening of October, 13th. Rajib's birthday, right? Rajib had recounted that he was in the market place, when he suddenly got a frantic call from his boss. And the next time he saw the "phantom"' was November 13th. We know the date because that was the day he was hospitalized.

'So naturally, on the morning of December 13th, Probhat babu has this weighing on the back of his mind: *The phantom is returning to haunt me tonight. My time is up.*

'My hunch is that this anxiety made him call up Biren Ghoshal that day. He was the only other person who knew about the incident, and perhaps Probhat babu simply wanted to have a talk.

'We also know that Probhat babu was displeased with Rajib for some reason. On the morning of December 13th, the two had an argument. Why would Rajib, a humble, docile chap who revered Probhat babu, argue with his boss on this particular day? Here is what I think happened.

'As a result of the anxiety that had been building up, Probhat babu, perhaps a little too impulsively, asked Rajib to marry his niece, Rumi. To him, it must have seemed like the best possible solution to his inheritance issue. If Rajib agreed to marry his niece, he could leave everything to him, and it would still remain with the family. Surely, his brother and his wife would be happy with such an arrangement.

'But Rajib refused. He probably had good reasons. Probhat babu was shocked at his insolence, a heated exchange followed. He might have even told Rajib that he had left his business to him in his will, and threatened to change it if Rajib did not oblige. Rajib still did not budge.

'If my guess is right, unknown to either of them, Rumi overheard the conversation. How do you think she would have felt at the rejection? Maybe she had been secretly harbouring romantic feelings for Rajib. She might have also been angry with her uncle, for proposing on her behalf without consulting her and for making it obvious that Rajib was not interested in her at all. So what does she do? The instant Probhat babu passes away, Rumi leaves the room saying she will call the doctor. Now, Probhat babu passed away around 8.30 p.m. Doctor Gupta, when did you receive a call from Rumi?'

'Around 9 p.m. I had just closed my clinic and was about to go home.'

'So then, what did Rumi do in this half hour? I will tell you what I think she did. She called Rajib. Informed him of Probhat babu's death. She might have even confessed her feelings. She would have told him that she had overheard the conversation that morning and that she understood why Rajib had refused. Her uncle was overbearing at times. It was bad enough to have him as a boss, but to have him as a relative! But now all that had changed. With the uncle out of the way, Rajib should not have any reason to turn her down.

'Rajib is not here with us today, but Inspector, if you question him, I think you will get the exact details. My guess is that Rajib was shocked. First, by the news of Probhat babu's death, and second, by the fact that his own niece seemed happy, almost relieved that her uncle was dead. It was this that prompted him to go see Biren, and eventually us. Something did not seem right to him.'

'But then...did Rumi...?' started Chandan Mukherjee.

'I dare you to make such an allegation!' yelled Probir Sanyal, his face red with anger.

'Please calm down, Probir babu. Please calm down. Allow me to finish, please.' Akhil Banerjee continued after a brief pause. 'Now Rumi, out of anger and hurt, wants her revenge. It is not clear just how she can manage this...but in a few days, a plan begins to emerge. The lawyer informed the Sanyal family that Rajib had been named in the will as a principal beneficiary. And everyone in the family knew about Probhat babu's argument that morning with Rajib, even though—unlike Rumi—they were not aware of the real reason, having caught the argument at a later stage, only when Probhat babu had flared up. When Probir babu further mentioned that his brother had been calling out Rajib's name in his dying moments, Rumi suggested to her parents that perhaps her uncle was accusing Rajib of murder? It seemed probable enough, and the more Probir babu thought about it, the more likely it seemed. He lodged an FIR with the police.

'Now, the problem was to convince the police that Rajib was indeed guilty. So, Rumi steals the first packet of arsenic oxide from the college chemistry lab...we all now know what happened next. So, my conclusion is simply this. There was no murder. There was only an attempt to make it look like murder and implicate Rajib of the same.'

Even as everyone heaved a collective sigh of relief, Inspector Bakshi said, 'You may have to face legal consequences, Ms Sanyal. My advice would be to hire a good lawyer right away.'

'There is one little thing that needs clarification,' said Akhil Banerjee. 'Probir babu, I want you to think very carefully before answering. At the time when your brother was having a heart attack, when he called out Rajib's name, was the window in his room open by any chance?'

Probir babu sat dazed and the question had to be repeated. 'I can't seem to remember,' he said finally. He thought for a while and added, 'Probably not. In these winter evenings, it is unlikely that the window will be left open.'

'Alright, then let me ask you this. Did you hear a sound? Like a rap on the window?'

Probir Sanyal's face lit up. 'Yes, yes! Now that you mention it...I clearly remember hearing a rap. I turned towards the window, then Dada called out, "Raj...Raj." I turned back to look at him. He was clutching his chest with the left hand and reaching out for me with his right. I rushed towards him, called out to Rumi and my wife. And then suddenly everything was over. He collapsed in my arms.' He paused. 'But how do you know about this, Mr Banerjee?'

'Hmm... Let me see if the last bit of the puzzle can be solved too. Today is January 13.' He glanced at the wall-clock. 'I think it is almost time for the ghost to pay us a visit.'

Puzzled, amused looks were exchanged as everyone got up to follow Akhil Banerjee. Probhat Sanyal's room was too small to accommodate the large gathering. A few stood at the door, peeking over the heads of others, unsure of what it was they were supposed to be seeing.

Akhil Banerjee checked his wrist watch. 'Almost time,' he said.

A minute or so later there followed a rap on the window. *Tap, tap,tap.* Inside the room, eyebrows were raised. Akhil Banerjee walked over to the window, pulled aside the curtains, and pushed the pane open.

A young lad, about eighteen or nineteen, stood there. The candle lit in his hand threw a soft light on his face. He was clearly north-eastern, with a flattened face, yellowish skin and narrow eyes.

'Ahrai?' asked Akhil Banerjee in English. 'Have you brought cake?'

'Yes, sir. Will you buy?'

'Yes. Come in to the house. I think we all want some.'

The Finer Points

Poltu bit his nails nervously backstage. His plastered arm on a sling still hurt when he tried to lift it. His mother's white sari was wrapped tightly around his body, the final yard covering the sling and then draped over his head. Bhombol had helped, tucking the inner edge of the sari into his jeans at the waist, then pulling and tugging at several places to make sure it did not fall off. But the attire made movement difficult, thought Poltu. He kept stepping on the pleats that hung in front of him. Bhombol had flatly refused to raise the sari any further for fear of having the jeans show from below.

Poltu had the sinking feeling that he would trip and fall flat on his face if he took a hasty step. His best bet, he calculated, was to step sideways only, like a heavy furniture that was being moved. Or perhaps to take steps with the left leg out, not directly in front, but a little to the left, followed by the right leg a little to the right and so on—like a Frankenstein dance step. At least, it would be less embarrassing that tripping and falling on stage.

His chest hurt every time he breathed. He had had to stick two Cambis balls inside the blouse to 'add volume' and these pressed hard against his ribs creating a most uncomfortable feeling. And as if all this was not humiliating enough, Biplab da added the final touch—lipstick and a bright red *bindi* on his forehead—'to complete the look'. Poltu thought he looked ridiculous, but the others hastened to assure him he had nothing to worry about.

Nonetheless, he felt deeply self-conscious at the way he was being ogled at—with that goofy look he knew only too well, the one that was reserved for when an unknown, pretty girl happened to cross your path. Only Bappa, he thought, acted normal. He offered Poltu a bitter tonic to help his nerves settle down. And he even asked Poltu if he was free the following evening. Bappa would take him out to the movies, as a gesture of thanks for accepting the role of Sita. It had almost felt like all this was worth it after all! But even he, Bappa, had stood so uncomfortably close during the conversation, that Poltu had felt compelled to retreat a step or two and sound evasive about his plans for the following evening.

There was a flurry of activities all around him. Wherever his eyes fell, Poltu saw clothes being put on or cast away, moustaches and unsightly moles being painted on faces, cardboard crowns being fitted on heads, cardboard swords wrapped in aluminium foil being brandished, Styrofoam cups—painted brown—being attached to noses with rubber bands, lines being read out for the last time, tabla being hammered to tune, opening bars of a Bollywood number being played out on the harmonium.

He peeped out of the wings to take a look at the scene outside. It was a chilly winter evening. A haze of gray fog covered the grounds of Sabuj Kalyan Park. Spectators with monkey-caps and shawls wrapped snugly over full-sleeve sweaters were beginning to fill up the seats. The first two rows, Poltu knew, were reserved for VIPs. Hand-written signs to that effect had been stuck on the chairs with cello tape. And if Bappa's 'sources' were to be believed, Piya and her family had paid premium price for the front-row seats.

Poltu wished he could simply run away from where he was, and join the spectators instead. He would sit there and laugh and applaud and whistle and boo along with others. Instead, he was backstage, trapped in a sari, being hit on by his friends and with butterflies running haywire in his stomach, getting increasingly nervous about the evening that was to come.

Ramu, the neighbourhood tea-stall owner had employed a few extra hands for the evening. The young boys went around calling out 'hot tea' and 'roasted peanuts'. Ice cream, cotton candy, roll and *puchka* stalls had been put up all along the perimeter of the park, and they seemed to be doing good business. Sound engineers went about inserting plugs and rearranging cables. One of them kept speaking, 'Hello, hello, mike testing, check…1, 2, 3…' continuously into the microphone in a baritone voice.

The seats had almost filled up now. Piya and her family were nowhere around. Maybe they will decide not to turn up after all, hoped Poltu. The thought made him relax a little. Behind him he heard Biplab da clap his hands for attention.

'Another five minutes!' He called out.

The butterflies returned—with friends and family.

*

In Akhil Banerjee's living room, far from the commotion of the Bollywood Ram Leela *jatra,* the All Bengali Crime Detectives sat sipping tea and discussing the finer points of the case.

'But, Joj Saheb,' asked Chandan Mukherjee. 'When did you start suspecting Rumi?'

'Well…the credit for that goes to you and Bibhuti babu. Had you not seen and heard all that you did at Probhat babu's residence, it would have been very difficult to connect Rumi to all this.'

'See, Joj Saheb, I had said this from the very beginning,' quipped Bibhuti Bose. 'Unless you go to the crime scene, it is impossible to get the vital clues.'

'Yes, yes,' said Chandan Mukherjee. 'But what vital clue did we get exactly?'

'Well…there were two. First, Bibhuti babu had overheard the inspector tell Probir babu's wife and daughter that he had received an anonymous call saying the murder weapon was hidden in Rajib's room. The fact that the police had searched the room and found nothing did not surprise me because, by this time I had already convinced myself that Rajib had to be innocent. But I asked myself the obvious question—why would anyone make this call unless he/she was convinced that there was something to be found? Otherwise, it would only help to prove Rajib's innocence.

'And that someone could make such a claim only if he/she had somehow managed to get inside Rajib's room and place the murder weapon there. I could not imagine under what circumstance Probir babu could get inside Rajib's house without raising suspicion. Then my thoughts went to the sales boys and girls Nilima Debi had mentioned. One girl in particular had made quite an impression on her. Could it be Probhat babu's niece? But then, what could be her motive?

'Also, I remembered that Nilima Debi had said that on the evening of December 13th, when Rajib got a phone call that informed him of Probhat babu's passing away, he had left the dining table and gone to the balcony and had spoken on the phone for almost half an hour. How long did it take to convey the news of someone's death? Five minutes at the most? Why would Manohar babu speak to Rajib for that long? Maybe, it was not Manohar babu who had called.

'Another clue, and this was most significant, was Bibhuti babu's discovery that Probhat babu's almirah was filled with perfumed candles. That is when all the pieces started to fall in place. It must have been his niece, I told myself, who would buy these fancy candles, hide them in Probhat babu's almirah as it was no longer being used by anyone, then disguise herself as a poor salesgirl and somehow gain access to Nilima Debi's home.

'The final clinching evidence was provided by Rumi herself, quite blatantly, when she stole yet another packet and did another bit of theatrics at Probhat babu's office. Then it became obvious what she had been trying to do all along. The reason could be anything, but some sort of romantic aspiration seemed most likely.'

'How did you know about the cameras installed in the lab? Kapil did not mention any such thing to me?' asked Debdas Guha Roy.

'There are no cameras,' smiled Akhil Banerjee. 'That was a shot in the dark, but she took the bait. Had she been innocent, she would have surely challenged me. *Show me the footage*, she would have said. But you noticed she kept quiet.'

'Joj Saheb, how did you find out about the ghost at the window?' asked Bibhuti Bose.

'Yes, how did you know about that, Joj Saheb?' asked Chandan Mukherjee. 'Frankly, the ghost episodes made me suspect Rajib even more. You see, he was the only person who knew about the incident at Kurseong. And he was never with Probhat babu when the ghosts arrived. So, where was he?! Na, I know what he has said...that the first time, he was shopping in a bazaar for his birthday dinner, the second time, he was on his way back from the movies and all that. But did he have a concrete alibi? That is what I kept wondering...'

'Well...what intrigued me about the phantom sightings was the punctuality. 13th of every month, around 8.30 in the evening! Did ghosts carry wristwatches and calendars?! Obviously, there had to be a simpler, more rational explanation. Then, I remembered the conversation about Bibhuti babu's colorful cap.

'A couple of days ago, I decided to pay a visit to the church myself. Sister Josephine was most helpful. A few casual questions later, it was apparent that the "ghost" that Probhat babu had been routinely seeing was none other than a young orphan boy from the church. I asked Sister to take me to the boys who went door-to-door selling candles and cakes. She readily obliged. When I met the boys—all of them about sixteen or seventeen, with their distinctive north-eastern features—I was sure Probhat babu had been mistaking one of them for the ghost. The boys were shy at first, did not answer any question at all. Then I told them I was a detective, doing undercover work for the police. And that they could be detectives too and help me solve a very important case. *Byas!* Immediately information started pouring in—who went to which street, what they found interesting, what struck them to be odd. I just let them talk freely...and soon enough, one of the boys by the name of Ahrai, said there was this house whose doorbell had not been fixed for months. And the TV was always turned up so loud that no one could hear the knock on the door, either. So I asked him what he did, and he replied, he simply went up to the window on the other side—not the window of the room with the television—and knocked on it. Once or twice an elderly man did pull aside the curtain, but he would immediately pull it back, before he had a chance to explain. He said he was not intending to visit that house any more, it was a waste of his time. But, I assured him that his next visit would not be disappointing.'

'So, Joj Saheb, are you saying that unknown to this young fellow, he was somehow the cause of Probhat babu's death?' asked Debdas Guha Roy.

'I'm afraid so,' nodded Akhil Banerjee. 'I think, for Probhat babu tension had been building up for a long time. It was the 13th of the month again. There was a strong likelihood that the ghost would return. That ill-fated evening, when Probhat babu was about to have his dinner, his brother came into the room. During the course of the conversation, there was that rap on the window. Probir babu, unaware of the "ghost", walked up to the window. It was then that Probhat babu had a cardiac arrest. Probir babu rushed to attend to his brother, but in a matter of seconds everything was over.'

'But, Joj Saheb,' asked Bibhuti Bose, shaking his head. 'Why would Probhat babu call out to Rajib at this time? I mean…he could call out for Probir babu who was right there, or even for a doctor. Why Rajib?'

Akhil Banerjee let out a long sigh before answering. 'If my guess is correct,' he said, 'He was not calling out for Rajib.'

'Then?'

'It would not be possible for me to confirm my theory—as the only person who had accurate knowledge of this is now no more—but my theory is that, when Probhat babu had recounted the story of the accident back in Kurseong, he had not been speaking the whole truth.' He took a sip and placed the cup on the table before continuing. 'My guess is that Probhat babu knew the person he had knocked over with his jeep. Do you remember, he had a servant who lived in his bungalow and took care of him? If I recall correctly, the servant had asked for leave and had promised Probhat babu his brother's service, a temporary replacement during his absence. I think, that night when Probhat babu was returning from the club, his servant was probably on his way to the village in his bicycle. Having been knocked down by Probhat Sanyal's he was not able to make it. Probhat babu must have surely recognized his servant, and panicked even more.

Maybe he threw the body over the cliff and then returned to his bungalow. For a couple of days, there was no news. The body had probably not yet been discovered. But then, one night, there was a rap on the window and Probhat babu was shocked…not just because there was someone standing outside, but because it was the very person he knew he had accidentally killed!'

'Let me guess,' called out Debdas Guha Roy. 'It was actually the servant's brother—the one who was to help out temporarily!'

'Correct, Debdas babu! He might have come to replace his older brother, or he might have come looking for the latter, since he had not arrived at the village as promised. The brothers would look very much alike, and in the state of mind that he was in, it was almost impossible for Probhat babu to think rationally.'

'What was the servant's name…?' asked Chandan Mukherjee. 'Was it Rajib as well?'

'His name was Raju,' replied Akhil Banerjee. 'I think that is what Probhat babu was trying to tell his brother.'

They sat in silence for a while, sipping tea and absorbing the facts of the case. A jangle followed by a loud crash in the distance pierced the stillness of the cold January night.

'Looks like the *jatra* has started, *moshai*. We should probably get going, otherwise the VIP seats will be taken,' remarked Chandan Mukherjee.

The remaining tea was gulped down, shawls were opened out and rewrapped tightly, monkey caps were pulled on over the ears. The All Bengali Crime Detectives were all set to face the long, cold night ahead.

'It's really interesting,' remarked Chandan Mukherjee, once they were out on the street. 'See how one thing leads to another. A young orphan boy comes to sell candles to your home, and that unearths events that happened fifteen, twenty years ago in another land! *Tajjob byapar!* Human life is the biggest mystery of all, *moshai*!'

'I heard a very interesting talk by one of the swamijis on television the other day,' said Debdas Guha Roy. 'He was talking about the immense organizational power of the universe—you could call it God or Nature or anything you wanted. But there was no denying that there is a supreme intelligence that runs this whole system. Just like a tiny seed has in it the entire programming of how tall the tree will grow, where the branches will come out, where the leaves will be, how the fruits shall be...our lives too are immaculately organized, he was saying, though it is not at all obvious. The Divine works behind a veil, he was saying. Perhaps, the mystery behind the servant's death would never have been solved, had not the orphan boy come knocking on Probhat babu's window! Two seemingly unrelated incidents, separated over space and time, and yet see how the two are interlinked!'

'Are you saying,' asked Chandan Mukherjee. 'That this (he spread out his hand to include his surroundings) has also been pre-planned? The All Bengali Crime Detectives were destined to meet one morning at the Sabuj Kalyan Park and henceforth their lives would be spent solving intriguing mysteries?'

'It may well be, Chandan babu. It may well be!' laughed Debdas Guha Roy heartily. 'And I must say, given our success rate, we might want to seriously consider opening a detective agency, *moshai*—what do you say? Maybe, have an office in one of our garages and put out an ad in the newspaper. Who knows how many puzzling cases out there are waiting to be solved? Of course,' he added hastily, 'Joj Saheb, being our President, will have the final say.' He touched Akhil Banerjee's shoulders in an affectionate hug.

Akhil Banerjee laughed, shaking his head. 'No, *moshai*, I

don't want to go down that route,' he said. 'We are no match for professional detectives with their sophisticated gadgets and rigorous training. Let us make no mistake there. Besides…if one keeps one's eyes and ears open, one will find so many things that arouse one's curiosity…so many questions that go unanswered. There is no need to go sniffing for mysteries.'

'*Moshai*, let me tell you one mystery that has been bothering me for a long time now,' said Bibhuti Bose. '

'What?'

'You know this boy…Bhobesh?'

'Bhobesh?'

'*Arrey*…that fat boy who comes to deliver the paper early in the morning.'

'Ah! You mean Bhombol.'

'Yes, yes, Bhombol, *kombol*…whatever his name is. Have you noticed, he wears the same sweater every day, a blue one? But on alternate days, he wears it inside out. I always think I should ask him why, but then, I'm a detective, I tell myself. I should be able to figure it out by myself. Till now, though, I have not found any plausible reason…other than the possibility that it is a mere superstition. Maybe, it's some kind of a lucky charm for him.'

'Hmm…there could be a simpler explanation,' said Akhil Banerjee, after some thought. 'Maybe, Bhombol is just plain lazy. His out-of-shape body is surely an indication of this laziness.'

'I still don't see how…'

'It could be like this. Suppose he wears the sweater right side out on Monday. When he takes the sweater off, it becomes inside-out, and he does not bother to correct it. So wears it inside-out the next day. Now on Tuesday, when he takes the sweater off again, it becomes right-side out, and so on.'

'Ah!' smiled Bibhuti Bose. 'Really…hats off to you, Joj Saheb.

What a simple and perfectly plausible explanation! It never occurred to me.'

They were quite close to the Sabuj Kalyan Park now. Loud clanging of cymbals and banging of drums suggested the *jatra* was well on its way. They produced their tickets and were shown to their front-row seats by a volunteer.

Debdas Guha Roy ignored the 'What took you so long?' from his wife, settled down on his chair and looked around. From the looks of it, the audience was thoroughly enjoying the show.

To his right, Bibhuti Bose was yelling at a bunch of volunteers. The VIP seats were clearly not to his liking. 'Why do you have the speakers so close to the seats,' he yelled to get his voice heard over the harmonium chords being bellowed out. 'My ears are going *jhala-pala*!'

'You can go to a seat at the back, kaku,' offered the volunteer.

'Why should I go to the back?! I have paid for VIP seats. You remove the speakers from here.'

The volunteers exchanged looks, shrugged, then scampered away. These old men were going to ruin their evening, it was clear. They'd have to find an alternate vantage point.

Bibhuti Bose glared at this show of insolence. 'Criminals! Bunch of criminals, all of them!'

'*O moshai!*' called out Chandan Mukherjee. 'Don't mind about the speakers. Let us enjoy the show. Looks like Sita is about to be kidnapped.'

Show Time

With the one arm that was still mobile, Poltu held on to the bamboo pole for dear life. His knuckles hurt, his face went crimson, the veins on his temples throbbed so hard he feared they would pop. But come what may, Poltu told himself, he was not going to let go of that pole.

Kaltu struggled to free his fingers. Jishu put his arms around Poltu's waist and pulled hard. Biplab da issued yet another verbal threat. 'Poltu, go on to the stage NOW! You have no idea what we're going to do to you if you stay here!'

'NO!' Poltu shook his head vigorously. 'I'm not going! You can't make me do this!'

The audience outside was getting restless. Biplab da could sense it. Raavan, an orange sari draped over his demonic outfit, had been standing outside Sita's hut for the past ten minutes, asking for alms. Some in the audience had even joined Raavan in his incessant call for a drop of water. *Bheeksham dehi! Bheeksham dehi!* They called out. If this was allowed to continue, it would be raining tomatoes and eggs very soon.

Biplab Maity breathed hard at Poltu. This boy has had it today. He snapped his fingers at Bappa, who immediately joined the army against Poltu. Bappa had a far more effective instrument than mere force. He began to tickle. It was becoming impossible for Poltu to hold on to the pole. He struggled, turned his frail body this way and that in an effort to avoid Bappa's fingers, but he knew he was fighting a lost battle. A momentary loosening of the fist was enough for his opponents. They pulled him away from the pole, and without a moment's hesitation, Bappa (in a monkey disguise) picked Poltu up on his shoulders, walked right up to the middle of the stage and deposited Sita. He waited a few moments, taking in the stunned and amused expressions of the audience, adjusted his belt, dusted his hands and walked smartly away to the sounds of loud cheering and whistling.

'*Bheeksham dehi!* A drop of water, and a handful of grains for this ascetic, ma,' called out Raavan for the last time.

Poltu stared in response. And gulped. Then stared some more.

'*Sure, swamiji,*' prompted Biplab Maity from the wings. 'Say it, Poltu!'

Poltu stood motionless. His stomach churned, his heart raced, his mouth went dry. He thought he was going to faint.

Biplab Maity grabbed a bamboo stick from backstage and poked Poltu from behind. The audience roared with laughter.

'Say your lines!' whispered Biplab Maity. 'Then get kidnapped, and get off the stage!'

It was clear that Poltu would not oblige. Biplab Maity yanked one of the extra mikes lying around, and said in a falsetto voice, 'Here you go, Swamiji.' Then gestured at Raavan to grab Sita and be off with her.

Raavan winked at Biplab Maity to show he had taken the cue. 'How can I take it from so far, ma?' he responded. 'Do step forward.'

Damn! This Raavan was stubborn. No! No! Biplab Maity gestured. Get him off the stage, get him off the stage!

Raavan squinted his eyes. The halogen lights were making it difficult for Raavan to see what Biplab Maity was trying to say, flailing his arms about, like he was chasing flies all around him.

'What are you saying, Biplab da? Can't understand,' called out Raavan and immediately bit his tongue. Biplab Maity buried his face in his palm. The audience roared with laughter. They were clearly getting their money's worth.

Meanwhile, Poltu's mind was completely blank. Where was he? What was he doing there? Who was he? Was he in a dream? He stared at Raavan. Was he supposed to give this guy something? Why did he stand there with his arm outstretched? And who were all these people, laughing their heads off? There, he could see Bolai Mama with his wife, and there was Habul da with his son, Shakespeare. And wait! He could see his mother and sister too…or at least, he thought it was them. He could not be sure, they were looking at the floor instead of at him. Why were they not laughing like the others, he wondered. And then his eyes fell on Piya—pretty as a rose, sitting right in front, clutching her tummy, her head thrown back in a wild fit of laughter. A sudden rush of warmth filled his insides.

And right then it all came flooding back.

Yes, he was a dude dressed in a sari, who had forgotten his lines and was being laughed at. But all that seemed insignificant when he saw how much Piya was enjoying this. *He had made Piya laugh.* In some form or fashion, he had played a part in making her happy. True, she was laughing *at* him rather than *with* him…but that mattered little to Poltu. Piya had noticed him. Finally. For once, he had Piya's undivided attention and he was determined to make the most of it.

'No!' called out Poltu, in a voice that surprised all, most of all Poltu himself. Biplab Maity barely dared to look up. 'I'm not allowed to cross the line.' Poltu was still looking at Piya. All his dialogues were for her ears only. 'You step forward, swamiji.'

'Ma, I cannot. If you cannot bring me the alms, please ask

your husband to do so,' said Raavan.

'My husband? My husband?' asked Poltu, gradually raising his voice. 'Do you even know who my husband is? He is the great Shri Ram Chandra of Ayodhya, who is greater than the greatest.' This was fun, thought Poltu. And he was not even stammering. Bappa's tonic must be working. 'So great in fact, that many, many television serials have been made on his life. So great is his glory, that when babies cry, mothers tell them "Sssh…*beta* sleep, or else Ram Chandra will come."' Poltu waved his right arm with flair.

Raavan looked desperately at Biplab Maity, raising his eyebrows as if to ask 'What's this now?' as Jishu and Bhombol rummaged through the sheets of dialogue. Biplab Maity signaled to Ravan to wrap up the scene.

'*Mata*, thank you for your generosity. I will now take the alms and leave,' said Raavan stepping forward.

'No, no! You cannot come here,' said Poltu, laughing hard. 'Can't you see, idiot! There is a line drawn on the stage! That's your limit. You cannot cross. Or else, you will burn to ashes.'

'Yes, yes,' said Raavan. 'You are right, ma. Please come forward, so I can take the alms from you.'

'Ha ha ha!' Poltu laughed a villainous laugh. 'Do you think I am stupid like all those other Sitas in the television serials? Don't I know who you really are? You are the evil King Raavan who wants to kidnap me and take me to that place far away… Sri Lanka.'

'Sri Lanka? No, no, you are mistaken, ma. I am a simple hermit. I do not know any Lanka.'

'Oh ho!' called out Poltu, stepping his right foot diagonally forward, and raising his arm. He swayed a little. Something inside him felt weird. Something seemed to be coming loose, but he could not put a finger on it. 'So you don't know about

Sri Lanka?' he continued, undeterred. 'LIAR!!' Poltu screamed. 'I saw you only yesterday watching the live telecast of the India–Sri Lanka test series. How do you explain that?!'

Raavan was close to tears now. Biplab Maity signalled for the curtains to come down.

'I don't know what you are talking about, *mata*. Why should I kidnap you? I don't even know who you are.'

'Very good! Very good!' said Poltu, slowly. He came forward and rested his arm on Raavan's shoulder. 'Well then…I will tell you who I am. Listen carefully. Listen very carefully!'

An instant hush fell in the audience. It was as if, everyone and everything around Poltu had frozen still. Biplab da's arms stayed in mid-air. Bappa, Bhombol, Partho and the others backstage blinked slowly. They stopped whatever they were doing, and turned to face Poltu. Bulti, the little girl in the front row, stared with her mouth left open, holding on to the peanuts she had wanted to munch. Habul da, a finger raised in admonition, halted his altercation with the person seated in front. The thick brown chocolate ice cream melted and dripped slowly down the fingers of the ice cream vendor, while he held out the cone for a customer. The popcorns that had flown out of the paper cup, when Balai collided with Bumba, froze in mid-air. Even the crow that had alighted from the branch of a nearby gulmohar tree, stopped flapping his wings. Piya stopped laughing. She had an eyebrow raised ever so slightly in disbelief, her fingers rested lightly on a cheek, and her deep, black, amused, almond-shaped eyes stayed on Poltu.

His vision was getting slightly blurred. Poltu tightly clutched on to Raavan's shoulders. The ground in front of him seemed to be swaying. 'This Sita…' he removed his arm, walked right up to the edge of the stage and thumped his chest with his free arm, then immediately cringed with pain. The Cambis balls hurt his ribs. 'This Sita...' he said recovering, '...is NOT a weakling! You may think she is just a girl, she will do anything you tell her to do. You can push her around, kick her about...' His tongue was getting increasingly uncooperative. 'make her...make her...dress up in a sari, put make-up on her, send her to get tea and biscuits and *chanachur*...while all you boys have fun in the clubhouse. You think, this Sita is a loser! She will spend her whole life sitting on top of a boundary wall while being devoured by mosquitoes. She will never be able to talk to a girl. She will never be able to say "I *lobh* you" to Pi...' The words died on his lips. The Cambis balls had slid down his blouse. His right arm still raised, Poltu watched in horror, as the balls bounced once...twice...thrice before rolling off the stage.

The audience erupted.

The curtains fell.

Debdas Guha Roy's Proposal

Debdas Guha Roy pressed the doorbell and waited, a packet of sweets from Horo Gouri Mishtanna Bhandar in his right hand. With his left hand he tapped his shirt pocket to ensure the photograph was still there. Sounds of footsteps followed the unlatching of the door in front.

'*Arrey*, dada?' smiled Nilima Guha. 'Come in, come in.'

'Uh…I hope I am not disturbing you.'

'*Arrey*, no, no! What are you saying? You are welcome anytime.' She gestured at the sofa.

Debdas Guha Roy held out the packet of sweets. 'For you, didi.'

'*E ki*? So much formality? Dada, you are like our family now. After all that you have done for Rajib. Tea?'

'No, no. Not necessary. I just had a cup before coming here.'

'So what?' exclaimed Nilima Guha. 'In this weather one can have as many cups as one wants. Give me a minute.' She left for the kitchen.

'Rajib will be so happy to hear you had dropped by,' she said, returning a while later with two cups of tea. 'Really, things had been terrible for us the last month. Had you and your friends not helped out, I cannot imagine what would have happened.' She continued to talk while opening jars and laying different biscuits and savouries on the plate in front.

'It was only our duty, didi. Please do not think too much

about it. Actually, the moment I saw Rajib, and heard him recount the story of his life, I was convinced he was a gem. Of course, much credit goes to you for raising him so well.'

Nilima Guha beamed.

Conversation rolled on. Finer points of the case were discussed. Nilima Debi wanted to hear everything. More than once, she expressed her disbelief at how much human values had slid.

'*Iye*...didi,' said Debdas Guha Roy, placing the cup back on the table. 'I had wanted to ask you something.'

'Yes, dada. Tell me.'

Debdas Guha Roy hesitated a moment, then took out the photograph from his pocket.

'*Bah!* Very pretty face,' commented Nilima Guha. 'Who is this?'

'My elder daughter, Anamika. She has an M.A. in English, and is now a teacher in a language institute. Very polite, gentle, well-mannered...'

'*Bah! Bah!* Very nice.'

'Didi...if you don't mind my asking...what do you think of an alliance between my daughter and Rajib? They would be perfect for each other, I think.'

'Oh...' said Nilima Guha.

'Uh...is there a problem?'

'No, no...not as such...well...yes. You see, Rajib's marriage has already been fixed...'

'Oh? Is it?'

'Well...yes. He told me about it only the other day. I asked him why he had refused Probhat babu's niece? She was pretty, well-educated, from a good family...really, Rajib should have just said "yes". But, then he told me about this girl he is friends with, right from college, it seems. They have decided to get married early next year.'

'Oh...oh...I see,' said Debdas Guha Roy, taking the photograph back.

'But do not worry, dada,' added Nilima Guha hastily. 'Your daughter is so pretty, and having met you I can only imagine what a wonderful upbringing you must have given her. There will be no dearth of good boys for her. Good families will fight with each other to bring her home. I give her all my blessings, she will find a wonderful husband soon...very soon.'

Debdas Guha Roy nodded.

He finished his remaining tea in silence and got up to leave.

'I will tell Rajib you had come. Please drop by again.'

'I will.'

Debdas Guha Roy thanked Nilima Guha and stepped out on to the cacophony outside. Buses, cars, rickshaws, autos were fighting for that one bit of space. He stepped back hurriedly as an auto whizzed past him, brushing against his sweater. Everyone was in a hurry, everyone had to be somewhere, everyone was busier than the rest of the world.

But not him, thought Debdas Guha Roy, as he once again felt the photograph in the safety of his pocket. There was no need to rush when one did not even know where one was headed. Such was life. Victory one moment, disappointment in the next. It was a package, and you could not choose only that which was favourable. Each event, however difficult and challenging, however unimportant, was needed to complete the full picture.

He would wait. He would wait for the perfect match for his daughter. And if God was willing, he would surely send him a good son-in-law. And if it was the divine will that his daughter remain unwed, he would learn to accept that too. There were plenty of girls these days who were unmarried, yet happy. Being married was no longer a compulsion, like it was in the earlier days. Piya could stay with them and teach, and study for as long as she wanted. *What you need will come to you at the perfect time. That is how the Divine has planned your life.*

Remembering those reassuring words of the monk from the television, Debdas Guha Roy hailed a passing taxi and called out, 'Haripada Das Lane.'

Acknowledgements

When I wrote the first book, *The All Bengali Crime Detectives*, my expectations were zero. I simply wrote a story about characters that are close to my heart. About a city, that *is* my heart. The response I got from readers all over the country was overwhelming. To a large extent, this second book in the series is a result of their encouragement and gentle prodding. They *needed* to know what happened next. To me, that was the surest sign that the characters I had created, had touched a chord in the readers' hearts. For a writer, there can be no bigger reward. I hope I have done justice to their long wait.

I thank my publishers, Rupa, and the team of editors, especially Sneha Gusain, for taking a special interest in the story and for ironing out the creases in the narrative; Mugdha Sadhwani and Sonali Zohra for the attractive cover design; my parents, Swapna and Aloke Chatterjee, my cocoon of unconditional love and support; my father's group of bridge-playing friends, for their unending supply of humorous anecdotes; my guru, Sri Sri Ravishankar, whose words of wisdom might have inadvertently crept into the narrative at times; Kanchan, my pillar of strength; and Urvi, my everything.